HAVEN

Center Point
Large Print

**This Large Print Book carries the
Seal of Approval of N.A.V.H.**

HAVEN

KAY HOOPER

CENTER POINT LARGE PRINT
THORNDIKE, MAINE

This Center Point Large Print edition
is published in the year 2012 by arrangement with
The Berkley Publishing Group,
a member of Penguin Group (USA) Inc.

The text of this Large Print edition is unabridged.
In other aspects, this book may vary
from the original edition.
Printed in the United States of America
on permanent paper.
Set in 16-point Times New Roman type.

ISBN: 978-1-61173-505-5

Library of Congress Cataloging-in-Publication Data

Hooper, Kay.
Haven / Kay Hooper.
p. cm.
ISBN 978-1-61173-505-5 (lib. bdg. : alk. paper)
1. Sisters—Fiction. 2. Family secrets—Fiction.
3. North Carolina—Fiction. 4. Large type books. I. Title.
PS3558.O587H383 2012b
813'.54—dc23

2012012335

AUTHOR'S NOTE

At the request of many readers, I decided to place this note at the front of the book rather than after the story, so as to better inform you of the additional material I am providing for both new readers and those who have been with the series from the beginning. You'll find some brief character bios, as well as definitions of various psychic abilities, at the end of the book, information that will hopefully enhance your enjoyment of this story and of the series. I promise to do my best to avoid spoilers!

This is #13 in the Bishop/Special Crimes Unit series, but I assure new readers that if this is your first experience with the series, you need not fear being lost in a sea of characters you're expected to already know or an ongoing plot whose threads were woven into the story six or eight books back.

This series is made up of trilogies, each connected not by plot but by a theme or idea I chose to explore, usually indicated by a keyword I use in each of the three titles. (The only exception to this rule is the Blood trilogy, which is connected by a single plot thread.) There are some recurring characters in virtually every book, but I trust I provide enough information in the text so that you're able to enjoy the story without the need for extensive background on those characters.

That said, if you are interested in reading the series from its beginning, a complete list of the titles, in order of their publication, may be found at my website: www.kayhooper.com.

If you are a new reader, welcome to the world of the Special Crimes Unit and of Haven, where psychic abilities are used and useful as investigative tools, and the people who live with those abilities are all too human, with strengths and weaknesses and the courage to hunt human monsters.

And if you've been with me from the beginning, or joined in somewhere along the way, welcome back. I know it's been a while, but let's go see what Bishop and the extraordinary people he's brought together are involved in this time.

PROLOGUE

In the first few minutes of Catherine Talbert's escape, she did her very best to be as quiet as possible. She thought he was gone, but she wasn't at all certain of that, and in her terror she just wanted to run.

But she crept instead, out into the darkness, not daring to take the time even to look for something to cover her naked body. If there was a moon, it was hidden behind a heavy cloud cover; either way, Catherine had no idea where she was. Strain her eyes though she did, she couldn't see any sort of artificial light anywhere that might have meant a house nearby.

Stupid. Of course there's no house nearby. Someone would have heard you screaming.

Surely someone would have.

She was dizzy, faint with hunger and exhaustion, and sore to the bone with bruises and internal injuries from the beatings, but all she felt was the desperate drive to escape. She chose a direction at random and struck out from her prison, moving as quickly as she could manage and still remain quiet. With no road to be seen— or, more accurately, felt—beneath her bare feet, she just made her way toward the deeper darkness of the looming woods, instinctively seeking the closest cover in which to hide herself from him.

There was a shallow stream she splashed through as quietly as she could, beyond worrying about snakes or mud or anything else the girly girl she used to be would have concerned herself with.

She wanted to live. That was all.

She just wanted to live.

Past the stream, the terrain changed, and she realized she was working her way up into the mountains. Mountains that had seemed so pretty to her when she had come to admire them. But now . . . Her bare feet were bruised and scraped by the granite jutting up unexpectedly here and there, and rough roots exposed by the heavy spring rains weeks before caused her to trip and stagger. Sometimes she fell.

But she kept getting back up.

Branches tugged at her as the undergrowth resisted her efforts to move through it, and she was vaguely aware that fresh wounds were being added to the cuts and bruises her body already bore.

The night was almost unbearably still and quiet, with not the slightest breeze to relieve the oppressive heat, and all Catherine could hear for what seemed a long time was her panting breaths. Then a brittle fallen branch cracked loudly beneath her foot, panic rushed through her in a surge of adrenaline, and she threw caution to the wind.

He might not have left. He might be right behind

me. And this is his place, his home; he knows it, I'm sure . . . oh, God . . .

Faster. She had to move faster.

As fast as she could.

As far as she could.

Her eyes had adjusted to the darkness just enough that she was able to keep from running headlong into a tree, but otherwise all she really saw were varying shades of black.

Still, she climbed as fast as she possibly could, grabbing rough, knobby branches and leafy bushes and stinging brambles to help herself along, at first not even feeling the slashes of thorns or the raw friction of bark and spiky leaves sliding through her fingers. Her breathing came in sobbing gasps now and her legs burned as she climbed and climbed and climbed. There was no path; there was just an unyielding steep incline studded with granite boulders and towering trees whose roots snaked out far and wide to anchor them to the mountain, and when she wasn't tripping over the roots, she was fighting her way through the thick underbrush.

She reached the top of a ridge, clung dizzily to a sapling for a few moments, then pushed herself onward. Downhill should have been easier but wasn't, because now she could feel the pain of her bruised and scraped feet, the hot pain all over that told her just how much the thorns and branches had torn at her naked flesh, and still she had to push on, through even more of the treacherous undergrowth. And now she had to fight to keep her balance because there was the danger of falling and rolling, of losing her footing and not being able to catch herself.

She lost track of time. She climbed to the top of one ridge only to stumble down with wavering balance and find another, again and again. She thought hours had passed, must have. Her breath rasped and muscles burned.

Gradually, the adrenaline of her escape wore off, and exhaustion pulled at her. She staggered, weaving left and right. Falling down, getting up.

Climbing.

Always climbing, maybe to the top of the mountain.

She didn't know anything except the drive to keep going.

Her raw hands grasped whatever might help her to climb, whatever might help keep her on her feet, but more and more often when she did go down, she stayed there for a while.

Resting, she told herself.

She breathed in the musty smell of the earth, her scraped cheek pillowed only by broken branches, rotting leaves, and sometimes granite. She was so tired she didn't really care. She might have dozed now and then before picking herself up and going on.

It occurred to her, finally, that her escape might

well leave her lost in these woods forever, lost and unable to find help.

That realization drove her to her feet again, and she grimly pulled herself up. Hours. Hours, which meant the sun would be up soon. And surely she could find help once there was light.

Surely.

Because she wanted to live. To survive this, and remake what had been a fairly useless life so far, a careless and unthinking life. She wanted more now. She wanted to have a family, have children and grow old and forget about horrible darkness and agony and terror, and the face of unspeakable evil.

She wanted to live.

She was working her way up yet another slope, squinting because she fancied she could see a lightening of the darkness. And the undergrowth seemed to be thinning out.

One step at a time, pulling herself with numb hands and leaden arms, she climbed. She thought she was near the top of the ridge, and told herself she would rest there, maybe sit for a while and wait for the sun to rise and tell her that, despite everything, she was going to live to see another day.

It caught her unawares even so. She pulled herself on, and a pale orange beam of light struck her in the face, blinding her.

It was warm, and so, so bright after the darkness

of hours. The darkness of days. It was wonderful.

She wanted to come fully into the light. To bathe herself in it.

She wanted to feel warm again.

If anything, she pushed herself harder, grasping another sapling to drive herself on, into the light, but this time the tree was stiff and snapped forward with more force than she'd expected, propelling her, almost launching her. And her numb feet gave her no warning that this time, a sharp granite edge meant more than the top of another ridge.

It was a cliff.

She didn't even have a chance to catch her balance, a chance to save herself. Catherine Talbert left the ground and flew, aware of a sensation of absolute, glorious freedom, and for an instant she almost believed it would be possible to land safely.

For an instant. Just that.

She fell, bathed in the light of dawn, making no sound because her terror of him was stronger than anything else, still. Her last thought was that even this was better than what she had escaped from.

Catherine Talbert was twenty-one years old.

ONE

Emma Rayburn shot bolt upright in bed, at first conscious of nothing except her heart pounding and the suffocating sense of being unable to breathe. Then she sucked in a gasp and slumped, her gaze darting around the room. Her room. Her bedroom, lit only by the pale light of dawn.

Not a dark forest. Not running and pain and terror.

Not a soaring end off the edge of a cliff.

Emma heard a soft whine, and leaned forward to pet the dog lying on the foot of her bed. "It's okay, girl," she murmured. "Just a dream. Just another bad dream."

Her heartbeat was returning to normal, but the oppressive weight of dread she felt had hardly diminished at all. She looked at the clock on her nightstand, saw that her alarm would be going off in another hour anyway, and tossed back the covers to get out of bed.

She went to her dressing table across the room and turned on one of the small lamps. With cold hands, she removed a journal from the top drawer and looked through several pages before turning to a fresh page and reaching for a pen to make a simple entry.

June 22
Another nightmare, in the woods this time.
Different: She was running. Trying to escape.
But the same ending. Always the same
ending.
Another dead girl.

Emma stared at the entry for a long time, then slowly looked back through the earlier entries. They went back nearly two years, with casual entries of a day lived in uninteresting habit interspersed with stark dates and brief descriptions noting a nightmare of death.

The death of a girl or woman she never recognized, virtually all of them taking place in a dark, featureless room. Not a room she recognized, and yet she was absolutely certain it was somewhere in this area, in or near town. Near home. She didn't know why she was so sure, but the knowledge was as absolute as the awareness of her own heart beating.

In less than two years, she had dreamed of a dozen girls and women dying. Dying violently.

Emma didn't need the first diary entry to tell her when the nightmares had begun. They had started after what had seemed a simple and fairly common accident.

Her family home, now a well-respected and popular inn known as Rayburn House, offered its visitors various means of exploring the

Appalachian Mountains surrounding this little valley where the small town of Baron Hollow was situated, and one of those means was guided trail riding on horseback.

Emma didn't ride often; she seldom had the time. But that day she had decided on the spur of the moment to go along with a group from Rayburn House. The trail ride had gone fine, just the same as it always did. Until . . .

Afterward, she had never been able to remember what had spooked her horse, but he had shied violently, catching her off guard, and Emma had fallen. Which wouldn't have done much harm, probably, except that her head had struck a granite boulder.

That casual decision to go riding had cost her more than a week in the town's small hospital, and gave her an almost invisible scar above her right temple that was easily hidden by her dark hair. The doctors had been concerned because she had been unconscious for hours. They had worried about bleeding into the brain, they'd told her. But that hadn't happened. The injury, they told her, had merely bruised a section of her frontal lobe.

Not like that had sounded scary or anything. Oh, no.

The list of symptoms she'd been warned to watch out for had been sobering, everything from difficulty concentrating or completing complex tasks she'd found easy to do before the accident, to changes in her personality or even loss of simple movement of body parts.

Paralysis.

None of that had happened, thank God, in the two years since the accident. Nothing had changed at all.

Except for the dreams. The nightmares.

"They're likely simple manifestations of the violence of your injury, Emma. That's all," Dr. Benfield had told her when she had finally found the nerve to ask him about it. "It's not uncommon after a head injury to experience in some sense a reliving of the pain and fear."

"But it seems so real," she had protested. "I feel the terror, the pain. The panic." *It doesn't just seem real. It is real. I know it.*

"Because it's what you felt when you had the accident."

"Yeah, but—" *I also feel them die.*

"Have you talked to Chief Maitland? Are there missing women being reported, bodies being discovered? Deaths corresponding with the nights when you dream?" His tone had been professional, but she had fancied a note in there somewhere of a doctor humoring his patient.

"No, nothing like that," Emma had answered reluctantly. "I mentioned it to Dan after that girl went missing last summer, even checked on the Internet *and* back issues of the newspaper at the

16

library, and other than her, there really hasn't been anything in the county. No reports of other missing girls or women who didn't turn up later somewhere. Anyway, I don't think I dreamed about that particular girl; there was a picture supplied by her boyfriend for the search parties. And he thought that she just hiked out of the mountains and caught a ride with someone after they argued. I heard later that was the case."

"Then your dreams aren't about real girls and women being horribly tortured and killed. Right?"

"Right. Right."

"They'll probably go away on their own, Emma. But if they don't, or if you start having real trouble sleeping, let me know. There are meds that can help."

That had been a few months before, when she had talked to Dr. Benfield. She hadn't returned.

Even though the dreams hadn't stopped.

Emma stared down at the journal for a long time, then closed it, her hand absently smoothing the leather surface. She wasn't sure which frightened her more—the possibility that her nightmares were just her still-injured brain on some kind of memory loop, replaying a potentially life-threatening accident again and again but giving the women in that terrifying little play different faces and torments, or that they were warnings to her that awful things

17

really were happening in this small, tight-knit town nestled in the mountains of Western North Carolina.

Bad things.

Things nobody else seemed to be aware of.

HAVEN
JUNE 25

"You know I usually don't ask," John Garrett said to his wife, Maggie, "but are you sure this is a good idea?"

"I'm sure Jessie needs something we can't give her, and whatever it is, it's interfering with her ability to work. Even her ability to live normally; the nightmares are hitting her harder each time, probably worse because she can't remember them."

They were standing in what the resident operatives referred to as Command Central: a large, open space at the center of the sprawling house, and one of the common areas open to all. It contained plenty of casual seating, numerous worktables and computer stations, and a huge rock fireplace surrounded by the sort of sofa you could curl up on for a discussion, to read a book, or just to take an afternoon nap. There was an entire wall of reference books, and various cabinetry and furniture pieces hid office necessities such as printers, fax machines, and files.

It was a work space, yet it managed to feel comfortable and welcoming for all its clearly utilitarian purposes.

This was Haven, a privately owned and run organization that provided trained operatives for various types of investigative work—operatives who were also psychics. They worked sometimes in tandem with law enforcement and sometimes entirely on their own, for clients. Haven was the name of the organization, and it was the name given by its operatives to this house and compound, which sat on a rather remote and highly secure five-hundred-acre spread just outside Santa Fe, New Mexico.

John and Maggie Garrett had founded and now operated Haven, and this was their home as well as their work space, a home they shared with resident operatives who occupied their own suites of rooms here in the main house or in cottages that were part of the compound. For some it was most certainly, between assignments, a family atmosphere, and even those not yet quite sure where they belonged admitted to feeling a comforting sense of community here at Haven.

For most of them, it was the first time in their lives they weren't made to feel like freaks, and were able to relax, living and working with others who also coped with both the highs and the lows of being "blessed" with special abilities.

At any given time, Haven could house as many as two dozen of their operatives. At the moment, there were twelve longtime residents, and four others spending a few months here in training.

Jessie Rayburn was one of the longtime residents.

"Do you know what the nightmares are about?" John asked his wife, whose psychic ability was an extraordinary empathy with the emotions of others and the unique ability to in some cases absorb and even heal their emotional and physical traumas.

Maggie shook her head. "Whatever the block is, it's solid. And I do mean solid. I can read more from her face about what she's feeling than anything empathically. She consented to having one of the telepaths try to get through again yesterday. He got nothing but a nosebleed for his trouble."

John frowned. "Maybe she didn't want him to get through."

"If so, either it's totally unconscious or else she's a hell of an actress, because she fooled me." Maggie shook her head. "Look, we knew from the beginning there was a trauma somewhere in her past, something buried deep. At first, she was so shut down there was no sense even in trying to get at it. And she could function, as a telepath and as a medium, so there was time to let her settle in, find her footing. Get used to the work. There was always a chance that would help. We both know it does sometimes."

John rested a hip on the corner of a desk and watched his wife sit down in the chair. They were, in this rare moment, alone in the room. "Well, you handle the operatives, but my impression was that you were being very careful with her in the work. Partnering her with operatives who had a lot more experience and who're a lot more . . . grounded."

With a slight grimace, her golden eyes amused, Maggie said, "You noticed that, huh?"

"Yeah. And I'm guessing she did too."

"Unfortunately. Jessie is . . . stubborn. And proud. And she doesn't like to feel she's being coddled or in any way treated differently from the other operatives. So she came to me a few weeks ago and said she wanted to break through whatever was causing her abilities to be increasingly erratic. Causing the nightmares she could never remember."

"Wanted to, or was ready to?" John wasn't psychic himself, but he had worked with psychics long enough to understand them better than most.

"Wanted to. I'm not at all sure she was or is ready to, subconsciously. But . . ."

"But you tried. And none of the usual tools worked."

Maggie shook her head. "Once you rule out

21

hypnosis, there really aren't that many quick ways to get at something in the human mind when the mind resists. A cognitive interview didn't work, because I didn't know where to start. Starting from when Jessie left Baron Hollow fifteen years ago was useless; she only remembered getting in her car and leaving, with the overwhelming sense that she had to go as soon as possible. And, like I said, another telepath didn't work. None of the psychological tests have given us anything."

"Did you call Bishop?"

Unit Chief and Special Agent Noah Bishop was the third person responsible for the creation of Haven; his own Special Crimes Unit of the FBI was a team made up of psychics, and his idea that such abilities could be useful as investigative tools had proven over recent years to be successful beyond even his hopes.

"I did."

"And?"

"And . . . he was typically Bishop. He said Jessie would know if it was time to go back to the beginning."

"Meaning back to Baron Hollow."

Maggie nodded. "Interestingly enough, Jessie walked in not ten minutes later asking if she could take her accumulated leave time and go back home for a visit."

John sighed. "So . . . did he just know she'd ask? Or does he know what fate has in store for her there?" One of Bishop's several psychic abilities was precognition.

"I don't know." Maggie paused, then added, "But she's packing to go back home. And even though I can't read her, I know damned well she's scared."

"I guess she wouldn't stand for it if we sent someone with her." It wasn't really a question.

It was Maggie's turn to sigh. "No. Her guard's always up with a partner, and there's no good way for me to send another operative otherwise."

John eyed his wife of several years. "Uh-huh. What is it you *aren't* telling me?"

"It's just . . . a bad feeling."

Having learned through hard experience to respect his wife's emotions and intuitions, John's only question was, "About Jessie? About her going home?"

Maggie hesitated, frowning, then said, "We have half a dozen operatives out in the field right now and three here who're going through difficult times emotionally and psychically; any of that could be responsible. I don't know what it is I'm picking up on. Or who it's coming from."

"So maybe not Jessie and her demons."

"Maybe not."

"Then all you can do," her husband reminded her, "is warn Jessie to be careful and to check in while she's gone."

"Yes," Maggie said. "I just hope that's enough."

23

"This is such a bad idea."

Jessie Rayburn pulled her car over to the side of the road and put it into park just at the top of the hill in front of the First Baptist Church. It was a spot always considered to be the start of downtown, a spot where most of downtown was visible.

She rested her forearms on the steering wheel, gazing down on Main Street, Baron Hollow, North Carolina. Almost picture-postcard perfect, a small town nestled in a valley of the Appalachian Mountains, a place where just about everybody knew everybody else. The locals, at least. Tourists were another matter entirely, passing through pretty much year-round with their cameras and curiosity, leaving no mark of their visit behind.

Jessie had done a quick Web check before setting out, curious to find out if there had been any important changes in the town she'd left behind.

With no major industry to support its work force, Baron Hollow's economic strength was its beautiful scenery and the charm of a small town where numerous shops and galleries offered locally created art and textiles and crafts, much of it renowned throughout the Southeast for its beauty and value. Mountain craftsmanship.

Well, all that and the reputed hauntings in various local areas, since ghost "hunting" had become so very popular in recent years. Baron Hollow had a long history of violence and odd events despite its peaceful, pretty appearance, which made it a prime location for paranormal researchers. Especially since so many of its buildings, commercial and residential, had been standing for a couple of centuries.

Once, the town had boasted giant textile mills, and a paper mill out on the river, and even a few plastics plants, and nobody had cared very much about ghosts or old legends, except to scare kids into behaving themselves. But the mills and plants had been dwindling even when Jessie had left. They were gone now, the paper mill abandoned and useless, and the textile mill buildings "repurposed" into pricy lofts or quaint arts centers where visitors could watch sculptures and pots and rugs and jewelry being made.

And any building or area that could claim even the hint of a ghost or some kind of paranormal energy had a sign out front now, advertising the fact.

There were even walking ghost tours.

Still, the appearance of downtown Baron Hollow hadn't changed all that much, Jessie thought. Quite a few of the buildings appeared to have undergone face-lifts of fresh paint or stucco or stone, and there were bright awnings and signs beckoning visitors, but otherwise it looked much the same. On the outside, at least.

Home. *Well, once. Not now.*

Fifteen years was a long time. A lifetime, really. She wasn't the seventeen-year-old girl who had fled Baron Hollow with all her worldly possessions stuffed in the trunk of her beat-up Mustang, a riot of wild emotions driving her, nothing in her mind except the need to escape.

Get away. Run away.

Escape something she couldn't remember except in fuzzy flashes that made no sense to her. Loud music. Voices and laughter. The smell of whiskey. The smell of sweat. Overwhelming shame. Guilt. The feeling of—

And it was gone. As quickly as that. Leaving behind it nothing except an urge to turn her car around and get as far away from this place as she possibly could.

It was an urge she could fight now. But not one she could ignore, as she had ignored the fear behind it for so many years. She couldn't pretend whatever had happened was only a dream. Or a nightmare. She couldn't block it out. Not now, not anymore. Fifteen years of blocking it out had left problems and scars she had to face if she had any hope of moving on with a normal life.

She wasn't even sure if she had consciously known, then, what she'd been running from.

Because all she clearly remembered was the need to escape, to run away.

"Damn. What the hell am I doing back here?" Her own voice startled her, but the question didn't. She'd been asking herself that all during the drive east.

It wasn't her inheritance; Emma could have that, and was welcome to it. God knew she'd earned it, staying here.

Jessie drew a breath and let it out slowly. Soon enough they'd talk about all that, if Emma wanted to talk. And that was a big *if,* since they hadn't been at all close as kids and Emma had been only fifteen when Jessie had left. Without saying good-bye.

To anyone.

But this whole trip was about . . . closing the door on the past. Letting go of baggage so Jessie could move on with her life. So she could sleep without nightmares and do her damned job.

Whatever she had to do in order to accomplish that, she would do. Had to do. Because she was happy in her life now, in her job; it was work she loved and which had, finally, given her an identity and a place in the world she was proud of.

That was worth risking a lot for. It was certainly worth risking a trip back to the town where she'd spent the first seventeen years of her life.

She pulled in a deep breath, then closed her eyes and let it out slowly, concentrating. Doing her

27

best to drop her guards so she could *feel* this place instead of just seeing it.

But . . . nothing. And she knew why.

She didn't want to feel what she knew she would feel here. Remember what she knew she had to remember.

Which meant she was buttoned up tight and sensing nothing.

For now, at least.

She gazed down on the busy scene that was Baron Hollow on a Saturday morning and drew another breath in an attempt to steady her nerve. No choice now. She was here. And she'd driven a long way.

And what was there to be afraid of, after all? She was hardly that frightened, defenseless seventeen-year-old girl now.

Far from it.

Whatever had driven her away from this place, she was certain she could handle it now. Certain.

She reached into her bag and found her cell phone, protected in its specially designed case from the sometimes erratic energy of a psychic. Not that Jessie had to worry about that at the moment, because she was all buttoned up. So tightly, in fact, that she was rather grimly certain she didn't even display an aura.

She hit a speed-dial button, and the call was almost immediately answered. "There so soon?"

"I didn't stop for much," Jessie told her boss.

"Maggie, are you sure this is necessary? The checking-in shit? I'm not on a case, after all, just a vacation. It's a little Southern town with almost no crime rate. Hell, I don't think there's ever been a mugging in Baron Hollow. Ever."

"Humor me, okay? Just a quick call every day to let me know you're all right. Going home is sometimes the hardest thing we ever have to do, especially when we're in search of memories. And you know me. I worry."

"Okay, okay." Jessie thought of her nightmares, the ones she could never remember, and her mind shied away. Determinedly keeping her voice light, she said, "I'll call. I promise."

"That's all I ask."

Jessie ended the call and dropped her phone back into her bag. She reached to put the car in gear, then froze, staring at her hand. For just an instant, so briefly she was . . . almost . . . certain she had imagined it, there had seemed to be the outline and faint color of a flower on the back of her hand.

A rose.

She stared at her hand, lifting it away from the gearshift to study what was now only smooth flesh.

But she was sure she had seen something. Almost sure.

"A rose," she murmured.

And she had no idea what that meant.

TWO

Jessie put the car back in gear and pulled away from the curb. It was only two short blocks to Rayburn House, built back in the days when this end of Main Street had boasted several large houses where the wealthy of Baron Hollow had lived.

Now, of course, the remaining wealthy families wanted larger lots and quieter streets, and built their mansions on mountain slopes to look down on the quaint little town. And what had once been large houses had mostly been turned into businesses of one kind or another, with a few divided into apartments or condos.

Jessie turned her car into the driveway of what was now an inn rather than the family home, reflecting that if it had been Emma's idea to turn Rayburn House into a paying proposition, it had been a good one.

Judging by the parking lot Jessie could see, off to the side and nicely landscaped so it wasn't ugly, Rayburn House was doing good business, at least on this weekend.

There was a rather unobtrusive sign that read VALET PARKING, so she left the keys in the car when she got out.

The long and wide front porch held several rocking chairs and small tables; one middle-aged couple was enjoying the summer morning with iced tea and a plate of cookies.

They nodded politely to Jessie and said hi, and she returned the greeting, equally polite.

It was warm, but not hot, so the big double doors were standing open, but the inn was protected from summer insects by a double screen door, decorative as well as practical.

The screen door was opened for her by a middle-aged man, neat in jeans and a crisp white shirt with a name tag that read DAVID. "I'll bring in your luggage, ma'am," he said, courteously. "And park the car."

"Thank you." Even as she said it, Jessie reflected wryly that she had left her bag in the car less because she'd expected someone to carry it for her than because she was still fighting the urge to bolt.

She could feel the pulse beating in her throat as she passed through the doorway and went into Rayburn House.

"Hi, welcome to—"

Approaching the registration desk, Jessie noted without surprise the other woman's surprise. "Hi," she said simply. "I'm Jessie Rayburn."

The woman behind the desk was about Jessie's own age, brown haired and brown eyed, and pretty in a pleasantly unremarkable sort of way. But her smile was friendly and her voice was innately warm, which undoubtedly made her the perfect innkeeper.

"Yes." She cleared her throat and looked apologetic. "I'm sorry, Miss Rayburn. I was just caught off guard by the resemblance. I mean, you're fair and Emma is dark, but otherwise . . ."

"Night and day," Jessie said, keeping her voice light. "People always said. I spoke to my sister a few days ago to let her know I was coming, so—"

"Oh, of course. I'm Penny Willis, the innkeeper, and we were certainly expecting you. Your room is ready. David will take your luggage up as soon as he parks the car."

"Thanks."

"You're up on the family floor, of course," Penny said to Jessie in that warm, friendly tone. She came around the desk and led the way toward the stairs. "I know Emma wanted to be here to meet you, but she's out right now. Every morning and afternoon, she walks to the park with her dog. I'll call her cell—"

"No, don't disturb her." Jessie softened that with a faint smile. "I'll take the chance to get settled in. We'll have plenty of time to talk later."

She followed the innkeeper up the curving staircase, wondering just how significant it was that Emma wasn't here when she had known exactly when Jessie expected to arrive at Rayburn House.

And Jessie was right on time.

IT HADN'T OCCURRED to him, when he'd first heard about it, that the homecoming of Jessie

Rayburn would cause him any problems at all. Why should it? He'd been a clumsy brute back then, true enough, and things had not gone according to plan, but it was a long time ago, and besides, he'd taken care to make sure anything she did remember would be . . . confused.

Assuming she hadn't simply forgotten the whole thing completely, pushing it into the back of her consciousness where she wouldn't have to deal with it.

It was a characteristic of hers, if he remembered correctly. Ignore what she didn't want to face. Pretend it hadn't happened. And if that failed, run away from it, as she had several times run away from home as a child.

She had definitely run away from something all those years ago. And if she had run because of what had happened at the party . . . if she was back now because she was beginning to remember . . . then she might just prove to be trouble, after all.

So when he saw her arriving on Saturday, he quashed the reckless voice urging him to pay a casual visit to Rayburn House and say hello to her.

No need to push his luck.

If he encountered her casually during the two weeks or so she was supposed to be here, then so be it. But seeking her out struck him as a bad idea. For now, at least.

Besides, he was a busy man.

• • •

EMMA RAYBURN CHECKED her watch for at least the third time, then threw the Frisbee again for her eager Sheltie to race after. They had the small park to themselves, which was a bit unusual on a Saturday in June, but since the new children's interactive "museum" was opening downtown this weekend, Emma assumed most of the kids were there. Snacks, entertainment, lots of interesting stuff to look at and do . . . It was any mother's dream summer destination for kids out of school.

The place was bound to be a hit.

Emma should have been there herself, she knew, to show her support both as a patron of the museum and as a community leader.

Funny how that label had stuck to her.

She wondered if Jessie would laugh.

They hadn't been close even as kids, not the sort of sisters who shared confidences and borrowed each other's clothes. Emma had been the tomboy, the one always out on a horse or hiking in the mountains or playing sports at school. Jessie had been more of a girly girl, interested in clothes and makeup and hair even before she hit her teens.

Outgoing when part of a team, Emma had otherwise been a bit of a loner and casual about friends, letting none get too close; raised to be self-reliant, her first impulse was never to confide in others or ask for help.

Jessie, on the other hand, had worn her heart on her sleeve. Impulsive and emotional, she had "run away" from home half a dozen times in childhood, and was always discovered hiking determinedly a mile or two from home, heading for anywhere but here. As a teenager, she had been flirty, with more male "friends" than girlfriends, always dressing to draw attention and seemingly comfortable handling that attention.

She and Emma had been very different in every way except their nearly identical faces set off by the night-and-day coloring; emotionally, they might as well have been strangers, or just teenagers who happened to live in the same house and saw each other only at meals, if then. Toward each other they felt a kind of detachment that mirrored their father's temperament, so perhaps that had been why.

Emma didn't know. Maybe that was it, that she and her sister had never been close because their father had expected them to deal with their own problems, to rely on their own smarts and strength rather than look to others. Even to each other. He had always traveled for business, sometimes gone for weeks at a time, and, an unaffectionate man, had viewed his daughters with something closer to detachment than even mild interest. And since their mother had died when Emma was eight and Jessie ten, that was all they had really known.

Besides, it had been fifteen years. People

changed. Emma knew she had. She assumed Jessie must have as well.

So maybe Jessie wouldn't laugh. Maybe she wouldn't find it at all amusing that her younger sister had become a respected businesswoman in the community.

Maybe she wouldn't give a damn.

Their phone conversation had been brief, and Emma hadn't been able to read much in her sister's calm, matter-of-fact tone. Jessie was coming home for a couple of weeks, just to visit. Just to see all the old, familiar faces and places. That was all.

She never had been a very good liar.

Don't borrow trouble. Wait and see what's on her mind.

Good advice to herself, Emma reflected with a sigh. Until she knew just why Jessie had really come home, it was useless to speculate. She checked her watch again, threw the Frisbee for a final time, and, as soon as Lizzie came racing back with it, called the dog to heel.

She met no one on the walk back home, which was probably just as well. It gave her time to practice her best pleasant, neutral expression, time to silently rehearse various things she wanted to say to Jessie.

As if she hadn't been doing the very same thing during the scant two days since Jessie's call.

Emma reached Rayburn House all too soon for

her peace of mind, but was reasonably sure none of her misgivings showed on her face as she greeted a couple of guests out on the porch and then went inside.

One glance at Penny's face told her that Jessie had arrived, so she merely said, "I lost track of time. Is she upstairs?"

"Yeah, for at least fifteen minutes. Said she'd unpack and settle in." Penny shook her head. "Wow, you two really do look alike. Dark and fair, but otherwise . . ."

"Night and day. We heard it since we were kids."

"So she said. She seemed very nice. Pleasant."

If there was a question in that, Emma chose to ignore it. "I'll go up," she said. "See you later."

"Okay."

Emma climbed the stairs, past the second-floor guest rooms and up to the third-floor family "apartment." There was a broad, wide landing at the top of the stairs, with several doors opening off it. One led up to the attic used only for storage; one was for linens and other storage for this floor; and then double doors led into the family apartment.

Beside the double doors was a discreet security keypad. Only Emma and Penny had the code. And now Jessie.

Emma punched in the code and let herself and her dog into the apartment. It was a lot of space reserved for virtually no additional family members, and Emma had been toying with the idea of reconfiguring the space so that the inn could boast at least a couple of third-floor guest suites with very nice views of downtown and the mountains.

Maybe next year. She hadn't decided.

Her dog headed for the kitchen and her water dish, and Emma was left there hesitating for a moment. Her suite was off the right-hand hallway, and part of her wanted to retreat there. Put off the meeting with her sister for another hour. Or two.

Idiot. She won't bite you.

Squaring her shoulders, Emma turned to the left and went down the hallway to Jessie's suite. She didn't let herself hesitate again, instead raising a hand to knock briskly and then barely waiting for the invitation to enter before opening the door and walking into the sitting area.

She left the door partially open behind her, knowing Lizzie would eventually come in search of her, but her gaze was fixed on the woman coming out of the bedroom to greet her.

A woman now, not a girl. Fifteen years was, after all, a long time. But she would have recognized Jessie, because that face and those eyes were very like her own, except that her sister was the fair one.

Night and day.

"Hey, Emma." Jessie spoke as though those years had not passed, as though they had greeted each other only yesterday. "I like what you've done with the place."

They had never been a hugging sort of family.

"Well, it was too big for just me to rattle around in," Emma heard herself respond just as casually. "This seemed the best idea."

"Clearly. I hear the tourists have discovered Baron Hollow."

"And just in the nick of time. With the mills gone and other industries deserting us, the town was in danger of becoming one of those sad places with boarded-up buildings and no people."

Jessie nodded slowly. "Good thing there are some artists and craftspeople to go with the nice scenery. And good that the old ghost stories can finally be useful for something other than scaring the kids." She walked over to the very compact and efficient kitchenette along one wall and opened the fridge. "All stocked. You?"

Blunt, Emma said, "I didn't know if you'd want to be on your own or if you intended . . ."

"Family time?"

"Something like that."

"I haven't been sure myself. Something to drink, Emma? I hear you've been to the park."

"I'll take a soda." Emma was, in a strange way, fascinated by the determined small talk. She took a few more steps into the room and sat down in one of the chairs flanking the sofa.

Jessie joined her, choosing to sit on the end of the sofa nearest her sister's chair, and handed over a frosty plastic bottle. "I'm sure there are glasses, but I haven't explored yet," she said.

"This is fine." *No rings. I wonder if she ever married.*

"I never did," Jessie said. "You?"

A breath escaped Emma, and she busied herself twisting the cap off her drink. "No. So . . . you can still do that. I wondered."

It was the only thing demonstrating a kind of closeness, a connection, that the sisters had ever known, existing since their mother had died. And it was purely one-way; Jessie had been able to read Emma's thoughts sometimes, but never the other way around—rough on the sister who was more private.

It had made both girls uneasy from the beginning, and it was something they had rarely ever mentioned. If anything, it had helped to drive an even deeper wedge between them.

Jessie frowned. "I shouldn't have, actually. I've built walls, guards, and they're all up. Nobody else's thoughts have slipped through. I shouldn't have been able to read yours."

"I guess some things don't change no matter how hard we try to change them," Emma said.

"I guess not," Jessie agreed, and her tone was grim.

• • •

HE WAS STARTLED when he saw her walking downtown. Jessie Rayburn. Startled not because he hadn't known she was coming home for a visit—everyone knew that—but because in his mind she was still seventeen.

She had been thinner then, her fair hair longer, and she'd walked with more of a pseudo-sexy swagger that had been very much for show. Now she walked with a confidence he had a hunch was real and hard-won.

Downtown was busy, so he didn't feel anybody would notice that he watched her for at least two blocks. He watched her because something about the searching way she was looking around, studying the buildings and the people she passed, caused a queasy unease to stir deep in his belly.

It had been easy to forget what they'd done all those years ago. Well, maybe not easy, not at first, but eventually he'd been able to push it from his mind and keep it gone. From his conscience. Because there hadn't been any consequences, after all, not even visible . . . damage. To her, at least. Their victim. As for the consequences to him, they had been manageable, especially when he pretended that none of it had been his fault, anyway. And as the years passed, the memories had dimmed so much that he'd almost convinced himself it had been nothing more than a drunken dream.

Nightmare.

But here Jessie Rayburn was, home again, walking with her head up, her shoulders back, and her gaze searching. For what? For whom? For him?

For them?

His mouth was dry, and the queasiness in his stomach made it a sour dustiness.

She could ruin him. She could destroy his life. Even now, even after all these years, she could punish him.

Them.

Because there was no statute of limitations on what they had done.

She could destroy them all.

DECIDING ON AN exploring walk downtown, Jessie had left Emma back at Rayburn House, both of them still stiff and a bit too casual with each other, both aware of an underlying discomfort that was more than their fifteen years apart.

Jessie hadn't picked up any more of her sister's thoughts, but she wasn't certain whether that was because of Emma's walls or her own. Interesting if it was Emma; what Jessie knew now that she hadn't known as a kid was that the majority of people who had mental walls had built them consciously or subconsciously because of psychic ability—active or latent.

Was Emma psychic, after all? Jessie would have said not. Had said not, as a matter of fact.

Part of her wanted to ask. Part of her didn't.

In any case, all she knew now was that there were too many unspoken things between them, too many years and too much differing life experience that separated them, and neither sister was willing to open that door.

Not yet, at least. Maybe not ever.

What if I'm putting us both through this for nothing?

The thought of returning to Haven no better off than when she'd left was depressing. Damned depressing.

Maggie had reminded her that she'd need to open herself up once she was here, and that was the one thing she'd resisted. She was still buttoned up tight.

Jessie's head told her that this was only her first day, after all, and that she had at least ten days, maybe two weeks, if she stayed as long as she'd planned. So there was time, surely. Time to let herself settle in, to talk to Emma—assuming she could. Time to feel more comfortable here before she allowed her walls to drop and her other senses to probe so that she could, finally, understand and face the truth of what had happened to her here all those years ago.

There was time.

"No. There isn't."

Jessie had been strolling past an interesting break between the buildings downtown, wider than an alley, that had been turned rather creatively into a park-like or picnic-like space with greenery and flowers and little seating areas, both chairs with small tables and larger picnic tables.

She stopped dead in her tracks and looked at the young woman standing near a stone bench maybe a dozen feet away from her. A young woman wearing winter clothing and a sad, anxious expression. A young woman Jessie could, faintly, see through.

A spirit. A spirit she could see with greater clarity than she'd ever been able to see one before. With all her walls up. Without even trying to see the dead, without even reaching out or opening a door.

The dead had come to her.

Jessie glanced around quickly, saw no one else near, and took several steps toward the spirit.

"I shouldn't be able to see you," she said, low and fierce.

"You see me because you have to. Because you're here, and you're the only one who *can* see. It's bigger than you and your memories, what's happened here. However it started, it's so much bigger now. Bigger than your pain and your shame and your guilt. You have to help me. You have to help us."

"I don't—"

"You have to stop him before he goes on killing."

"YOU'RE SURE?" MAGGIE Garrett asked calmly.

"Oh, yeah." Jessie struggled to keep her own voice steady. "A young woman, dressed for winter in clothes about a decade out-of-date, sad face, almost transparent, creepy stuff to say. Definitely a spirit. And I wasn't looking for one. At all." Jessie had walked back to Rayburn House and managed to make it up to her room without encountering anyone who wanted to talk to her. Which was a good thing, since she felt jumpy as hell and doubted she was hiding it.

She had always envied Emma her outward serenity.

"Do you believe this spirit is connected to why you went home? Why you needed to?"

"I don't know. I don't see how, but since I don't really remember what happened except in flashes that make no sense to me, I can't be sure of anything. All I can tell you is that she asked me to stop a killer, and I gather whoever she was referring to has killed more than once." She kept her voice low, more out of habit than because she had any expectation of being overheard.

"But there's no evidence of a serial killer operating in Baron Hollow?"

"I got on my laptop as soon as I returned here,

and checked the Haven and SCU databases; there's nothing about an active serial in this area, not even the suspicion of one. I also went online and checked the local newspaper archives, but they're still working on getting most of the back issues digitized; for that older stuff, I'll have to physically go to the library. Online, I could only go back a year or so."

"And?"

"People go missing around here all the time. I mean in the mountains all along the Blue Ridge, not specifically Baron Hollow. With all the tourists, the hikers . . . Jeez, I'm betting some of them never show up in any record because they hike in and out, just passing through on their way from somewhere to somewhere else. Often without family, or with family six states away who have no idea where they've been for years. Unless something happens to cause a disturbance, none of the locals would even notice; new faces just passing through is the rule around here, not the exception."

"A perfect hunting ground," Maggie said.

"The thought had occurred. I haven't narrowed down the area, but a quick check showed me there are more than eighty people currently listed as officially missing in North Carolina, and those are just the ones on the record; God knows how many have really disappeared without a trace. Men, women, and children. But the only thing I found local was a bit on a girl who went missing last summer. Big news, major search and rescue that went on for days. And then her boyfriend, who had reported her missing, seems to have rather sullenly admitted she probably hiked out of the mountains and hitched a ride back home after they'd fought. The chief of police followed up, and turns out that's what happened. Case closed."

"So, no killer."

"Well, none that I've been able to find any evidence of. But we both know spirits don't show up just to yank somebody's chain. Pardon the pun."

"Mmm. You're on vacation, Jessie. Hunting a killer wasn't part of the plan."

"Tell me about it."

After a moment, Maggie said, "I'll do some checking on this end and get back to you if I find anything. In the meantime, why don't you spend some family time, like you planned."

"Unless and until another spirit shows up?"

"The only investigating you should be doing is trying to figure out—or remember—why you ran away when you were seventeen. That's all for now."

"Yeah," Jessie said. "That's all."

THREE

Nathan Navarro walked into Command Central with a cup of coffee in hand, yawning. "Christ, I feel like I've been asleep for a week," he told Maggie.

"Nearly twenty-four hours. But after that last case, you were overdue. Have you eaten?"

Navarro couldn't help but smile inwardly. She was his employer and he respected her more than just about anyone else in his life, but it never failed to amuse him that Maggie just naturally mothered everyone around her.

She looked at him out of serene golden eyes in a sweet face surrounded by an unruly cloud of reddish hair, nothing about her appearance offering any indication of the very sharp and oddly calculating mind capable of juggling many operatives and usually several assignments at any given time *and* of making some extraordinarily tough-minded decisions.

"I'm not mothering," Maggie said. "Just testing the readiness of one of my operatives for a new assignment."

"Stop reading me."

She smiled. "Your emotions are easy to pick

48

up on, pal. I don't even have to try. Which sort of fascinates me, because you're very, very good at masking them visibly and maintaining an unemotional facade."

"One of my many strengths." He changed the subject. "I'm ready for another assignment. Put me to work."

"By rights, you should have a week off, at least."

"I don't want a week off. I want to work."

"Mmm." She studied him for a moment, seeing a big man with obvious physical strength and an unmistakably military stance, and wondered fleetingly if Bishop was right and Navarro would eventually end up in the SCU. There was nothing to disqualify him, after all—except for his reluctance to too quickly re-up with the US government again after years with Naval Intelligence.

Well, that plus the fact that he was still dealing with the traumatic event that had awakened his latent psychic abilities. And learning to deal with the abilities themselves, at least one of which was most certainly emotionally unsettling. And possibly emotionally damaging; Maggie wasn't sure about that yet.

"Put me to work," he repeated. "What've we got?"

"A bit of a mystery." She caught him up, quickly and concisely, with Jessie's trip home, the reasons for it, and the spirit she had encountered warning of a killer hunting in that small, isolated town.

Navarro frowned. "I've never worked with Jessie. Is she a strong medium?"

"Erratic. Same with her telepathy, though that's tested as definitely a lesser ability."

"But you believe she saw a spirit?"

"Oh, yes. Jessie has a . . . singular lack of imagination in many ways. It's helpful in some cases, and a disadvantage in others. But one thing you can be sure of is that if she says she saw a spirit, then she saw a spirit."

"So I'll be looking for the remains of that victim—and possibly a few more."

"That's the idea. *If* there's a killer operating there, he has a wilderness in which to dispose of his victims once he's done with them. And there are plenty of isolated homes and other places where he could hold them. Torture them. Use them however he does to satisfy whatever his particular twisted needs are." Her voice, always gentle, made the matter-of-fact words sound more chilling.

"Do we know that's what he's doing?"

"As soon as Jessie reported in, I knew. Because, somewhere deep down inside, unconsciously, Jessie knows too. I don't know how or why, but she knows."

"Maybe picking up on the negative energy of months or even years of murders?"

"Maybe. She's capable of that."

"Have you told Bishop about this?" Navarro asked.

"I have. Just talked to him before you walked in. For now, all we have is the word of a spirit that something's been happening there. No evidence. Not only have the local police not asked for outside law enforcement help; they clearly have no awareness that anything unusual might be happening there. The FBI can't show up and launch an investigation without being asked, unless they have evidence a federal crime has been committed or the crimes have crossed state lines. So far, no evidence."

"So, it's Haven. I look until I find something to convince the locals they have a problem serious enough to call in the feds, or else find something that makes it clear we have a federal crime on our hands."

"Exactly."

"Will I be working with Jessie?"

Maggie didn't hesitate. "No. Jessie needs to concentrate on what she went there to do—find out about and remember the trauma in her past. Unless and until either you or she finds a connection between that and this possible killer, I want you working separately. You've never met, right?"

"Never, oddly enough. Every time I've come back to base, she's been off on assignment."

"It's not so unusual," Maggie told him. "We

have dozens of agents based in other states now. Since you live in Chicago, you're only here briefly, just like many of our other operatives. Nathan, are you sure you want to go straight into another assignment?"

"I'm sure."

Maggie studied him a moment longer, then nodded. "Okay. I've e-mailed what info I've got to your tablet. Also the dossier on who you'll be in Baron Hollow."

"That's the name of the town? Odd."

"Odder still, it used to be *Barren* Hollow." She spelled it. "Apparently someone along the way decided that was redundant."

"Or just plain unsettling. I'm guessing the place has a history?"

"Oh, yeah. I've also e-mailed you what background I have; you'll have to dig for the rest yourself, on the way or once you're there."

"Copy that. So who am I this time?"

"You'll be using your real name, so that's a plus—unless Jessie happens to recognize it."

"And if she does?"

"Play it by ear. Confide in her if you see the need. But I'm betting she'll be preoccupied with her own concerns. If she doesn't ask any questions, or you two don't cross paths, keep your investigation separate until you have something worth sharing."

"Copy that," he said again.

"This time around, you're a writer. Go start reading up on the file, in case you have questions. The jet's standing by. Wheels up in three hours. That should put you in Baron Hollow late this afternoon, and you're booked into Rayburn House for the next two weeks."

"Two summer weeks in the southern mountains looking for a killer. Just my idea of a good time." He lifted his coffee cup in a rather mocking salute, then left the room.

Almost immediately, Maggie picked up one of the office phones and hit a speed-dial number.

"Bishop."

"Nathan will be on his way shortly," Maggie said without preamble. "Listen, are you sure this is the way to go? Sending him in there without telling him about Emma Rayburn?"

"I'm sure."

"And I don't suppose it'll do me any good to ask why?"

"Some things have to happen just the way they happen." Noah Bishop, an exceptionally powerful telepath and seer, possessed a normally cool and virtually always calm voice that gave away nothing he didn't want it to. So, as usual, he gave away nothing. Especially when reciting what had become the SCU mantra.

"Nathan's going to be pissed when he finds out," she said.

"Oh, I think not," Bishop replied. "In fact, I

53

think that by the time he finds out about Emma, Navarro is going to have far too much on his mind to worry about . . . trifles."

"Trifles? Bishop, one of these days either one of your people or one of mine is going to stumble over one *trifle* too many and come after you with blood in their eye. Better watch your back."

"Oh, I do," Bishop said. "I always do."

"SERIOUSLY, WHAT'S WITH us and the weather?" Special Agent Tony Harte of the FBI's Special Crimes Unit stood at the window, frowning as he stared out at the heavy rain. "No matter where we land, the weather invariably begins to suck. Are we carrying around our own dark cloud?"

"Do you really want me to answer that?" Bishop asked absently. He was half sitting on one end of a long conference table as he studied crime scene photos, suspect photos, time lines, and other notes on an evidence board in front of him.

"It's been raining for three days straight, Boss."

"It's Seattle, Tony. It rains here. A lot."

Tony sighed and moved away from the window. "Yeah, yeah. At least it's just rain now and not a storm. I hardly slept a wink last night. The storms just kept rolling through, hour after hour."

"I know."

Not for the first time, Tony reminded himself that if he, only a second-degree telepath and so relatively weak in terms of sensitivity, had been disturbed to the point of wakefulness by the energy of the storm, then Bishop, whose abilities were redefining the limits of power even within the SCU, must have been driven nearly mad by it.

Then again, he was Bishop. So probably not.

Tony said, "Well, it makes things difficult. The rain. If there was any evidence at that murder scene, it's been washed away, same as with the first two." He frowned as he sat down at the conference table near his unit chief. "Do you think that was deliberate? Waiting for the weather to help him?"

"I think there's very little about this killer that isn't deliberate," Bishop responded.

"But it's gotta make it harder for him to hunt," Tony said.

"Maybe somewhere else. But in Seattle? If people stayed inside to avoid the rain, they'd never go anywhere. He's chosen spots that aren't well traveled but do serve as handy shortcuts for people who live and work downtown. Pedestrian shortcuts."

"Good point. I guess that's why they pay you the big bucks."

Bishop turned slightly to look at his agent. "Something on your mind, Tony?"

"You don't already know?" Tony frowned, then said, "Oh. You're shielding."

Bishop didn't change expression, his face remote in a way that might have made someone who didn't know him uneasy. "Miranda is working that serial case outside Chicago."

Tony did know his boss, and nodded in understanding. "Then you two are taking the threat against her task force seriously."

"Yes."

"And you believe the serial they're after is psychic."

Bishop nodded.

So he and his wife had closed down the link between them as much as possible, the two of them shielding their abilities, both for their own protection and to safeguard what information both knew about their investigations.

Tony wondered, not for the first time, what really would happen if one of them was—He shut even the wondering down, remembering instead what had happened only a few months previously, on a painfully bright street in a terrorized small town, Miranda lying there bleeding while her husband, ashen-faced, held on to her hand and to the telepathic link between them with all the considerable strength at his command.

Psychic connections could be lifelines.

They could also be very, very dangerous.

"Tony. What is it?"

Pushing that horrible memory aside, Tony said, "What's going on with Haven?"

"What do you mean?"

"I mean all the e-mails and phone calls and other communication between Haven and the SCU. Between you and Maggie. I know what's normal, Boss, what's usual. And I know what's unusual. This is unusual. What's going on?"

Bishop didn't question his agent's knowledge of communications that were, to say the least, sensitive. Within the SCU, it was commonly recognized, however wryly, that there were few if any secrets inside a unit made up of psychics.

Instead, he merely explained the situation with Jessie, her homecoming, and what she had seen there.

"So we've got another killer? Who've we got checking it out?"

"There's no evidence of a crime, Tony. Jessie saw a spirit. No name, no good description, no idea when the woman died. Even the most open-minded of small-town police officials are going to have a hard time justifying an investigation into something like that."

"But we're not doing nothing." It wasn't a question; Tony knew his boss very well.

Bishop's shoulders lifted and fell in a faint shrug. "Haven doesn't have to wait for an invitation, so Maggie's sending in Nathan Navarro, with a solid cover story."

With a frown, Tony said, "Now, that's a name I know. He's a bit like Lucas, isn't he?" Lucas

Jordan, another SCU team member, specialized in locating missing persons. And Haven operatives tended to "mirror" SCU agents when it came to their abilities. With a few extras and oddities thrown in, of course.

"A bit like him. Except that Navarro's unique ability is to find the dead."

"But he isn't a medium."

"No, not as we define mediums. He doesn't see the dead, but he's able to locate their remains. He says he feels pulled in the right direction. Starts with a map or a logical place to search and just . . . follows his instincts. His secondary ability is clairvoyance, also useful but nowhere near under his control yet. He came out of Naval Intelligence with considerable investigative skills as well."

"Another ex-military operative."

Bishop nodded. "They do seem to find us. Or vice versa. In any case, military training means additional survival skills that are likely to come in handy. Especially in this case, since Navarro is in a small town surrounded by the closest thing we have to wilderness."

"Something else that sounds familiar. I know we often work in cities—such as now—but we do seem to end up in nice little towns surrounded by wilderness and inhabited by a human monster or two an awful lot more often than chance would dictate."

"True enough."

Tony brooded for a few moments while his boss returned to studying the evidence board for their current case. Finally, Tony said, "If Maggie sent in Navarro, she must be pretty sure whatever Jessie saw is just the beginning."

"I'd say so."

"But the beginning of what? New murders—or the uncovering of old ones?"

"That," Bishop said, "is what Navarro is there to find out."

BARON HOLLOW

"I think I want to go to church today. Do you go to church?" Jessie asked suddenly at breakfast.

"Sometimes. Not every Sunday."

"Still the First Baptist?"

"Yeah, like half the town."

"Good," Jessie said. "Want to come along today?"

"Why not?"

"Then let's get ready. If that clock over there is right, preaching starts in about an hour."

Emma might not know her sister very well as an adult, but it didn't take sisterly knowledge to look at the closed, almost secretive expression on Jessie's face and know that she was going to church for a good reason, and it had nothing to do with prayer or singing hymns.

Emma just wished she knew what that reason was.

She was no wiser nearly an hour later, except in her realization that Jessie intended to visibly *be* at church. Not only was she wearing a dress, she was wearing a red dress.

A very red dress.

Emma wasn't embarrassed or otherwise bothered by the display, just curious. She was even more curious when Jessie led the way to the front of the church, to the "family" pew, and took a seat there. As if she wanted every person in the packed church to know that Jessie Rayburn was back home.

And afterward, during the customary socializing out in the church's front yard, Jessie asked Emma to reintroduce her to people she had known, or who had known the family when she was a teenager.

Which meant just about everybody, or at least those who lingered to talk.

Emma didn't know what her sister was up to, but she had a strong feeling that she wasn't the only one who viewed Jessie's calm smile and curiously flat eyes with unease. Worse, she thought Jessie knew exactly the effect she was having on those around her, and that it was very deliberate.

"Jessie, what are you doing?" Emma asked as the sisters walked the short distance back to Rayburn House.

Without denial, Jessie merely said, "Stirring the pot."

"Okay, but what's in the pot?"

"The past. And maybe something that carried over into the present."

"Am I supposed to understand what you're talking about?"

"No. Not yet." For the first time, Jessie's smile held the hint of a real apology. "The less you know, the better, at least for now."

"That sounds foreboding." Emma kept her tone light, but she began to feel seriously alarmed.

As they turned onto the walkway to the front door of Rayburn House, Jessie was shaking her head. "Don't worry. I'm not sure it's even about me anymore. At least . . ."

"At least what?"

Seemingly half to herself, Jessie said, "At least maybe I can help stop something that started with me. Even if it wasn't my fault. Even if I— Never mind, Em."

"Never mind? Jessie—" But Emma never finished the question, because her sister's face had closed down again, and if she had learned one thing about this woman her sister had become, it was that she didn't give away anything she intended to keep to herself.

She didn't give it away to anyone.

NORMALLY, HE WOULDN'T have been on the hunt again so soon. He tended to be satisfied and satiated after enjoying himself with his prey,

61

able to go on about his normal life without the dark urges tormenting him. For weeks, usually, even months sometimes when he needed to stretch it out because of the dearth of prey in the winter.

But the last one . . . The last one had escaped before he had finished with her, and that had left him unsatisfied. He had tracked her, of course, and he had found her—and left her as he found her. She was far, far off the trails in the area, and he didn't anticipate anyone else finding her.

The scavengers would finish off the remains quickly enough.

He had considered briefly and then discarded the idea of bringing her back to his garden. She didn't deserve to be there, he decided. She was unworthy of that very precious and beautiful resting place.

She deserved what she'd gotten, sprawled out on the hard, bloody ground for animals and maggots to feed off.

He had been enraged by her escape, but he had learned long ago to channel his anger into something constructive; this time it had been repairing and strengthening his trap so that his prey would never escape him again.

Now, calm once more but highly conscious of the hunger inside him, he began to hunt. Watching the tourists, the hikers, those transients who passed through his town on a regular basis.

Noting who was alone or apt to wander away from their group, noting which ones found rooms in town and which preferred to truly rough it in the woods with tents and sleeping bags.

Looking for vulnerabilities.

It was half the fun of the hunt, choosing his next prey.

He didn't lurk, but came and went casually, making a point not to spend very much time in any one spot. He talked to those he would be expected to talk to, but otherwise kept himself in the background as much as possible, something he was very good at doing.

And watched.

A small voice in the back of his mind warned him to wait, to keep an eye on Jessie Rayburn and find out for certain just why she was back here after so many years, but that voice was drowned out by the dark urges driving him.

He needed to hunt. Now. And if, later on, Jessie proved to be a problem he would need to deal with, well, he knew how to handle her. Nobody would be surprised, after all, if Jessie ran away from Baron Hollow again.

Nobody at all.

FOUR

"So, what's Victor up to these days?" Jessie kept her voice calm and her eyes on her plate. Sunday lunch after church had been a family custom back in the day, usually silent, since their father had had little to say to them. But now it was just Jessie and Emma alone in the family suite dining room, with only Emma's attentive Sheltie—lying near Emma's chair and politely not begging—for company.

"Well, he's as charming as always," Emma replied dryly, about their older cousin. "To most people. You know I've never cared for him; that hasn't changed. I mostly avoid him, except when he persists in trying to buy land I don't want to sell. He's been fairly persistent lately, so things have been even more tense than usual." *Never did learn to take no for an answer.*

Jessie frowned just a bit, trying to shore up her walls so stray thoughts from Emma didn't keep slipping through.

Unaware, Emma sipped her coffee, adding, "He wants to buy some of your land too, by the way. That piece out by Willow Creek Church; what we both have in the area are parcels that adjoin land he already owns."

"I'm not interested in my inheritance, Emma. You can have the lot, and you're welcome to it."

Emma didn't look surprised, but shook her head. "Trent Windell is still the family attorney, and he's looked after your share of what Dad left us. There's income from the inn, from several rental properties, plus investments, and it's added up over the years. He and a financial advisor have managed your money as well as they have mine." *Don't be an idiot and turn down what belongs to you.*

Jessie frowned again.

"Look, if you don't want the properties, we'll work something out, but that money is yours. It won't make you rich, Jessie, but it's a nice nest egg for retirement, or to buy yourself a house sometime in the future, or whatever. Trent will transfer it to any bank or investment outfit you want to use."

"You're the one who stayed here and took care of Dad," Jessie pointed out, still frowning.

Emma was shaking her head, her expression wry. "He didn't change after you left, you know; he was perfectly capable of looking after himself, and preferred to. Practicing what he preached to us. We had staff to take care of the house and cook, and Dad occupied himself with the business. He sent me off to camp so I wouldn't be underfoot in summer. I went away for college, and even after I came back here I traveled every summer to get away, see something of the world. And Dad was healthy right up until that stroke killed him. So if you're thinking I deserve more of the inheritance than you do, think again. Dad's will was fair, Jessie."

"I'm surprised he thought I'd ever come back." She wondered if she had been missed at all, but inside she knew the truth, and so she didn't bother to ask it out loud.

"We both know he wasn't sentimental. There's a provision in the will that says if neither you nor any legitimate heirs you might have claim the inheritance within twenty-five years, your share is divided between me and Victor and/or our heirs."

"Well, I sure as hell don't want Victor getting anything." Jessie heard the muted anger in her own voice, but was powerless to control it.

After a moment, and in a neutral tone, Emma said, "You were angry with him when you left Baron Hollow. That last couple of months or so. I remember it." *And I've always wondered about it.*

Jessie hesitated, then said, "He'd been hitting on me. Said I . . . blossomed that summer. I was seventeen and he was twenty-five. *And* he was my cousin. It was gross."

"Jessie, he didn't—"

"He and his friends liked to party. Even though I was mad, I was also flattered by the interest, the attention. He was considered quite a catch, remember, even then, and my friends at the time kept track of that sort of bullshit." Jessie shrugged. "We were idiots, but teenagers tend to be. That's the only way I can really explain . . . I was stupid enough to get talked into going to some of their parties. There was a lot of drinking."

Emma was frowning now. "Jessie—"

"I'd sneak back into the house late, so you and Dad never knew. Anyway, it's not something I like to remember. And not something I want to talk about. Besides, a lot of it's still fuzzy. Most of it, really, if I'm honest about it." She looked across the table at the sister who was a stranger, and asked herself again if Emma needed to know any of this. Her life was here, and what right did Jessie have to ruin it for her?

"Are you saying . . . something happened between you and Victor?"

"No, I'm not saying that." Jessie shook her head, avoiding her sister's gaze. "I drank too much and barely remember any of it, but there were a lot of people at those parties. Not just Victor. He was usually there, but . . . I don't want to talk about it, Emma. I'm sorry I brought it up."

"Why didn't you tell me about all this then?"

"I didn't tell you then because you were only fifteen and because . . . because we didn't confide in each other. We weren't close and you know it. Sisters don't have to be; it isn't an immutable law."

Emma was frowning. "Whatever we were then,

I hope we can at least talk now. Jessie, did someone hurt you at any of those parties? Take advantage of you?"

Jessie uttered a shaken laugh. "An old-fashioned phrase. Like I said, Emma, a lot of it is fuzzy. I'm not sure what are memories and what are . . . things I might have seen or heard. All I really know is that I *feel* something bad happened that summer, at one of those parties. That's why I came home, to try to sort things out."

Emma was certain there was a great deal Jessie either knew or suspected and simply wasn't willing to share. Yet, at least.

She wanted to ask more questions, but the set of Jessie's mouth told her it would be useless. Her sister was stubborn. That, at least, had certainly not changed.

IT AMUSED HIM to hunt on a Sunday.

Such a good little God-fearing town, with many a hypocritical ass planted in a pew come Sunday morning.

He wondered if they had any idea at all how many "secrets" were no such thing.

He saw it all. Knew it all. Who had financial problems. Who was sleeping with whom. Who lived in neat little houses disguising highly dysfunctional families. Who had committed crimes. And definitely who had committed sins.

He enjoyed knowing their secrets. Having that

power. Knowing that he could destroy them if he chose.

He had been tempted, more than once, to do just that, out somebody with a secret. But that wouldn't do, of course. That was just the sort of stupid mistake that was likely to backfire and cost him more than he wanted to pay. Because he had the biggest secret of all, and it was one he intended to protect at all costs.

But that was second nature, after all these years, and he didn't worry about betraying himself as he hunted.

There were plenty of tourists about, uninterested in church, some marking time in the downtown restaurants and cafés until the Main Street stores opened up, while others were preparing to hike or ride up into the mountains. He found it easy to move among them. To blend in. He did not, honestly, expect to find his prey quickly; it usually took him several days of hunting at least, and sometimes weeks, before he settled on a target.

But he found her almost at once.

She was a hiker, carrying a big-ass backpack with the ease of someone who had carried it a long distance. She had that slightly grungy appearance of someone who had bathed in streams, if she had bathed at all, for at least some days and possibly weeks; her short reddish hair looked clean, but her jeans were worn and the cotton shirt she wore open over a tank top boasted a few rips and tears that didn't seem like they were there for a designer look.

Most important, she appeared to be alone.

He managed to get close enough to overhear as she sat at a picnic table outside JP Mann's place, two streets back from Main. JP owned and operated the largest stables in the area, and the one closest to the easiest access up into the mountain trails, so he got most of the tourist business. Being a sharp man, JP also had an arrangement with one of the cafés in town to supply box lunches and other goodies, and did a fair business selling maps and hiking supplies as well.

The target—whom he was already thinking of as his June Rose—had bought herself a box lunch and was eating it, exchanging what sounded like small talk with a couple of other hikers and two people who were excited because they were about to join a horseback ride up into the mountains.

He had an uneasy few moments as his Rose talked to the other two hikers, but it eventually emerged that she was heading north while they wanted to head west. She was meeting friends up near Virginia, she said, all of them hiking in from different directions: It was their Summer College Challenge, a version of some sort of physical contest that they dreamed up and executed during their summer breaks every year.

"But you shouldn't hike alone," one of the other

hikers, a young man, told her. "Find somebody else who's heading north and buddy up. Much safer."

"Oh, I'll be fine." Her voice was easy and confident. "Once I get up to the main trail, there'll be other hikers and forestry people all over the place, plus rest stops and campsites. I've hiked that area before."

"Okay, but that's miles away. It's the from-here-to-there part that's a little hairy."

"I'll be fine," she repeated. "I have plenty of rations, all the right equipment including pepper spray, and even"—she lowered her voice—"a little gun, just in case."

"Bears don't take much notice of little guns," one of the other hikers said dryly.

"I know how to be safe from bears. The gun is for any two-legged trouble." Her voice was still easy and confident.

He made a mental note about the gun, pleased rather than discouraged. It was usually so easy. Maybe this time it wouldn't be. Maybe his Rose had a few thorns to make things interesting.

He noted how far she had progressed with her lunch, and decided he had time to go make a few preparations for the hunt.

As he moved away, he could feel his heart beginning to pump, feel the adrenaline flowing through his body.

He loved the hunt. It was almost the best part.

• • •

STUBBORN SISTER OR not, Emma wouldn't have been human if she hadn't tried. "Jessie, you can talk to me, you know. Even if we've never been close, we're still family. And I know this town and its people better than you do, at least now."

"Well, when I figure out what questions to ask, maybe I'll take you up on that. In the meantime, I'm more or less fumbling in the dark, just looking for something that sparks the right memories. I need to do that alone, Emma. You can't help me."

"Jessie—"

"I need time. And I'm asking you to give me that. Just . . . don't tell anyone I'm trying to remember what happened that summer."

"Because you know it was bad?"

"Because I don't know. And I don't know who was involved if it *was* bad. And we both know what a small-town gossip mill can do to reputations, especially if it only has speculation to work with. I don't want anybody speculating about the past, not until I have a handle on it myself. They can be curious about why I came home, but I can make it look like it's the property I'm interested in, my inheritance, and that should satisfy most people and won't surprise anybody. I need you to go along with me on this, Emma. I'm asking you to promise me. I'm betting you still take your promises seriously."

"I do. But—"

"Listen, I came back here to finally close the door on the past. I have to do that my own way. Promise me."

"All right. Dammit. I promise."

"Pinkie swear."

Emma smiled for the first time, if a bit wryly, and held a hand across the table so her little finger could hook briefly with Jessie's. "Pinkie swear."

Jessie hadn't realized she was so tense until she felt herself slump. She managed a smile in return. "Thank you. We all have to deal with our own baggage, you know. That's just part of mine."

Emma leaned back in her chair and sighed. "I've a feeling I'm going to regret that promise. I thought I heard you last night. Did you have a nightmare?"

"I don't remember. Maybe. I have them sometimes." She was gazing almost absently at Emma, and was surprised to see a fleeting reaction cross that familiar face. She wasn't sure what it meant, and for the first time she wished she wasn't trying so hard to keep Emma's thoughts from slipping through her walls.

"About?"

"I don't remember what they're about," Jessie said. "By the way, this house? Definitely haunted." Her tone was matter-of-fact.

Emma recognized a deflection when she heard

one, but she was too interested not to follow. "Seriously?"

"Oh, yeah. I've seen half a dozen of the dearly departed in various places, especially downstairs. Judging by the clothing, from more than one era, going all the way back to Civil War days."

"So all the way back to when at least parts of this house were built."

"Yeah. A couple of spirits in more recent dress, but I didn't recognize them. Probably not surprising."

"And they didn't . . . communicate with you?"

"Not so far. Sometimes spirits don't need help from the living; they just don't want to leave, for whatever reason. But if it's any comfort, they seem totally benign."

"You used to say the place was haunted, but it was something you just felt; you never said you saw anything. You see ghosts all the time now?"

"I see them. But here . . . they're clearer than I've ever been able to see them before. Maybe because I grew up here; I don't know. Still, it's a little surprising, because I've never been unusually strong as a medium *and* because my walls are still up."

"Walls you learned to build at this Haven place you told me about, where you work."

Jessie nodded. "It's a sister organization, privately run but also linked, unofficially, to a unit inside the FBI, and what those people don't know about psychic abilities isn't worth knowing. Neither the mainstream nor the fringe element has a clue, believe me."

"Seriously?"

"Oh, yeah. Way more things in heaven and earth than most people can possibly imagine. Things being studied and used in the field by the Special Crimes Unit and by Haven. And the first thing we're taught, whether Haven operative or SCU agent, is how to build or use our walls—or shields, some call them. So we have some sort of control over our abilities and can protect ourselves."

"Protect yourselves from what?"

"Negative energy. Usually from other psychics, bad guys. They're as likely to have psychic abilities as the good guys are, maybe more so." As her sister continued to look questioningly, Jessie went on. "It's all based on energy, the energy the human body and the human brain produces. Think of psychics as having a receiver they can tune to certain frequencies. On one frequency, maybe you tune in spiritual energy, and so you see or hear spirits. On another frequency, maybe you tune in the energy of someone's thoughts."

"The way you do mine."

Jessie nodded. "According to SCU research and experience, the reason no telepath can read a hundred percent of the people around them isn't because of anybody's shields or even the strength and control of the telepath, but because every human mind is unique: tuned to its own frequency. And a psychic's . . . range . . . of frequency is naturally finite. Limited, like any other sense, and varying from psychic to psychic. I can read you sometimes, but not always, and even that doesn't mean every other telepath you encounter would be able to. And there are lots of people whose thoughts I'll never hear. Really lots, in fact, since my range appears to be very narrow."

"But you're worried about how well your walls are working here. Or not working."

"Well, they're not working the way they're supposed to. As tightly buttoned up as I thought I was, I shouldn't be picking up your thoughts, but they keep slipping through. I shouldn't be seeing spirits—and they're everywhere. This really is a very haunted town."

"Most of the ghost hunters who come here tell us that, but the locals generally seem to humor them rather than believe them."

"I'm not surprised. What most *ghost hunters* tend to view as evidence is pretty damned thin. Once you get involved in the real thing, though, it stops being about proof and starts being about how you can control your abilities and use them productively."

"So you build walls."

Jessie nodded. "We build walls."

"So why aren't your walls holding things out?"

"That is the question. Unfortunately, I don't know the answer. Yet, anyway." She hesitated, then said, "Emma, have there been any murders in Baron Hollow?"

Emma started visibly. "What, recently? Not that I know of. You know there've been killings over the years—hence some of our better-known ghosts. But crimes like murder don't really happen in Baron Hollow, not these days." She frowned. "Why do you ask?"

"Just . . . curious. Thought I might be able to help out the police chief if there were any local unsolved homicides. Who is the police chief, anyway? Anybody I knew?"

"He's closer to Victor's age than yours, I think. Dan Maitland."

"Doesn't sound familiar."

"And he's not crazy about ghost hunters, who we see a lot of and who he has to be polite to because they're paying tourists. And he's also not very fond of any kind of nonpolice investigators. So it might not be smart to tell him you're basically a private investigator who's also psychic."

"I don't plan to tell anybody that," Jessie responded lightly. "Do me a favor, and keep it to yourself. In spite of the fleeting idea I might be able to help the local cops, I didn't really come here for a busman's holiday."

Exactly why did you come? How do you mean to

*go about closing those doors on the past? And
what are your nightmares about? Those parties
you say you don't really remember? Or something
else?*

But Emma didn't ask out loud, and Jessie
pretended that more thoughts from her sister
hadn't slipped through walls designed to hold
them out.

THERE WASN'T A lot to do in Baron Hollow on
a Sunday, and Jessie was too restless to stay at
Rayburn House, so she went out for another walk
after lunch. She knew that virtually all the
downtown businesses, excepting a couple of
restaurants routinely open since breakfast, opened
up shortly after church let out, but were seldom
busy, and she wanted to explore a bit in less
crowded conditions than those she had experienced the day before.

As she strolled, pausing now and then to study
the contents of a storefront window, she told
herself that she neither expected nor wanted to
encounter another spirit. Her walls, after all, were
as solid as she could possibly make them, and at
least half her concentration was fixed on keeping
them that way.

At the same time, what the spirit had told her
yesterday was also very much on her mind. A
killer? Here? Jessie had been with Haven too long
not to have learned that killers could be found in

the most unlikely of places, often hiding in plain sight in unsuspecting little towns just like Baron Hollow, tourist towns, and her knowledge of that made it all the more worrisome.

And despite Maggie's instructions for her to concentrate on why she had come here, Jessie was nagged by the possibility of a killer hunting in this small town, and nagged even more by the uneasy worry that if that was happening, it was somehow connected to all the buried stuff that had finally brought her back home.

If she had learned anything in recent years, working with Haven, it was that true coincidences were rare, and that the universe tended to put you where you were for a very good reason.

Was she here to uncover more than her past? Would uncovering her past also expose a killer?

Her imagination? Or trained psychic intuition? She wasn't sure; that was the problem. Almost from the moment she'd hit town, she had been nagged by uncertainty and doubts.

But was that so unusual? Coming back after years to a place that held negative memories and even triggered stronger nightmares was bound to mess with her head, and she'd learned that psychics were especially vulnerable to that sort of thing, being influenced by their surroundings.

And by the baggage banging against their heels.

So maybe her mind had simply conjured a spirit warning of a killer because as much as she wanted to deny it, as much as she'd *tried* to deny it for years, she was afraid of this place.

Afraid to remember—

"Jessie? Damn, it is you."

Despite being caught off guard by the timing, this was a meeting Jessie had prepared herself for. She turned to face her cousin Victor Rayburn, who was physically more impressive at forty than he had been at twenty-five, but who still wore on his handsome face the lazy half smile that had caused more than one teenage girl to melt into a senseless puddle at his feet.

Jessie didn't melt. This time.

"Victor. I'm surprised you weren't in church."

"Because I needed to be or because the town expected me to be?" He looked and sounded amused.

"Six of one." Jessie shrugged and slipped her hands into the front pockets of her jeans. "I hear you're the man here in town. That must make you happy."

"It makes life pleasant," he admitted, still smiling.

"Yeah, I'll bet."

"And what about you, Jessie? What have you done with your life since you left Baron Hollow?"

"This and that. Jobs. School. Career. Usual stuff."

"Career? Funny, I never imagined you having a career. You never seemed to have a specific interest when you were a kid."

"Well, we all grow up, don't we?" Jessie had no intention of telling Victor one bit more than she had to about her life, so she changed the subject abruptly. "Emma says you want to buy some of the land Dad left me."

"Yeah, that parcel out by Willow Creek Church. Even the flat land so close to the mountain slopes isn't good for much, not farming or even pasture, but it adjoins land my family's owned for generations. I'll pay the fair market price, Jessie. Get your own appraisal if you want."

"Maybe I'll do that."

"Well, I'd appreciate it if you make a decision before you leave town again; otherwise the whole thing will stay in limbo. Emma won't part with an acre, and Trent isn't going to sell off anything of yours without specific instructions to do so."

"I'll let you know, Victor."

"Good enough. See you around, Jessie. And—welcome home." He reached out to grasp her bare arm, squeezing it briefly, then went on his way past her.

FIVE

Jessie stood there for only an instant, then made herself continue walking, outwardly calm. But inwardly, her stomach was churning, and she felt very cold.

Hot breath on her face, stinking of cheap wine and whiskey. Dim lights and shadows. Noise coming from another room and laughter in this one. Hands touching her roughly, pulling at her clothes. A heavy weight bearing down on her. A sharp pain, and she tried to cry out, but there was a hand over her mouth now, other rough hands holding her wrists and ankles.

More pain, feeling her flesh tear, the hot wetness of blood. And then the pain was bearable, and she was whimpering so quietly she barely heard it herself, so the hand lifted away from her mouth. She turned her head to escape the foul breath, and through tear-blurred eyes she saw a muscled forearm.

She blinked, trying not to think about the panting and heaving, the raw soreness, the acrid smell of sweat, just waiting for it to be over. She concentrated on that forearm, on the muscled strength of it, strength she surely couldn't have fought even if she hadn't drunk too much.

And on ... the marks. Scars? No ... there was color.

A tattoo. A rose tattoo.

Her nightmare. Some of it. Maybe the most important parts of it.

Half under her breath, Jessie heard herself mutter, "A tattoo. He had a tattoo."

She had no idea whether Victor had a tattoo; today he'd been wearing a crisp white long-sleeved shirt, and hard as she tried she couldn't remember whether he'd had one fifteen years before.

He didn't seem the type to consider a tattoo appropriate decoration or expression on a body he worked hard to keep in shape, but she was unwilling to trust either her judgment or her memory about that, not after so many years away.

But what if it was him? He was at those parties, almost always. And he was always egging me on to try all those different kinds of drinks. I remember that.

I think I remember that.

But had he done more?

He had been the one refilling her glass even if all she was drinking was beer; she remembered that clearly. Flirting with her. Touching her casually and yet in a possessive way that thrilled her because he was so much older and all the girls wanted him. And then there was the forbidden-fruit aspect of it.

Her father would have had a fit if he'd found out, and all the church biddies would have been appalled—and that had added to her excitement.

She didn't want to cull through that flash of memory, but forced herself to. Three of them. At least three of them. Four? Laughing. Pouring whiskey into her mouth as they held her down. And then tearing at her clothes—

Jessie could literally see the curtain in her mind drop, cutting off the memories with an abruptness that was almost a shock.

She wasn't ready. Not yet.

Not ready to remember all of it.

Absently reaching up to rub her bare arm where Victor had touched it, frowning, Jessie walked on.

CAROL PRESTON WAS a confident young woman and an experienced hiker. She had hiked all over the country, even in this general area near Baron Hollow—though it was the first time she had actually gone down into the town.

She didn't linger. She'd been raised in a small town, and knew how boring Sundays tended to be. Very. So after enjoying her box lunch and the casual conversation of other hikers, she set off again.

She hiked with several others for maybe a mile or so, then bid them good-bye, with more reassurances that she really could take care of herself and would be fine hiking on her own. She struck off alone to the north, as planned. She'd gotten off to a late start because of the lunch and conversation, pleasant though it had been, so the afternoon was well advanced, and she'd hiked no more than another couple of miles over the rough terrain before deciding to make camp for the night.

She found a likely spot and went through the

familiar motions of erecting her small tent and building a safe fire. Not that she needed it for warmth, but a campsite just wasn't a campsite without a fire. And besides, she wanted coffee and her supper, and she wanted both hot.

She enjoyed solitude, and nothing happened to mar her experience that night. She enjoyed her coffee and her supper, and after sitting for a time gazing into the flames, she banked the fire for the night and crawled into her tent.

It was a warm night, so she didn't zip the tent or her sleeping bag. The quiet night sounds of the forest were familiar to her, and lulled her quickly to sleep.

Nothing disturbed her rest or her dreams, and she never felt the presence of something that drifted into her campsite sometime after midnight and stood for a long, long time just watching her.

JUNE 29

She woke at dawn, as she'd expected to, and once again built a fire and cooked herself a meal. She cleaned up after herself and packed up her things, leaving the campsite nearly as pristine as she'd found it, with only a ring of rocks surrounding warm ashes to mark the spot where she had paused to rest.

Despite the narrow, twisting trail that was for long stretches often more imaginary than real, and the rocky terrain, she moved at a comfortably brisk pace. The bet with her friends this year included a nice little payoff for the winner: a good dinner that was *not* pizza every night for a semester.

She wanted to win.

Carol liked being alone, and liked hiking alone. Unlike some of her friends and fellow hikers, she never listened to her MP3 player while hiking; she liked listening to the sounds of nature all around her. Besides, she was no idiot; if you were listening to music, you could hardly hear any warning signs of danger.

And there were always warning signs. Or sounds.

It was probably a good hour or more after she'd left her campsite behind when it dawned on Carol that what was nagging at her and had been for a while now was the *lack* of sound. The forest was too quiet, and a nameless unease stirred in her. She stopped walking, listening intently, but heard nothing. Not even birds.

She looked around, turning in a slow circle so she could see all around her. There was nothing out of place. Nothing unusual that she could see.

And yet . . .

The hair on the back of her neck was standing out, and she felt herself growing gradually chilled despite the almost oppressive heat of the still, summer air.

All her instincts were screaming at her that there was something wrong here, something dangerous. Yet her senses told her nothing except that it was unnaturally quiet.

Trying to think quickly and clearly, Carol went over the map in her head and realized that she was probably as close to the main—and undoubtedly more populated—trail north of her location as she was to the trail back at Baron Hollow. She could make it within a few hours, she thought, well before dark. If she hurried.

So—push on, then.

Carol remained where she was long enough to shrug out of the backpack and get her pepper spray and gun out. She slipped into the straps of the backpack once again, settling it comfortably to distribute the weight, then did a quick but thorough check of her .22 Smith & Wesson revolver and clipped the holster to her belt. The pepper spray she carried looped around her wrist.

The precautions should have made her feel safer.

They didn't.

The forest was still too quiet, way too quiet, and she felt too chilled for the summer air.

But she walked on, more quickly now. So quickly, in fact, that within only a few minutes she had to stop to catch her breath. At first, that was all she heard—her own panting breathing.

And then a twig snapped.

Somewhere close.

EMMA STOPPED JESSIE in the reception area as her sister was apparently on her way out on Monday morning. "Look, should I take it personally that you've spent as little time as you possibly could here at the house so far?"

"I told you I'd mostly be wandering around town." Keeping her voice low so as not to frighten any of the guests, Jessie said, "Besides, it's not you; believe me. Right now, if I look past you into the living room, I can see a Prohibition-era woman standing near the fireplace, smoking. Using one of those old long cigarette holders. Jeweled. Did you know, by the way, that this house was the equivalent of a small-town speakeasy back in the day?"

Emma blinked. "There's a mention in family archive records that an ancestor of ours was famous for his ability to get good whiskey even when it was outlawed. He claimed he just had a good cellar from before, when it was legal, but his neighbors didn't believe it."

"Probably because they helped transport it."

"Jobs were hard to come by in those days," Emma noted. "I imagine people took what work they could get, even if that meant the illegal transport of liquor. Besides, it's not like it was a popular law with broad support."

"True enough. And at least that ancestor of ours had the sense to share the wealth with the town.

Anyway, given the . . . temperament . . . of those times, I'm guessing this house saw a fair amount of violence." She drew a breath, and let it out in a quick sigh. "I'm told spirits generally don't bear the marks of whatever killed them, and that's been my experience up 'til now, but that woman has a bullet hole over her left breast." Jessie paused, then added dryly, "I find that unnerving, and I'd rather not look at it."

"Which is why you're going out again."

"Well, that and the practical need to look at the rest of the properties on this list Trent gave me and decide if I want to keep any of it. My reasonable excuse for wandering around, remember? Penny had the cook pack a lunch for me in case I'm out the rest of the day." She lifted the lightweight backpack at her feet and shrugged into it.

"You're going alone?"

"Sure. It's a nice day for a hike, and none of this property is all that far from town. And since the houses are farther apart and we can't claim a war battlefield in this area, I'm not quite as likely to encounter more distracting spirits while I ramble around."

Frowning again, Emma said, "This psychic stuff really is bothering you, isn't it? I thought working for Haven had helped."

"So did I."

"Maybe you should call them, tell them what's going on."

"I've reported in." Jessie kept her voice casual. "But we learn to control this stuff by being exposed to it, so maybe it's a good thing that Baron Hollow is so . . . haunted. Anyway, Maggie told me to concentrate on what I came here to do, and that's settle with the past."

"You said you talked to Victor."

"Yeah, nice and civilized." She hadn't confided in Emma about the flash of memories that meeting had triggered, and didn't intend to. Not, at least, until she could clearly recall what had happened at that particular party; she wasn't about to leave Emma here in what should be her safe home with the certain knowledge that three or four men she quite likely knew had brutalized her sister fifteen years before, *especially* not when she couldn't be sure just who had been in that room.

"Jessie—"

"I'm okay, Emma. Just jumpy today, and a long walk sounds like a good idea."

"Just be careful, will you, please?"

Jessie looked at her curiously. "Now you're sounding as jumpy as I feel. Any special reason?"

"No. No reason. Just . . . there are a lot of tourists in town, a lot of strangers."

"I'll be fine. See you later, probably by suppertime."

Emma watched her sister walk out of Rayburn House, and bit back a sigh. They were still strangers, or as good as. Jessie was restless inside the house, quick to leave on her own to "ramble" around elsewhere, and she never had much to say when she came back. On top of which, Emma was positive she was having nightmares.

She had nearly confided her own nightmares more than once, but the timing had never seemed right. Besides which, she hadn't had a nightmare since before Jessie had come home, and had already half convinced herself that it was just as the doctor had said, her recovering brain reliving a traumatic event.

Which was why she had been so caught off guard when Jessie had asked her about recent murders.

I should have talked to her about the nightmares then. But she had let that moment pass because the nightmares had seemed so . . . insignificant. Just dreams, and with a logical explanation for them— her accident. How could they be anything else?

HE HAD ENJOYED tracking her. He knew the forest, the mountain trails, like the back of his hand, so it was a simple thing to shadow her, to move parallel to the trail she followed.

He didn't need a trail.

All late Sunday afternoon, he had shadowed her, staying far away so as to not attract her notice. When he judged there was enough distance between her and the hikers and trail riders who had chosen a different trail, he moved closer, still easily able to blend with the forest. He was close when she made camp for the night, and though he toyed with the idea of taking her then, he decided to wait a bit longer, to draw out the anticipation he felt.

He hadn't been able to resist coming back up here hours later just to watch her sleep. His June Rose.

She didn't know he was there, of course. They seldom did, unless he wanted them to.

A methodical man, he went over it in his mind, the plan for Monday. It would be a busy day for him, so he'd have to catch his prey in the late morning, not too late. Then take her to his trap and leave her there, to be enjoyed later on.

She was actually making it easier for him, since she was hiking in the right direction. When he caught her, he wouldn't be very far from his trap. Not very far at all.

Smiling, he drifted away from her campsite, leaving her to peaceful dreams he knew would be her last.

He was back very early on Monday, pleased to find her already up and about as well. She had clearly already had her breakfast, and was now briskly packing up her little camp in preparation to move on.

Good. That was good. He had a busy day ahead, with appointments elsewhere, and couldn't afford to spend too much time shadowing her today.

Not too much time. Just enough to savor.

It annoyed him when she stopped suddenly, frowning as she gazed around her, and yet he was also aware of a thrill of excitement. She might not know it consciously, but some animal instinct was warning her that she was in danger.

Good. Good.

He saw the gun she removed from her backpack, coolly calculating how close he would have to be to surprise her, to make sure she never got the chance to fire that gun—or use the pepper spray.

Close. Unless, that was, she froze in the moment.

She didn't look the type to freeze.

Good. Good. Worthy prey.

He waited until she walked on, then shadowed her again, his mind racing ahead, following the topography of the mountainside. There was a place he knew. Farther along. A place where he could get close without her seeing him.

A place where the distance between them would be, he judged, just close enough.

He wanted the struggle, hungered for it, but he didn't want to give her a chance to get off a shot. A gunshot in these woods could easily go unnoticed; he knew only too well how many hikers and campers carried a rifle for protection. But the sound of a handgun was different, and he couldn't take the chance of the wrong person hearing and noticing that difference.

He had to get his hands on her quickly.

Aware of his heart beating faster, of adrenaline rushing through his entire body, he quickened his silent steps, moving faster so as to get ahead of her. And get in position.

JESSIE HAD A rough map of the area she planned to explore; Trent had sketched it out for her, basing it on the land surveys in his office. Some of it she found vaguely familiar, experiencing a few flashes of memory that were blessedly uncomplicated. Childhood stuff. Walking with friends, swimming in a broad creek in the heat of summer, picking berries.

Pleasant memories.

But, gradually, despite the bright summer day, she found herself shifting her pack as though the light weight was uncomfortable. Nervously tucking a strand of hair behind one ear. Looking around her in a different way. That was when she recognized her own skin-crawling uneasiness.

Someone walking over my grave.

Now, *there* was a disturbing thought.

And the sensation wouldn't go away. If anything, it got stronger as she walked. Jessie stopped, looking around to orient herself. The land she'd set out to explore lay at the base of the mountains, in one of the many small valleys—some would say mere ravines—that dotted the area.

Though she hadn't consciously chosen to do so, she realized she was following, through sparse trees, something a little more than a trail. It was a road. Not much of a road, to be sure, but a road nevertheless, where cars had traveled in the not-too-recent past.

Jessie stood there for a minute or so, her hands gripping the straps of her lightweight backpack. Gripping and easing, gripping and easing, in a rhythm she recognized as a poor outlet for tension. She frowned down at the two faint ruts with grass and weeds growing between them. It wasn't, she thought, an old road now no longer used and being rapidly reclaimed by nature; it was a road that was used sporadically.

Not exactly an uncommon thing in the area, between teenagers looking for places to park and other teenagers learning to drive—and old roads that simply no longer led to any place of interest.

Frowning, Jessie took another step, and felt the tingly unease increase.

She could have sworn she caught a glimpse of movement from the corner of one eye, but when she turned her head, there was nothing unusual to be seen. Maybe just her nerves . . . except that it happened at least three times, and by then what she was feeling was that she was definitely not alone out here.

It was strange, and unsettling, and though training told her to open herself up to whatever energy it was she was feeling, a deeper instinct told her not to.

It was Bad. Whatever it was, it was Bad.

Wherever it led, whatever lay at the end of it, this road was . . . something to fear. Something she feared.

Jessie didn't remember the road, but her memories of many things about Baron Hollow were still fuzzy. Still, as she forced herself to walk on, the cold unease grew stronger, colder. And there was something creepily familiar about it. She *knew* this somehow, knew this feeling, where it came from and even what it meant.

It was . . . Her mind tried to shy away, and she fought to stay focused. This feeling, this coldness, this . . . awareness of evil. It was familiar because . . .

Because it was in her dreams. It was the way she felt when she woke, unable to remember anything except this horrible feeling of having looked at evil, right in the face.

It was broad daylight on a warm summer day, and Jessie's skin was cold and clammy. The sun beat down on her, yet she was shivering. There was no sign of anything amiss, and yet she wanted to turn and hurry back the way she'd come.

That compulsion was so strong, finally, that she did stop with a jerk, and turn—and nearly jumped out of her skin.

"You can't run away from this." It was the same

anxious-faced female spirit who had spoken to Jessie in town. The only one, so far, who had spoken to her.

"Why the hell not?" Jessie heard herself demand, hating the spooked sound of her own voice.

"Everything happens for a reason; you know that. You came back here for this."

"I came back here to settle with the past."

"Yes. You did."

Jessie shook her head. "Nothing happened to me way out here—that much I'm sure of. What happened to me was—it was in town. A house in town."

"That was the start. His first. But he was younger then, and even if he'd been ready, he didn't dare kill. Not a local girl, someone easily connected to him. He was smarter than that. Even then, he was smarter than that. And he was always in control, always had his monster on a leash."

If she had believed she felt cold before, that was nothing compared to how Jessie felt when she heard those words. Through dry lips, she heard herself say something she hadn't been sure of until this moment. "How am I supposed to find out who he is? How, when I don't remember who was even in that room? There were four of them. That night. That last party. At least four of them. Who—Which one—"

"You can't turn back now. Follow the road. Follow your instincts. Stop him, Jessie."

The spirit vanished, there one instant and gone the next.

Which one of them became a killer? How can I single out one when I can't remember who any of them were?

For what seemed a very long time, Jessie stood there, staring at where the spirit had stood. More experienced mediums had told her about this, about the spirit world's often enigmatic "help" for the living. For whatever reason, whatever universal rules dictated, direct questions were seldom answered and the information that was offered too often sounded like riddles.

But this . . .

Jessie shrugged out of her backpack and dug into it for her cell phone. It was dead, despite being wrapped in the protective casing developed by the FBI's Special Crimes Unit; psychics tended to have strong electromagnetic energy, and that energy tended to play havoc with electronics, especially those worn close to or on the body like cell phones and wristwatches.

The casing was usually effective, at least to a point. But Jessie had forgotten to charge her phone the night before, so what energy it held had been even more easily depleted than normal.

"Dammit. Dammit to hell."

Slowly, she replaced the phone in her backpack, her panicked urge to call for help slowly fading. What was wrong with her? She was a trained investigator, and experienced. And this was just the sort of situation she was expected to know how to handle.

Spirits. And, possibly, murderers.

But . . . never before on her own.

The question was, was she *supposed* to handle this on her own, investigate on her own, because the spirit was right? Had the horrible experience in her past truly been the beginning of something even more horrific involving other women? Was it somehow her fault? Her responsibility? Would things have been different if she'd been stronger that night, if she hadn't drunk so much or had been able to put up a fight?

If she had reported it, had told someone?

Was there innocent blood on her soul?

Everything in Jessie cringed from that thought, but it had to be faced. Because the universe was about balance; that was another thing she'd learned. And if her own weakness had been some kind of trigger, some catalyst for a killer, then . . . maybe she *was* meant to stop him, here and now. Maybe the dead phone was as much a sign as the spirit had been. Maybe it was intended to show her that she had to do this alone.

Some things have to happen just the way they happen.

Their mantra, both Haven and the Special Crimes Unit.

Jessie had joined Haven with no belief in

destiny, in fate, but she'd had a total change of mind and heart within the first months in what had become her new life.

Destiny existed. Fate existed.

And some things had to happen just the way they happened.

"Okay," she said aloud. "Okay."

She drew a deep breath and swung the backpack over one shoulder. And continued walking along the road, fighting to ignore the dread that grew stronger with every step.

SIX

"They say they're afraid."

Emma looked up from her paperwork and lifted an eyebrow at her innkeeper. "Wasn't this the couple who *wanted* to see a ghost?"

Penny grinned. "Yeah, our honeymooning couple. But I gather they expected a brief vision of some sort of ethereal figure floating down a hallway. Waking up to strange scratching noises in the walls was a bit more disconcerting."

Emma wondered briefly if the spirits Jessie kept seeing were quite as benign as she said they were, but dismissed the idea. She'd lived in this house all her life, and she guessed that if anything *not* benign had existed here, she would have seen or felt something by now—psychic or not.

So, mildly, she said, "Uh-huh. Sounds to me like

Jax isn't doing her job." Jax was the resident cat of Rayburn House, and a locally famous mouser.

"I thought the same thing," Penny said, adding, "but everything she catches seems to be in the basement, not any of the rooms. Besides, the last time we had Ed here spraying to make sure the bugs stay outside, he checked for rodents too. Even went up into the attic to make sure no squirrels had chewed their way in since the last check. We came up clean. If there are mice in the walls, I don't know how or where they're getting in."

Since Emma, like her ancestors before her, was meticulous in doing whatever it took to maintain the more-than-a-century-old house, she wasn't surprised the pest report had come back showing no problems. From cleaning out the gutters and power-washing the stonework to touching up paint on trim and replacing worn rugs and carpets, maintenance was on a carefully planned schedule year-round and kept the old house in excellent shape. Two of the eight guest bedroom suites were completely redone every year on a rotating basis, just to help keep everything looking fresh and updated. And Emma had shut down for nearly six months a few years previously to completely update both wiring and plumbing.

So . . .

"We shouldn't have mice in the walls." Emma shrugged. She hadn't confided in Penny about what Jessie had seen, so she kept her voice casual when she added, "But maybe we do have ghosts. More than one guest has reported seeing or hearing strange things over the years. And there are the family legends, people killed or dying here in the house."

"Yeah, I keep hoping, but so far no luck. I mean, I've had no luck seeing or hearing anything paranormal."

"Well, I didn't think you wanted to be listed among the family legends as a ghostly presence," Emma said dryly.

"Hardly. I plan to die peacefully in my sleep at a hundred and one, after having completed every single thing on my bucket list."

"A hundred and one?"

Penny grinned. "More than a century."

"Ah. Well, I'm not going to ask what's on your bucket list." Without giving Penny a chance to respond to that, Emma said, "As for our guests, maybe they were just imagining things. They came here expecting a haunted inn, and what the mind expects, the imagination tends to create."

"More than likely," Penny agreed. "I thought I'd suggest they can move to the other side of the house if they want; the Topaz Room is vacant now."

Emma nodded, but said, "Better warn them any sounds they hear in there are likely to be from a wandering writer in the room below theirs. Didn't you put him in the Garnet Room on the ground floor?"

"Yeah, because he's going to be coming and going, and didn't want to disturb the other guests. He did promise to be quiet about it, and judging by the way he moved, I'd say he's not likely to bump into the furniture or anything like that. He's more catlike than Jax is."

Eyeing her innkeeper, Emma said mildly, "I see he made an impression."

"Well, yeah. I mean, come on, Emma—we don't exactly have an excess of unattached men around here. At least none that you or I haven't known forever—warts and all. Navarro is an unknown element. You have to admit, even his name sounds . . . exotic."

"He's a writer. We've had them stay here before."

"Not like him, we haven't." Penny grinned. "Wait'll you meet him."

"Uh-huh. Well, just remember that he's only visiting. Men like that don't put down roots in places like Baron Hollow."

"And innkeepers don't dally with the guests. Yeah, I know. Don't worry—I doubt I'll get the chance to dally. Between my schedule and his apparent determination to explore the town *and* the wilderness all around us, I'll be lucky to catch just enough glimpses to fuel my fantasies. Which is probably all I can handle anyway."

"You're probably underestimating yourself, but when it comes to guests, I'd say that's the way to go."

Penny laughed. "True enough. Okay, I'm going to go and get our honeymooners moved."

"See you later." Emma made a mental note to ask Jessie if she'd noticed any spirits in the vicinity of the Topaz Room. She caught herself chewing on a thumbnail, and forced herself to stop. But the anxiety she felt was still very much with her.

Whatever Jessie said—or didn't say—Emma was convinced that her sister's urge to reopen the old wounds of her past was something that could very well have consequences Jessie hadn't considered.

Assuming Victor had, in fact, been involved, Emma was certain he would go a long way to protect his reputation. If Jessie confronted him, if she asked the wrong question—or the right one— if whatever had happened even all those years ago reflected badly on him . . .

For the first time, that struck Emma as odd, the fact that whatever had happened to Jessie had *not* gotten around town all those years ago, had not become the subject of gossip. That was just the sort of gossip the town thrived on, and Emma most certainly would have heard about it, especially once Jessie had left—or run away from—Baron Hollow.

What that told her was that Jessie had not awakened in somebody else's house after a party, disoriented and disheveled after whatever had happened to her, forced into a dazed walk of shame past others to get herself out of there and home.

She had somehow gotten home, on her own or with help, and no one had seen her—or noticed anything unusual if they had.

Had someone snuck her into the house? Because it would surely have been very late, and for all his preaching of individual responsibility and self-reliance, their father had kept his teenage daughters under a strict curfew: Jessie might well have been able to sneak in past curfew if she hadn't been drunk or hurt, but if either had been true, could she really have gotten into the house without waking anyone?

Unless . . . it had been during one of their father's regular and sometimes lengthy business trips out of town. By then, he had been accustomed to leaving the girls on their own, with only the middle-aged housekeeper/cook, a live-in widow who had taken no more than a cursory interest in either of the girls and was there more for form's sake than to exert any authority over Jessie and Emma.

It occurred to Emma, not for the first time, that there were a lot of questions she should have asked herself when Jessie had left—and since then. And even more since Jessie had come home.

For the past, she had no excuse for not asking if something had been wrong, if something had happened to hurt or frighten her sister; all Emma remembered was that after weeks of behaving oddly, practically hiding in the house and keeping to her room, Jessie had abruptly run away, that time for good, and though upset and even angry, there had been little Emma could do about the situation.

Angry? Why had she been angry? Because Jessie had left without even saying good-bye? Because she had escaped and left Emma to endure a small-town life with little change and even less excitement? Maybe. Maybe that had been it. Emma wasn't sure.

But she was sure that, for the present, she hadn't asked Jessie more than a few questions because Jessie had made certain she wouldn't. It wasn't only her psychic walls that were up; Jessie had put even more distance between herself and her sister, and it was all too clear she didn't want that gulf crossed.

For whatever reason.

Emma realized that she had exchanged one anxious habit for another; she was absently fingering the small scar in the hairline over her right temple. It told her that her anxiety level was intensifying.

What it didn't tell her was why.

* * *

HE WAS ABLE to get ahead of his prey easily and with enough time to get himself set and ready for her. After so many years as a hunter, he knew what he was doing. And he was very, very careful to make no mistakes.

He settled in and waited, and within fifteen minutes or so, he saw her coming toward him. One look told him she had relaxed her guard somewhat; it was virtually impossible to be guarded for an extended length of time, and that was something he often took advantage of.

She was already questioning herself, doubting what she had felt or sensed earlier. Convincing herself there was no good reason for her to be jumpy.

Good.

He was so perfectly camouflaged in the brush beside the trail that she came within two feet of him without seeing him. In the last instant, as he leaped, he thought she sensed danger, but by then it was too late for her to react effectively.

He had the gun holster unclipped from her belt and tossed out of reach before she could even make a move for it, and was so adept with his razor-sharp knife that the loop holding the pepper spray around her wrist was severed before the gun hit the ground. He cut through the nearest strap of her backpack, and as that weight fell away from her, he had her in his arms, trapped.

107

She struggled for only a moment, instinctively, before the knife pressed to her throat drew blood. Then she went still.

"Make a sound," he breathed, "and it'll be your last. Got it?"

Her chin barely moved in a nod. She was breathing in terrified little gasps, and, held tightly against him, her body shook.

He had her bound and gagged with duct tape and with the hood over her head in a matter of seconds, so practiced in his art that she never even got the chance to plead for her life.

That would come later.

He gathered up the gun and pepper spray, zipping both into her backpack, then hoisted her over one shoulder, picked up the backpack, and set out through the forest, away from the trail.

She smelled like fear.

He liked that.

JUNE 30

Nathan Navarro had settled in nicely over the past couple of days. Baron Hollow had at first seemed no odder to him than most small towns and rather more welcoming than he had expected—though that could have been due to his ostensible reason for being here. He'd been warned; people were intensely curious about writers.

The locals hadn't wasted much time. He had

patiently answered the usual questions about his surname—yes, Spanish in origin but generations back, and really quite a common name in the US and, yes, he was aware that he looked more black Irish than Spanish, a trait for which he credited or blamed his mother—and quite a few about his supposed job.

"Where do you get your ideas?" seemed to be the most popular.

He'd been warned about that too.

But all in all there had been only polite, casual interest in him and only a cursory interest in his movements.

Which was just as well.

It had given him at least some time and opportunity to get the lay of the land, both literally and figuratively. He was more resigned than surprised to find both cell service and high-speed Internet spotty at best, and the terrain surrounding Baron Hollow was difficult, remote, and had a well-deserved reputation for having sheltered for generations more than one fugitive from the determined searches of cops and feds.

There was more than a little bit of bad history here, rather famously so, back during Prohibition and even further back to the Civil War, and bad feelings about various wrongs lingered even today, which was one reason he was undercover.

One reason.

The dense mountain forests surrounding Baron

Hollow had, in fact, swallowed up a few fugitives and never bothered to spit them out, somewhat ironically since most of it was federal land. In any case, it was always possible that some of those people were still hiding up in the mountains somewhere, or maybe they had walked out at some point and just stayed off the grid.

Or maybe they had put a hurrying foot wrong and tumbled off a cliff's edge on a narrow mountain trail to their deaths; bodies left exposed to the sometimes harsh elements, predators, and scavengers were likely never to be found. And if they were found, there generally wasn't a whole lot left to identify.

Like this one.

Navarro stood in a small ravine, looking down at human remains spread out across a relatively level area beneath a granite outcropping that formed a cliff high above, frowning as he studied the scattered bones, a few with tendons and shreds of muscle still attached.

And there was the smell he recognized. Blood soaked into the earth, and decomposing flesh.

Death.

Not much was left of her. Not much at all. He didn't even see a skull, just a few strands of blond hair clinging to a shriveled bit of scalp at one end and tangled among sticky briars at the other. He imagined some animal grabbing the skull and tugging, making off with all but the few pitiful hairs anchored to the briars and the patch of scalp that wouldn't let go.

With an effort, he shook off the image, hoping it *was* just his imagination and not a flash of what had actually happened. As a matter of fact, something about that image bugged him, and when he knelt to look closer, he realized what it was.

Her spine around the base of her neck had been severed, and the cut was too clean to have happened naturally. Nothing had wrenched her head free of her body.

Someone had cut off her head. And though there was no way for him to know for certain if she had in fact been running and had fallen to her death, every instinct he had told him that was what had happened. Which meant that someone—either an unspeakable ghoul or an unspeakable murderer—had found the remains later and had removed her head and taken it away.

His money was on the killer. The question was, had the killer left the rest of her because this was the way he always disposed of his victims, letting the weather, scavengers, and nature clean up after him? Or had he left her here as some kind of punishment for escaping him?

Or for some other reason entirely?

Navarro rose to his feet and continued to frown down at what was left of the victim. He never got used to this. No matter how many times he found himself looking down at some variation of this too-familiar scene, he never got used to it. Which was probably just as well.

Getting used to unnatural death was probably a pretty good indication that it'd be time to hang up his spurs.

For now, however, this was still his job, or part of it. So he looked, making various mental notes. One such note was that it didn't take a forensics expert to know that these remains had been out here at least a week, and possibly a couple of months.

No, not that long. Between the heat, summer rains in the last week or two, and wildlife hungry after a rough winter, human remains would be consumed and/or decompose and be scattered in a fairly short amount of time.

If he was looking at a victim of a possible killer in the area—and one glaring omission from what he was looking at told him it was more than possible—then she had died recently.

Navarro pulled out his cell phone, figuring it was worth a shot since he was so high up and possibly near one of the cell towers he had spotted earlier in these mountains, but was still mildly surprised to find he had a signal. He hit a speed-dial number.

"Didn't you just check in?" Maggie asked by way of a greeting.

"This morning. Right now I'm hiking in the

mountains west of town. And I've found something. Someone."

"Send me a picture," she said immediately.

Navarro got the best angle he could and snapped a shot with his cell, sending it back to Haven.

"There isn't a lot to see," he told Maggie once he'd done that. "I'd say the animals got to her quickly. Probably drawn here fast because of the blood from the impact. The drop from the cliff above me is at least seventy-five feet, and underneath the fallen leaves and shit here is mostly granite. She hit hard."

"You think the fall killed her?"

"I think somebody could have dumped a body off the cliff, but this is a pretty damned inaccessible place, and why bother? If he planned to leave her out in the open for the animals to clean up, I've passed dozens of ravines off the main trails that would have done the trick. One good shove and she would have rolled down a rocky slope, into some fairly nasty underbrush and, for all intents and purposes, vanished. The animals would have gotten to her before the smell of decomp attracted any attention. No, I think she was running, trying to escape, maybe at night, and fell."

"No chance it was an accident, a hiker who put a foot wrong?"

"Take a closer look at the picture."

There was a moment of silence, and then Maggie said, "Ah. No sign of equipment. Or clothing."

"Yeah. I doubt a naked woman was running through these woods by choice. Even a teenager wouldn't be that stupid."

"I don't see a skull."

"Neither do I. And there's a clean cut through the spine I'm guessing means he found her here and removed it. Maybe to delay identification through dental records; unless her DNA is registered in one of the national databases, identifying her is going to be a bitch."

"Meaning military, medical, law enforcement, government service, criminal—or missing persons."

"Those are the choices. And your average tourist or hiker doesn't fit into any of them."

"There was no news locally of anyone missing?"

"No. I have to say, though, the place is crawling with tourists, which is one reason I'm guessing she was a hiker or somebody else just passing through. Down in town, up on the trails hiking and on horseback, pretty much everywhere you look are people who don't live here. I talked to a couple of hikers not an hour ago who didn't even go near town, nor planned to. They were just hiking up along the Blue Ridge." He paused, then added, "It'd be easy as hell for somebody to go missing

114

up here without any media or law enforcement in the area knowing about it."

"That," Maggie said, "is not going to make your job easier. Any other feelings I should know about?"

"Yeah," Navarro said. "I could feel it down in town some, but up here . . . There are some very bad vibes in these mountains. The whole place stinks of death."

Something Navarro, of all people, would know. Because when he came hunting, he was hunting the dead.

SHE HAD TRIED to get his attention, without success. At first it had baffled her, because she recognized what he was and knew he could sense what others could not. He had, after all, left the trail and gone almost directly to all that remained of—

Of her.

She kept her gaze averted from all that remained of herself, of her mortal body, because she wasn't ready to face that. Maybe she never would be.

Then again, maybe "never" was a useless concept wherever she drifted in between these attempts to break through to the world she had so recently inhabited.

Why can't you see me? Feel me?

He appeared oblivious to everything except

what his normal five senses observed. So maybe he couldn't see or sense her. Maybe this was a wasted effort. Or perhaps it was simpler than that. Perhaps her fight to stay alive had exhausted her spirit to the point that she couldn't yet gather enough energy to *make* him see her.

Somehow, without really understanding, she knew that energy was a factor. That she needed it, needed to focus it in order to break through to . . . the living.

Frustrated, she watched as he studied the remains, his face showing little emotion. Not unexpected, that; something else she knew without wondering how she knew that he was here searching for a killer, her own killer, and those who hunted monsters tended to be made of very tough stuff indeed.

But would that make it harder, despite his abilities, for her to reach him? Her energy was all emotion; she knew that. For now, at least. All wild emotion, regret and anger and bitterness for a life cut short, all of it without focus. And worry for those left to face what she had. And if he couldn't *feel* that, how could he feel her? How could she warn him of the danger?

How could she warn any of them?

She hesitated, then concentrated, staring at his face, willing him to look up, look at her. Willing him to see her. But instead of that, she realized he was growing fainter and fainter, and she recognized the pulling sensation that told her she had been here too long.

She resisted instinctively, because there was still so much to do before she could go, before she could rest.

But she'd pushed herself too much already, and as he and the forest around him grew more and more distant and blurry until they finally disappeared into a cold, gray twilight, she wondered in despair if she would be able to do anything at all to stop the monster when those all around him were oblivious to just how close he really was.

SEVEN

Jessie didn't know quite what she felt when she eventually discovered that the old road that filled her with such cold dread led to a shallow creek, on the other side of which was a neat-looking little cabin.

It had red-and-white-checked curtains hanging in the two front windows. It had a wooden rocking chair on the front porch. It had flowerpots on either side of the front steps. With flowers in them.

Surely somebody wasn't living way out here, with no sign of electricity run to the place. No . . . because the "driveway," such as it was, would surely show more signs of regular usage. Wouldn't it?

She stayed well back, taking what cover she could behind a cluster of slender pines. She still felt cold and deeply uneasy, constantly fighting the urge to get away from this place as fast as she could.

Weird. Because it looked so damned *normal.*

It looked like some old lady lived there, she thought.

But it didn't feel that way. It felt cold and dark and not a place anybody would want to visit. It made her skin crawl unpleasantly.

Jessie could feel that with her walls *up;* even the thought of lowering them to sense more was so stomach-churning she knew it would be impossible. So she tried instead to use her normal senses.

She watched. She listened.

For a long, long time.

The yard that sloped down to the creek wasn't exactly neatly manicured, but nor was it choked by weeds; there were patches of red dirt and more than one half-buried granite boulder, but the grass, such as it was, had been cut recently.

She didn't see anyone; nor was there a sound coming from the cabin. No car or truck was within her sight, but she obviously couldn't see the rear of the cabin and whether there was a second drive or roadway leading to it.

After that long, tense waiting, Jessie finally made herself move. Keeping the same distance between herself and the cabin, which was probably around fifty yards, she began to circle it, crossing the wide, shallow creek with ease and quiet because it was filled with granite slabs that were stable enough to hold her weight and near enough to one another to provide a path across the water.

On the other side, she found the same sort of ground, with pines and poor soil sporting little else but briars and weeds—until she came parallel to the side of the cabin. Someone, she realized, had gone to the trouble of bringing in tons of rich topsoil at some point, spread so thickly it was almost a sprawling berm, and had then planted the sorts of bushes and trees commonly found in suburban yards.

It hadn't been recently done, but she guessed it had been only a few years ago.

From one side of the cabin, around the back, and—as far as Jessie could tell from her position—wrapping around the other side was this thick layer of rich soil, heavily planted. There were hardwood trees that appeared to her to be at least ten years old, perhaps more. There were azaleas, most past their spring blooming season, and other flowering shrubs. There were beds of flowers separated by a winding footpath of flat slabs of flagstone. There were big garden urns, here and there, planted with flowers, and Jessie could see at least one rustic bench placed to afford the best view of the odd little garden.

Odd because this place was out in the middle of nowhere. Odd because the single "road" she could see didn't appear to be used regularly, and yet the cabin was cared for, as was its roughly two-acre yard. And odd because, unless she had badly misread her sketched map, this place was on the edge of land she owned; this land belonged to Victor.

And unless fifteen years had changed him a great deal, this was definitely not a place Victor would have for himself. Not his style *at all.*

Unless . . . a love nest? A meeting place kept so pretty and homey by some woman hoping Victor would finally settle down?

Possible, she supposed. Likely? She didn't know. But the fact remained that this place existed; it was here.

So . . . what were the alternatives? Squatters? That didn't make sense. Squatters settled down but were prepared to grab a few things and run when they had to; whoever had built this place put down roots. Money had been spent here, and a great deal of time and effort. And who would go to all that trouble on land they didn't own?

Despite the silence, Jessie had to believe that someone occupied the cabin, and was perhaps even now inside.

And she wasn't about to just go up to the door and knock.

She hesitated, but a glance at the sun told her that the afternoon was nearly gone, and that she needed to head back toward Baron Hollow if she hoped to reach Rayburn House before dark.

She really didn't want to spend any time at all wandering around in the dark. Not out here.

Reluctant, but relieved as well, she began to cautiously retrace her steps. Tomorrow, she thought, was soon enough to return. Soon enough to explore further and try to determine who lived way out here in this odd little cabin on this oddly cultivated patch of "useless" land.

And find out why the place filled her with dread.

"FOLLOW PROCEDURE," MAGGIE told her operative. "Study whatever you can of the scene, photograph for later study, then report it to the local police."

"And then keep looking."

"Well, one victim doesn't a serial killer make. She could have been running to escape an abusive husband or boyfriend; it happens. You'll have to see if you find more, or if the local police are worried enough by this one to call in reinforcements." Maggie paused, then added, "And watch your back, will you? *If* you've got a local killing, and he's been doing it for years, he'll either be very complacent—or hypervigilant to threats. You poking your nose around is likely to be construed as a threat."

Navarro sighed. "Yeah, it usually is."

"Just be careful."

"I will. Talk to you at the next check-in." He ended the call, frowning a little.

Maggie had a bad feeling about this whole situation. Bad feelings Navarro understood. Bad feelings he took serious note of, especially when they were voiced by people he trusted and most especially when his subsequent activities, such as this rapid but seemingly casual exploration, turned up a body very quickly.

Or what was left of one.

He eyed the scattered remains a minute or two longer, certain this was a fresh kill, someone who had been alive no more than a week or two ago. And still certain she had died while trying to escape . . . something or someone.

His extra senses were offering him no more than that.

Navarro's strongest psychic ability was in locating the dead—their actual physical remains; he wasn't a medium, had never seen a spirit, and barely understood how his own ability worked, especially since he'd come to it recently in life. What he did know was that he could look at a map, or just start walking, and . . . somehow . . . that extra sense led him to what he was looking for.

But locating the dead wasn't his only psychic ability. Haven and the SCU called it clairvoyance, though his understanding of the term was that it covered a rather broad range of different ways of sensing one's surroundings. Some clairvoyants heard information as if listening to nearby whispers, some had visions or dreams, and some simply . . . knew.

Things they couldn't possibly know. Except that they did.

He looked down at what was left of this woman, this young woman, and in his mind's eye he could see flashes of a desperate, dogged race through a dark forest—and the sudden plunge off a cliff that had ended it. Clairvoyance or simply imagination—he didn't know which.

Not fair at all, of course, that she had escaped a twisted killer only to die here, like this.

But life wasn't fair. And neither, more often than not, was death.

Navarro returned his cell phone to the case clipped to his belt, hesitated, and then shrugged out of his backpack and retrieved his camera. It was a good one, and he was adept at using it. He took numerous shots of the remains, then added a few of the surrounding area. He knew this wasn't a crime scene but, for want of a better phrase, it was most certainly a dump site, and he wanted to look over the photos later at his leisure and after he e-mailed them back to Haven, something he would have done even if it wasn't part of Haven's normal procedure in such situations.

Finished to his satisfaction, he put his camera away and shrugged into the backpack, then remained where he was for another several minutes, carefully studying his location.

He was a considerable distance off the trails, so he'd have to think up a plausible reason why he had ended up here; stumbling over a body tended to focus police attention rather sharply on details like that one. He set a part of his mind to formulating and answering likely questions such as that one even as he noted landmarks that would lead him—and the police—back to this place.

Then he adjusted the straps of his backpack and began to make his way back to the trail. It was uphill.

As he climbed, he continued to study the area, both to fix landmarks in his mind and because he was pondering the location of the remains and wondering how she had ended up where she was.

Escaping, he knew. But what that told him was that she had been kept somewhere in the area, likely not too far from where her remains had wound up.

Panicked and injured as she'd certainly been, in shock and desperate, it was almost certain that she had not run as far away from wherever he'd kept her as she'd probably thought she had. People lost in the woods rarely traveled a straight path, and given all the dips and ravines and winding trails in the area, the chances were good she had wandered around quite a lot without actually moving any great distance from her prison.

She had probably fallen more than once, injuring herself even more, and that would have slowed her. If she had been climbing, as she likely had been given where her remains had been found, that also would have slowed her. If he had kept her without food or water even for a brief amount of time, that also meant she wouldn't have had much strength or speed once the adrenaline rush wore off.

So she had probably been held nearby, at least as the crow flew. "Nearby" meaning within a three- to five-mile radius, most likely— and assuming she had escaped from where she had been held, and not during transport.

That still meant a lot of territory, virtually all of it incredibly rugged terrain.

Navarro ticked off the possibilities in his mind, detached because he had to be, because feeling too much for a victim's life cut short was a sure route to burning out quickly and being unable to do his job.

Whoever she had been, the girl deserved justice, and whoever her killer was, he deserved . . .

Well, to Navarro's way of thinking, he deserved a bullet in his brain, with no further human resources wasted on him. Navarro didn't believe in rehabilitation, not when it came to twisted killers.

But Navarro wasn't a cop, and he was no longer a soldier, so that sort of decision wasn't his to make.

Not unless he was defending his own life, of course, or someone else's, and that was always possible.

There were even ways to make it possible. If, that was, he was able to identify and find the killer.

"Not my job," he muttered. Well, not exactly his job. His job was to find more victims, or find some other evidence that a serial killer was operating in this seemingly nice little town.

The town that felt rotten to him, somewhere down deep, and not just out here in the mountains.

"SO YOU WERE just hiking up here and found the body?" Police Chief Dan Maitland eyed the tall man standing with him several yards away from where his small forensics team worked over remains that could hardly be called a body.

"That's right."

"A fair bit off the path, weren't you?"

"I like to explore. Paths are there because the exploring's already been done."

"Dangerous in these parts, to wander off on your own."

Navarro's wide shoulders lifted and fell in a faint shrug. "I'm no novice when it comes to hiking in remote areas. I've a good sense of direction plus a compass, and picked up a map of the area yesterday to study before I set out. Besides, I know how to live off the land, and I always hike with enough supplies and equipment to see me through a week or more if necessary. Just in case."

"Boy Scout?"

"Military."

Well, that explains a lot. It explained how the man was able to carry the obviously loaded backpack now at his feet with a deceptive ease. It explained the way he walked and the way he stood. It even explained the crisp report he had offered when he'd turned up at the Baron Hollow Police Department nearly an hour before.

He hadn't wasted words, and he hadn't seemed particularly disturbed by his grisly discovery. And he had led them back here without taking a single wrong turn, which would not have been an easy thing even for a hiker with years of experience in these woods.

I'd never have pegged this guy as a writer. Not that Maitland had ever met one before, not a book writer anyway, so for all he knew they all looked like recently ex–Special Forces guys who had played quarterback in college.

Maitland said, "So you weren't planning to return to Rayburn House tonight?"

"Hadn't made up my mind, to be honest. I let the innkeeper know I'd be coming and going, out here as well as in town, so they gave me one of the ground-floor rooms with its own entrance. That way I won't disturb any of the other guests no matter how late I'm out or how early I come back." He paused, then added, "With storms forecast most afternoons for the next week or so, I decided to get in some hiking before the weather got temperamental. I wanted to get a solid feel for the area. Lot of stories attached to these woods."

"Lot of tragedies," Maitland said. He hesitated, then added, "Not everybody is happy about a writer nosing around looking under rocks. In case you weren't warned about that."

"I was." Navarro smiled faintly. "When you write fiction, nobody much cares how many rocks you turn over; when you write nonfiction, people tend to get a little more nervous."

"Is that why you use a pen name? And why there's no photo of you on the books?"

"Not really. More for my own privacy than anything else. As a general rule, writers don't like celebrity. So Colin Sheridan gets all the fan mail—and the occasional threat—and I don't have to listen to long, drawn-out stories on airplanes from wannabe writers."

"Threats?"

"There have been a few along the way, when I was writing about something controversial. Goes with the job."

"I guess everybody has stuff hidden under rocks they'd rather stayed there."

"It's human nature," Navarro agreed. "But this time around I'm more interested in older history, in legends and local mythology, and the kinds of stories I've dug up so far here in the South usually aren't much of a threat to the living."

Maitland reached up to wipe away a trickle of sweat from his brow, and the gesture prompted by the usual oppressive June heat also prompted a thought. "Still, I'd be careful if I were you. Here in Baron Hollow, I mean. Many of the families in the area have been here since this place was nothing more than a footpath through the mountains, and with families like that, old secrets can sting even after generations."

Navarro studied him for a moment, head slightly tilted, then said, "I do my best never to make enemies, Chief, especially when it's needless. Baron Hollow has quite a history, most of it already well documented, and the ghost stories of Rayburn House *and* Baron Hollow are already well-known enough to draw tourists."

"And ghost hunters," Maitland said rather sourly. "Constant parade of them now that it's the sort of show really popular on TV. So they come here. With boxes of equipment and cameras and a tendency to scare themselves silly when a gust of wind slams a door shut or century-old wood pops and cracks because the weather changes."

"They give you trouble?"

"Not all of them, but a few. I can hardly send them packing when they aren't breaking any laws *and* they bring some much-needed tourist dollars to the community. And they're mostly harmless, if incurably nosy." He shrugged. "Still, a lot of the locals haven't been very happy to see their homes show up on some of those cable programs, even in background shots. Enough so I was surprised when Emma agreed to your visit."

Navarro offered the "official" version of events, even as he wondered about the real author and how persuasive Maggie had had to be in order to arrange for someone else to come in his place. Then again, perhaps she had simply doubled his book advance; Haven got what it needed, and being privately funded by a multibillionaire like John Garrett meant money was always on the table.

A lot of money, when necessary.

"When we spoke by phone months ago, I told Miss Rayburn I wouldn't make either Rayburn House or the town look ridiculous, and offered to let her read the manuscript before my editor sees it. That seemed to satisfy her. She'll get approval of any photos I decide to include as well."

"Uh-huh. And how does your editor feel about that?"

"I don't talk much to my editor until a book's done." Navarro shrugged, hoping he wasn't denigrating editors everywhere. "What she doesn't know, we won't argue about."

"I guess when you're as successful as you are, you get to call a lot of the shots."

"A few, at least." His gaze tracked across the several yards separating them from the remains he had found, and he changed the subject abruptly. In a sober tone, he asked, "Do you think there's any chance of making an identification?"

"God knows. Unless my people find a skull, we won't even have dental records to work with. All I can tell you is that she's been out here at least a week, maybe longer."

"She?" Navarro asked, reminding himself it was information he wasn't likely to know, even as he focused his attention intensely on Maitland; he didn't believe in mind control, but he had noticed that when he concentrated on the questions he was asking, most people tended to provide him with information. Even normally hard-nosed and close-mouthed cops.

Whether it was part of his clairvoyance or something else, Navarro neither knew nor cared. He simply used it as another tool to do his job.

"According to my ME, enough of the pelvic bone is intact to determine sex. Definitely female, probably young. No fingerprints, of course, and just about all the labs servicing law enforcement are so backed up on toxicological and DNA tests that it isn't practical even to submit a sample except in an active homicide investigation. With what's left here, I doubt very much Doc will be able to determine cause of death, and that means we play the odds and list the death as unexplained, probably accidental."

He paused. "Or a potential homicide."

"Homicide?" Navarro's voice was mildly curious.

"Well, I have to consider it until I have evidence to the contrary. So we ship the remains to yet another backed-up lab in Chapel Hill. Might hear something back in a month. Or three. And even then the report will as likely as not tell us little more than we know right now." He shrugged, wondering with faint irritation why he was being so forthcoming with this stranger. "We'll go through the motions, do what we can to try for an ID, but we have open files on dozens of missing people."

One of Navarro's dark brows lifted, giving his pleasant but unremarkable face a momentary and rather unsettling sharpness. "So many?"

"Over the last dozen years. And within a hundred-mile radius, most of it wilderness like this peppered with a few small mountain towns like Baron Hollow. Not a lot of residents to the acre, but plenty of tourists passing through, including a lot of campers or hikers who don't exactly introduce themselves. And too many of them do something careless or just don't understand how easy it is to get lost up here. So they do.

And sometimes I doubt we even know about it, so the numbers of actual missing are probably higher.

"I was just looking at those missing-persons files no more than a week or so ago, because unresolved cases bug the hell out of me." He shrugged. "We're far enough off the Blue Ridge Parkway to provide hikers with the same thing you were looking for—unexplored territory. Mostly federal land, lots of it, and pretty damned unexplored. As in remote and dangerous. The terrain aside, there are bears, wild boar, at least a couple packs of feral dogs, and even sightings of big cats have been reported. Which is why I'm glad you have a rifle. And thanks, by the way, for stopping in when you got here to let me know that. Most don't bother."

"Like I said, I don't see the sense in making useless enemies; registering a firearm with the local police is a reasonable and sensible precaution." Not that he had mentioned his handgun, of course.

"True. So is carrying a letter from your law enforcement back home declaring that you can be trusted not to panic when a twig snaps and shoot another hiker—or yourself in the foot."

Navarro smiled. "I assume you called him."

"Naturally. You got a glowing recommendation." The chief paused, then added dryly, "And I got a warning that when you dig, you tend to find things you weren't looking for. Like this, I suppose."

"It's happened a few times, I'm afraid. Maybe just because I tend to explore off the beaten paths."

Maitland grunted. "Well, too many of the usual hikers in these parts set out to explore without being as prepared as you obviously are."

"Maybe I should put a chapter about that in my book," Navarro offered wryly.

"God knows we put it in all the guidebooks and on the maps. People just figure it won't happen to them." The chief turned his own gaze toward the remains of the unidentified young woman, and added slowly, "I don't know, though. This one really doesn't feel to me like a careless hiker."

"Why not?"

"Two major reasons, the second one a lot more troubling than the first. Because she was apparently hiking alone, unusual for a woman, although we do get a few every year. And because there isn't a scrap of clothing or equipment anywhere around her. Even out in the elements like this, we usually find some rotted cloth, the rubber or leather sole of a shoe or boot, part of a backpack. Something. But not this time. Not so much as a button off her shirt." He shook his head, adding almost absently, "And if this was an accident, there should be, you know. There really should be."

EIGHT

Emma didn't sleep well. At all. Supper with Jessie had been strained, to say the least. Or, rather, Emma had been conscious of strain; her sister had appeared to be in a world of her own, and Emma had no idea how to join her there.

Or even if she wanted to.

More than once, she opened her mouth to at least attempt to talk about something serious, but in the end always stopped herself. The closest their conversation came to being serious was when they briefly discussed news of the poor woman found up on the mountain.

"I thought you said there hadn't been any murders," Jessie said abruptly.

"There haven't been. I mean, obviously if that woman was killed . . . But it could have been an accident. In fact, it's more likely than not. People die from falls in the mountains all the time. Well, often enough that all the trails are posted and any hikers warned. We even leave brochures in the guest bedrooms warning them about the dangers."

"Discreetly, I imagine. So as not to alarm the guests who *do* want to go hiking."

Emma frowned at her. "We do what's required of responsible innkeepers, Jessie."

Jessie looked at her sister, also frowning. And then her frown cleared and she shook her head.

"Sorry. I guess my mind was up there on the mountain. I've investigated a few suspicious deaths. They tend to stay with you."

"Are you going to—"

But Jessie was shaking her head again. "Stick my nose in? I don't think so. Vacation, remember?"

"I remember. I was wondering if you did."

Jessie's gaze slid away from Emma's. "And wondering if I'm still fumbling my way through fuzzy memories? Well, I am."

"No luck clearing anything up?"

"Afraid not."

Emma opened her mouth to ask where Jessie was spending so many hours away from the inn, but then closed it. If Jessie wanted her to know, she'd tell her, after all.

Clearly, she didn't want to tell her sister anything of importance.

Emma went to bed with a headache.

She didn't think she'd sleep at all, but eventually did, though the pounding in her temple followed her into dreams.

Nightmares.

She thought he must have injected her with something, because it felt as if she had slept for a long, long time. When she woke, not even sure her eyes were open because it was so very, very dark, her throat was dry, her head pounding, and she felt sick to her stomach. In those first confused moments, she thought it was because of fear.

But then she realized . . . it was the smell.

Dirt . . . and blood . . . and death.

Until that moment, she hadn't realized that death had a smell, a stench, but it did. It smelled of copper and rotten eggs and old leather and desperate sweat.

She tried to move sluggish limbs, only to hear a cold metallic rattle and feel something hard encircling one of her wrists. She managed to get her free hand moving, and felt around the other to discover what seemed to be a bulky metal cuff. She swallowed hard, and slowly moved her fingers up the heavy chain to where it was bolted to what felt like a stone wall.

Chained. Like an animal.

She grasped the chain and pulled as hard as she could, knowing she had little strength and probably wouldn't have been able to free her-self even if she'd had more.

She kept feeling around, trying to get some idea of where she was. Chained to a wall, yes. On some kind of small bed or cot, she thought. Cold iron frame, not wood. One hand was free, but her ankles were bound with what felt like duct tape, far too thickly for her to have any hope of breaking free.

It was dark, so dark. The kind of dark that human eyes could never get used to, a blackness that awoke a primal terror in her, born in ages past when only a fire kindled by primitive man kept the darkness and all its dangers at bay.

She had no fire. No light.

Only terror.

She thought she was underground, but it was only a feeling. She thought the space in which she lay chained was small—but it was only a feeling. She was cold, her skin clammy, and her stomach heaved so violently that she only just stopped herself from being sick.

In a small, still-sane corner of her mind, she told herself she didn't want that smell added to the rest.

And in that same tiny sane part of her mind, all she knew for certain was that she was in trouble. Bad, bad trouble. She put her free hand down on the cot's mattress, bent on pushing herself upright if possible, and felt wetness under her fingers. There was a lot of wetness, she thought.

She brought her fingers up to her face, and when they were still inches away, she could smell it.

Blood.

In the terrible silence of her prison, Carol

Preston heard an animal-like whimpering sound, and realized it was coming from her.

EMMA WOKE IN a cold sweat, a sour taste in her mouth and terror black in her mind. She found herself sitting up in her bed, in her pleasant bedroom visible in the faint moonlight filtering through the windows' curtains, the white-noise machine on her dresser softly playing the soothing sounds of ocean waves.

Home. Safe.

Gradually, her heart stopped pounding, and the sour taste in her mouth almost went away. She soothed Lizzie automatically as the dog whined, picking up on her owner's emotions. Neither one of them was getting much sleep these days. Nights.

It was three a.m.

She threw back the covers and got out of bed, going to her dressing table across the room. She turned on one of the small lamps, and with shaking fingers removed her journal from the top drawer, looking through several pages before turning to a fresh page and reaching for a pen to make a simple entry.

July 1
Another nightmare. But this time, she was still alive.
Being held captive . . . somewhere.
Terrified.

And this time, I have a name.
Carol Preston.

Emma closed the journal and smoothed her hand over the leather, frowning. Her mind kept telling her that it was just a nightmare, like all the others. Not real. There was no woman being held captive in a terrible, dark place that smelled of blood and death.

But . . . there was a name.

She'd never gotten a name before, maybe because in those earlier nightmares the women were virtually always enduring physical and emotional torture so horrific that they'd had no sense of self, of identity. All they had felt or thought about was agony and terror.

But this one . . . She hadn't been tortured.

Yet.

A hiker ambushed, her attacker concealed so expertly he'd been on her before she could react to defend herself. The hot breath of a whispered warning, a razor-sharp knife against her neck—and then the tape over her mouth and binding her wrists and ankles, and the hood that had prevented her from getting a good look at her abductor and seeing where he carried her through the woods.

Emma kept telling herself it was just a nightmare, not real. It was like a mantra in her mind, probably because the alternative was so awful to contemplate. But she had to.

Because maybe there was a real woman out there, a real woman named Carol Preston, and she was being held captive in a dark, dark place that smelled of blood, chained to the wall like an animal.

Maybe.

Tell Jessie. Because Jessie was, after all, a private investigator of sorts. *Tell Jessie, and then—*

Emma's mind shied violently. *Tell Jessie and get her killed.*

However experienced and effective Haven was, however experienced and well trained their operatives, the bald truth was that Jessie was here alone, on vacation, without backup of any kind.

Emma didn't even know if she had a gun.

And however much she might have, must have, changed in fifteen years, what Emma had seen so far was a withdrawn, distant, and rather secretive sister preoccupied with troubling questions about her own past, most of which Emma had a hunch Jessie hadn't reported to her boss, at least not in anything but the vaguest of terms.

Adding a possible killer into that mix . . .

No. Too dangerous.

However much Jessie's secretiveness, moods, and attitude bothered Emma, she was more disturbed by the thought of her sister setting out to find a killer and his victim. Or to find out whether there really was anything to Emma's dreams, his victims.

One body—or what was left of it—had been found up on the mountain, and though Emma had no way of knowing for certain if that poor woman had been one of those she'd dreamed about, the fact that she'd been found in the woods, reportedly with no clothing in the area around the remains, fit at least one of Emma's dreams all too well.

A terrified, naked woman running for her life.

Emma stared down at her journal, trying to think clearly. Tell Dan? Tell him what—that she'd had another nightmare? Ask him to check all the police data banks for a missing woman named Carol Preston?

What little she'd told him about her dreams had elicited the same sort of reaction she'd gotten from her doctor. They were just dreams, just nightmares that were the last vestiges of trauma from the fall she had taken.

There, there. Don't worry your pretty little head about it.

Emma wasn't anxious to see that reaction again. But she didn't intend to do nothing at all.

But what could she do? Even assuming the woman existed, and was being held captive, Emma had no idea where or by whom; nothing she had seen during the abduction before the woman's head was covered had looked at all familiar. And not a clue as to how to go about searching.

All she had was a name.

"Carol Preston," she murmured. "Who are you? Where are you? And what kind of monster is holding you?"

JULY 1

"So no luck?" Maggie asked.

Navarro had quickly located the areas of downtown Baron Hollow that offered the best cell reception, and luckily one of them was outside a little café where umbrella-shaded tables and chairs occupied a side courtyard.

They offered a selection of very good sandwiches on the lunchtime menu, and he had just enjoyed one.

"It's like I told you—the vibe of this place is really off. I'm sensing something, but it's . . . diffused. Impossible to bring into focus. The longer I'm here, the worse it is. Thing is, every time I think about going back up into the mountains, it's like coming up against a wall."

"As if you're not supposed to be up there?"

"That's the way it feels."

"Because something is blocking you, or drawing you elsewhere?"

"I don't know. Not yet." Navarro reached up to rub his temple. "And there's a damned storm on the way, so that won't help things."

Not all psychics were strongly affected by storms, but Navarro, unfortunately, was.

"Look, don't push yourself," Maggie said. "Do whatever you can to minimize the effects of the storm and wait for better timing. You'll be no good to anybody if you go down."

"Yeah, copy that."

"Have you encountered Jessie yet?"

"Not unless we passed in the street or at Rayburn House. I've been out and about or else in my room, and as far as I know haven't seen either of the sisters."

Maggie sighed. "I hate investigations when nothing seems to be happening. We almost always find out later that lots was happening; we just didn't know about it."

"That's another of the feelings I've got," Navarro told his boss. "That the victim I found yesterday wasn't this killer's first and won't be his last." And what he hated most was that, chances were, he'd learn the truth of that only by finding more bodies. Or remains.

"How's the town reacting?"

"Well, the police chief did his job and got her down off the mountain without upsetting the tourists. His official report is accidental death until evidence proves otherwise—despite the lack of clothing and other personal effects up there. From what I've heard today, the gossip mill beat him and the body down the mountain, with most of the facts well-known by now. The townsfolk are accepting the accidental death

144

theory. None of their own are missing, after all."

"That's a fairly cynical thing to say."

"I'm feeling fairly cynical. And more than a little useless, which is not a feeling I like." He paused, then went on. "With so little to go on, the chief couldn't match up the remains with anybody on his missing-persons list. Plus, his ME agreed she died hardly more than a week ago, and there's nobody on the list in that time frame."

"Nobody on the national list, either, not that matches what little info we have. I checked. The state ME will give us the DNA results, and we'll run those."

Navarro was mildly surprised. "Give us?"

"John called in a favor."

"Ah. Well, I'm glad. But it'll still take weeks, won't it?"

"Just to get the DNA through the lab, yeah, probably. But I've also tagged all the missing-persons databases, so if any woman fitting the parameters we have is reported missing, we'll know about it."

"Good." He winced as his head throbbed suddenly.

"Storm close?"

Navarro had stopped asking how she knew things like that when she was hundreds if not thousands of miles away. "Yeah. I'm going to head back to the inn and wait it out. I'll report again on schedule, sooner if anything here changes."

"Copy that. I'll be here."

NAVARRO HAD QUICKLY realized that coming and going by his suite's private entrance was practical only at night or very early in the morning. Since the entrance was at the back of the house and nowhere near the guest parking area—which, with thoughtful and artful landscaping, didn't at all resemble a parking lot—using it by day seemed to him unnecessarily . . . stealthy.

Being known as a somewhat reclusive writer with his mind on a book-in-progress was one thing; he didn't want anyone wondering why he felt the need to sneak in and out of his room during the day when the front door was much more convenient.

Of course, it also exposed him to the comings and goings of the other guests.

He hadn't yet decided if that was a good thing or a bad one.

No more than three steps into the reception area, he had to detour around a jumble of luggage, and boxes that presumably held equipment of some kind. He chose to move toward the reception desk rather than the other way, which would have taken him into the middle of what looked like a quiet but spirited argument between three people—two men and a woman.

Innkeeper Penny Willis, looking faintly harassed, said to him in a low tone, "For God's sake, don't tell them you're a writer. They'll find out eventually, but let's delay it as long as possible. I'm betting they have lots of stories to tell."

He paused by the counter, lifting a brow. "What kind of stories?" He too kept his voice low.

"Ghost stories. Unless they're the sort always looking for demons or evil forces instead of ghosts. These groups tend to lean one way or the other." She sighed. "Paranormal researchers from up North. We get them from time to time."

"So Chief Maitland mentioned yesterday."

"Oh, yeah, this little group is all excited because of that body found yesterday. They're trying to decide if they want to hike up into the mountains today or wait until tomorrow. You might not want to mention to them that you found the poor woman."

"Thanks for the warning." Navarro felt another kind of warning twinge in his head, and added, "Unless they enjoy hiking in stormy weather, they won't be going anywhere today. I'd say we've got about fifteen minutes until the skies open up."

"You can feel storms coming too? They make me jumpy as a cat."

He wondered absently if she was a latent, but another, stronger twinge made him say, "The low barometric pressure of a storm affects a lot of people in different ways. Trivia," he added rather dryly. "Writers tend to know a little bit about a lot of things."

"Probably comes in handy at party trivia games," she said with a smile.

Navarro almost said he wouldn't know about that, but instead returned her smile, lifted a hand slightly in farewell, and continued on past the common rooms to the hallway that would lead him to the two ground-floor guest suites Rayburn House boasted.

The Garnet Room and the Opal Room. All the guest suites in the inn were named after precious or semiprecious gems. He had no idea why, though he supposed the names were more welcoming than simple numbers.

He had almost reached the hallway when he heard Penny call out from the desk, "Oh, Emma, Dylan's here, in the kitchen. He wants to talk to you about that new stove."

Navarro felt another twinge in his head. But, even stronger, he felt something else, a tugging deep inside, a compulsion he couldn't ignore. He stopped and turned, just in time to see a woman emerge from another rear hallway of the big house, this one leading to Penny's office—and the office of the owner of Rayburn House.

She was a tall woman of maybe thirty with a voluptuous figure, dark hair, and striking blue-green eyes. Her face wasn't beautiful, but it was curiously memorable with its almost sculpted high cheekbones and vulnerable mouth.

Navarro certainly remembered it. Her.

She saw him, her features tightening briefly in an expression he wasn't certain was shock or some kind of anger. But it passed quickly, and though she waved a hand at Penny in acknowledgment of the message, she didn't turn toward the kitchen, but instead took several steps toward him.

"So you're the writer," she said, her voice pleasant, almost musical.

"And you own the place." His own voice was rougher than he wanted it to be, and he couldn't look away from those eyes, couldn't stop searching them for . . . something his head told him wouldn't be there. "Emma Rayburn."

"Yes."

"You had a different name in St. Louis."

She didn't blink. "So did you."

Navarro was highly conscious that they stood on the edge of the common areas, quite probably under the observation of more than one pair of curious eyes. The inn was having a busy Wednesday, and this was neither the time nor the place to go into all the questions and explanations tumbling through his mind. So, in the end, all he could say was, "We need to talk."

"Do we? Well, maybe later. Enjoy the rest of your afternoon, Mr. . . . Navarro." This time she did turn toward the kitchen, her movements as graceful as he remembered.

He watched her until she turned a corner and vanished from his view, then forced himself to continue toward his suite. He thought he did a pretty good job of keeping his expression pleasant and neutral, at least until he got into his room and closed the door.

Then he leaned back against the cool wood and drew in a deep breath, letting it out slowly. It didn't help.

A relatively simple investigation had just gotten a whole lot more complicated. And a whole lot stranger.

NINE

JULY 2

"It's the what?"

"The Arts Festival," Emma repeated patiently. "On July Fourth. Day after tomorrow. Saturday."

Jessie looked at her with a curiously blank expression for an instant, then blinked and appeared to actually *see* her sister. "The Arts Festival. I take it this is the sort of event where they block off Main Street and there are booths and tables and tents and every possible kind of junk food imaginable?"

"Well, I hadn't thought of it quite like that, but,

yeah. Pretty much the whole town turns out, plus tourists. The artists that don't have storefront space can display and sell their stuff, and there's always some kind of raffle and other prizes, and live music, fireworks at night, of course, and . . . You're really not listening to me, are you?"

Jessie blinked again. "Sorry. My mind was wandering. What do you do at this festival?"

"This year I'll be the Band Nazi."

Jessie frowned at her. "Excuse me?"

Emma sighed. "There's a lineup of local and regional bands that play all day and into the evening. On the courthouse steps. I'm responsible for making sure each band is ready to go on when the last one is done with their set, that they have everything they need. It can be fun, or it can be a pain in the ass."

"Sounds like the latter to me."

"I did it last year. It wasn't so bad." Emma shrugged. "Anyway, I wanted you to know what'll be going on, in case you want to not disappear that day."

Jessie didn't attempt to deny her frequent absences over the last couple of days; she merely said, "There's been a lot of land to check out. I had no idea."

"I hope you at least took cover yesterday during that god-awful storm."

"What? Oh, yeah. Of course. It gave me a head-ache, though, so that's why I went to bed early."

Without seeing or speaking to her sister.

Emma said, "I thought maybe the spirits of Rayburn House were still bothering you."

With a fleeting look of surprise, Jessie said, "You know, I've hardly noticed the last day or two. Other things on my mind, I guess."

Aware of her sister's barely masked impatience to be on about her business—whatever that was— Emma said, "I guess. Should I expect you back for supper?"

"Well, back by dark, at least. Whatever you want to order in is fine with me."

"Okay."

Jessie didn't appear to notice anything odd about Emma's voice, but just waved a casual hand and left the inn, shrugging into her ever-present backpack.

Crossing from the reception desk, Penny said sympathetically, "If you need a shoulder, I'm here."

"That obvious, huh?"

"You mean obvious that you and Jessie haven't exactly connected since she's been here? Afraid so."

"Well, I don't know why I expected it to be otherwise. We weren't emotionally close as kids, and we took two very different paths in growing up. Fifteen years is a long time."

Penny frowned. "Yeah, but . . . Look, it's none of my business and you can tell me so, but if you ask me, Jessie didn't come back here to connect with family. There's something else going on with her, and whatever it is, it's very, very important to her. She's a woman on a mission."

The word choice didn't strike Emma as at all odd. She thought about the little Jessie had confided about the fuzzy but clearly disturbing memories of something happening to her that last summer all those years ago, and nodded slowly.

"You didn't live in Baron Hollow then," she said, "but . . . it was an odd, tense kind of summer, even before Jessie left. I can't really explain it, but I felt it, and I was only fifteen. As for Jessie . . . I don't know all of it, but I do know she went through something traumatic. Traumatic enough that it drove her to run away for good. I think this trip is about healing."

Blunt, Penny said, "If she was hurt here, then I think this trip is about evening the score. Or at least about something a lot less benign than healing old wounds. Emma, even someone who never knew her can see that Jessie is driven, and that there's a lot of anger in her. *And* it's like she's only got so much time and she knows it. Maybe it's just that her vacation is ticking away and she's got to do this before she leaves; maybe she knows she'll never come back to Baron Hollow again. But whatever it is, she's pushing herself to get *something* done, and I don't think it's healing."

"Yeah." Emma sighed. "Look, I have a couple

of errands this afternoon. Can you hold down the fort?"

"Sure. I'll watch Lizzie if you like."

"No, I'll take her with me." She usually did, especially since most of the downtown businesses had no problem welcoming a well-behaved dog on a leash.

One of Emma's appointments was at the family lawyer's office, but that was later on; right now, she had a restless need to be out of the inn, and knew she had to obey the nagging urge to tell *someone* about her latest dream.

Even if he did pat her on the head, metaphorically, for her trouble.

Police Chief Dan Maitland didn't quite do that, but he also couldn't quite hide his impatience. "Another dream? Emma—"

"I know, I know. We've talked about this before. But this time I have a name, Dan. Carol Preston. Could you at least check and see if she's on a missing-persons list somewhere?"

He jotted down the name on a notepad by his phone. "I'll check it, but I can tell you she isn't on any local or statewide list, not unless she was just added. I've been poring over those lists since the body was found up on the mountain."

"No luck yet, I take it?"

"No. And, honestly, I'm not expecting any. Even when the lab gives us DNA, chances are high that hers isn't in any database because most people's isn't unless they're known criminals, government, or military. Hell, I'm just now getting my people registered into the law enforcement database, and in some small towns they aren't bothering to do that. Still a lot of debate about the information being misused." He shrugged a bit wearily.

Knowing he had undoubtedly put in some long hours since the remains had been found, and had more long hours to come because of the festival, Emma got to her feet. "I know you have things to do. Just . . . If that name should show up in any of your searches—"

"I'll let you know right away," he promised, also rising. "In the meantime, why don't you and Lizzie go enjoy the preparations for the festival. She's giving me that look again."

Emma glanced down at her dog, who was standing by his desk and was indeed staring up at him, and laughed. "Sorry, but you know she doesn't like many men. She growls at Victor, and I think he takes it as a personal insult."

"Because not everybody loves him?" Dan suggested wryly.

"I think that's it, though he just says animals always like him and that Lizzie is the problem."

"Uh-huh. Figures. Well, I won't blame her for not liking me, but that stare is a little unnerving. If not before, I know I'll see you at the festival. You're in charge of the bands again this year, right?"

"For my sins, yes." Emma lifted a hand in farewell and left his office. She said hello to a few of the officers and staff she knew, but kept moving through the building and outside.

She checked her watch and frowned to find it had stopped, but didn't think much about it since a clock on the corner of a downtown bank told her what time it was. She still had some time to kill before her appointment at Trent's office, but she was too restless to return to the inn.

At least, that was what she told herself as she set out for what she trusted appeared to be a leisurely walk with her dog.

She was just restless. It had nothing to do with Navarro.

Nothing at all.

SHE HAD THOUGHT—hoped—that her eyes would accustom themselves to the darkness and she'd be able to see at least some details of her prison. At least, part of her hoped that; another part of her didn't want to see.

But as the hours passed, Carol Preston discovered that there was a darkness so absolute that human eyes were not designed to penetrate it. There was no light in this place, absolutely no light.

If she was going to explore her prison, it would have to be by touch.

Everything in her shuddered at the idea.

She would never have called herself brave, but she always had been confident. She clung to that, telling herself that she needed to do her best to figure out just how bad the situation was. After all, maybe her captor had slipped up and left something within her reach that she could use to free herself.

It was possible.

It was all the hope she had.

Bracing herself mentally, she began to slowly feel her way around the entire cot. The mattress had many wet spots, plus the stiffness of material that indicated it had been wet once but had dried.

As her nose had adjusted to the smells of her prison, she had identified both urine and feces, and with her own bladder beginning to be uncomfortably full, she had been conscious, absurdly, of the entirely human, shameful fear that she would wet herself. Or worse.

Now, feeling the wet and damp and stiff areas of the mattress, she had a good idea that she wasn't the first with that problem. She hunched over to smell the mattress here and there, and definitely smelled urine as well as blood.

With an effort, she put that out of her mind and, with an almost overpowering reluctance, eased off the cot and onto what felt like a hard-packed dirt floor. The chain that fastened her to the wall allowed her to move only that far, only off the cot and onto her knees. She couldn't even maneuver herself to get her taped ankles in a position so she could get to her feet.

In fact, her feet felt numb, and for the first time she wondered if the duct tape was so tight it was cutting off the circulation to her feet.

Nifty little way of keeping your captive from running.

Kneeling there, terrified, she slowly reached out, inching her fingers along the dirt floor.

Wood. It felt like the leg of a chair or something, but when she felt all the way to the bottom, she realized it was sunk into the ground. She didn't know how far, only that the leg hardly moved at all when she wrapped her cold fingers around it and pulled.

She felt a bit more, and discovered a second leg. This time, she slowly, very slowly, worked her fingers up until she felt the edge of a seat.

A chair. She was almost sure it was a chair.

Almost at the limit of her reach, she probed a bit farther and felt . . . hair. Long strands. Sticky.

Sticky with blood?

Her stomach heaved, but once again Carol managed not to vomit. Instead, she stretched out as far as she could, barely feeling the pain of her manacled wrist, and forced herself to follow the trail of hair across the chair's seat.

She felt something else. At first, because her fingers were so cold, she thought that was why what she touched seemed so very cold. But then, as she pressed, then slowly explored, she realized she was touching human flesh that had been refrigerated. Or frozen.

She was touching a terribly beaten and swollen human face, and it was turned toward her.

A face. A head.

No body.

Carol Preston scrambled back onto her cot, not even aware now of the high-pitched keening sounds coming from her own throat.

NELLIE HOLT STRETCHED luxuriously, gauged the lack of reaction from beneath half-lowered lashes, then sighed with more impatience than hurt. "You really are a bastard, Vic; you know that?"

"Why this time?" Victor Rayburn asked absently.

"We just had hot monkey sex in the middle of the afternoon, and both your hands are on your BlackBerry instead of my boobs."

"Well, 'had' being the operative word," he said, still without looking at her. "We *had* hot monkey sex. We're done now."

Nellie threw a pillow at him.

He ducked, proving both eyes hadn't been on his cell phone, and tossed the small device aside as he reached for her, grinning.

She evaded him. "Oh, no, not now, you don't. I've been insulted. No more hot monkey sex for you, buster."

"How about hot doggie sex? Or even—"

"I'm sorry I started this," Nellie announced, cutting him off before he could become even more outrageous.

He pushed her back onto the remaining pillows and let her know in no uncertain terms that hot sex of any variety was still very much on his mind.

"Okay," she said at last and somewhat breathlessly, "I'm game if you are. But it *is* nearly four, and—"

"Oh, hell," he said, sitting up.

He hardly sounded out of breath, Nellie noted ruefully. "Appointment?" she asked.

"Yeah; sorry." He ran his fingers through dark hair and sent her an apologetic look from blue-green eyes. "I have a meeting with Emma at Trent's office."

Nellie banked pillows behind her as she watched him moving around the room, naked and unself-conscious, gathering his clothing. "How come you and Emma can only talk with a lawyer in the room these days?"

"You know Emma."

"Yeah. And I know you. Better than most, I dare say. So what's going on with you two?"

"Usual family shit."

Since he hadn't confided what sort of "usual family shit" was going on between him and his cousin, Nellie opened her mouth to ask. But before she could frame the question in some innocent, undemanding way, he asked an entirely normal question of his own, so normal that she tried not to think he had deliberately cut her off before she could ask him anything more.

"Do you mind if I take a quick shower?"

"No, of course not. Go ahead. I left out clean towels for you."

"Thanks, love." He disappeared into the bathroom, pushing the door to behind him, but not closing it all the way.

Lying among tumbled sheets, Nellie thought about that. And about the careless endearment. He'd steam up her bathroom and half her bedroom before his "quick" shower was done. And as for the endearment, she was neither young enough nor naive enough to take it at surface value.

She was not Victor Rayburn's love.

A month ago, even a year ago, she would have said with confidence that his love was himself, pure and simple. Vic Rayburn thought a lot of himself. It was part vanity, part arrogance, and an awful lot of confidence. He enjoyed being a Man to Be Reckoned With in Baron Hollow, a man with money and influence, a certain amount of power. A very good-looking man with charm and sex appeal oozing out of his pores.

A lucky "catch" if the woman wanted a fun time in bed.

But a very elusive lover if she expected anything more.

He suited Nellie perfectly.

A man who drove the right car and wore the right clothes and knew just how to make himself agreeable.

Nellie had wondered, once upon a time, what kept such a paragon in a fairly boring little backwater town like Baron Hollow. But she thought she knew now.

Because here he was Victor Rayburn, and his opinion on just about anything mattered. He was from an old, established family highly respected in the area, with parents who had left him a couple of reasonably thriving businesses that other people ran for him, plus a very large house and enough land that it could almost be termed an estate, and numerous rental properties that brought in nice income.

But even with all that, most anywhere else he would be just another good-looking, charming man with a fair amount of money and an aversion to matrimony and other long-term relationships. Which meant he would be rather ordinary.

So Victor had chosen to be Someone Special in Baron Hollow rather than being Someone Ordinary in another place.

She was pretty sure that at forty he had thoroughly enjoyed his life to date, and that he had no regrets. But she was also pretty sure that something had changed recently, and even though Nellie was only a part-time reporter for their small local daily—and did that mostly for kicks—she'd caught the whiff of some kind of interesting story over the last week or so.

Though they'd never been on especially close terms, it was obvious that Vic and his cousin Emma were both harboring a new tension these days. Since . . . since sometime around when Jessie had arrived, now that Nellie thought about it.

Nellie frowned, trying to decide if the hostility between the cousins had begun since Jessie's visit. She wasn't sure. Nellie had barely been aware of Jessie when they were kids, and she'd caught only a glimpse or two of the other woman around town in the last few days.

Not that she'd expected anything else; Jessie hadn't viewed her as a friend fifteen years ago, so it was highly unlikely she would view her as one now, and the feeling was mutual. Nellie had always been casual friends with Emma, but this being a small town and the both of them small-town women, they tended to see each other at various committee meetings or town events; theirs wasn't the sort of friendship that involved lunches out or other deliberate social plans.

In any case, there was really no way for Nellie to know for sure whether Jessie had been the cause of tension between Victor and Emma unless she managed to corner Emma and ask her about it outright. But Emma had been uncharacteristically elusive, even slippery, in recent days, and Nellie had been granted no opportunity to satisfy her curiosity.

Especially since Victor had been evasive as well.

Nellie leaned forward, looping her arms around her upraised knees, and stared absently toward the bathroom door, watching steam curl out and begin to reach upward for the ceiling.

Jessie. Was she still the irresponsible, dramatic troublemaker she had been when she'd put her little Ford Mustang in gear and Baron Hollow in the rearview mirror at seventeen? Or had Jessie Rayburn changed as they had all changed in the ensuing fifteen years?

EVEN WITH THE driven determination to break through, it took more strength than she thought she had left to do it again—and she had the suspicion that it would cost her.

She decided to think about that later.

When she did break through, she was more than a little surprised to find herself where she was, though she wondered why she should be. She had worked out for herself that Jessie's walls were up and reinforced with all her considerable will; for whatever reason, Jessie had closed herself to the spirit world.

This one was more open, even if she didn't know it.

She had never even met Nellie Holt, but in this in-between place where she found herself, she knew this woman. At least up to a point. She knew who she was, her name, odd little facts about her.

She knew she could trust Nellie.

Even so, she hesitated. To find, in such a small, interconnected town, people she could be absolutely sure weren't in some way involved . . . that was hard. Finding somebody who might actually care and help Jessie—and Emma—before it was too late was even harder.

So far, he had gotten away with killing for a long, long time; if that didn't change, if he wasn't stopped, he'd only grow bolder. He might decide he was truly beyond the law, that he'd never be caught.

Especially if he felt threatened, felt that he had no choice except to move swiftly to protect his secret. By taking the chance of changing his hunting methods.

By going after someone local.

Like Jessie. Jessie, who was busy uncovering a past that threatened his secret.

Jessie, who had a history of running away, and was so very vulnerable because of that.

Because who, really, would be surprised if Jessie disappeared, if she "ran away" again?

Not even her sister.

The spirit drifted closer, frustrated yet again

because she knew her presence was unseen, unfelt.

It was humbling to watch the world go on without you, she had realized. Even in the best of times, it had to be that. But this wasn't the best of times, and, dammit, she needed *help.*

Someone had to stop him, and soon. Because once he got rid of Jessie, and perhaps even Emma . . . he could go on killing for years without anyone being the wiser.

This town needed help. All his future victims needed help. Jessie and Emma needed help. They needed someone or something to stand between them and the monster.

At the very least, they needed someone who *knew* the monster existed.

It would be so much easier, she thought, if she could just explain things. Lay it all out. Ten minutes of straight talk, even five minutes, would do it. Hell, two minutes and she could get an important point or two across. But even if she'd had the strength for that, and even if someone opened a door for her so she could have had those five or ten minutes, there were things the universe just didn't allow.

Both the living and the dead had their own roles to play—and some things had to happen just the way they happened.

Still, she wasn't entirely useless, even now. There *were* a few things she could do.

So she focused, concentrating as hard as she'd ever concentrated in her life, and did all that she could to offer what she knew all too well was a dangerously enigmatic warning.

TEN

Well, to be fair, Nellie mused, Vic hadn't changed all that much in fifteen years.

In his entire life, really.

And she didn't think Emma had changed. Despite going to the other side of the country to college, with scant visits home during those four years, she had returned to live in her family home when she could easily have gone elsewhere, still the friendly, sweet-natured, small-town girl she had always been, with a pleasant sense of humor and a career as a teacher that allowed her to take regular summer trips exploring the country and even the globe. But no matter where she went, she always came home. And she was still the girl who kept her mother's single strand of pearls as a treasured heirloom.

She almost never wears them, though. I wonder why.

It was the sort of niggling question that had driven Nellie to write for the local paper even though she didn't have to earn her living; she certainly wasn't wealthy, but frugal parents had left her a nice little inheritance and a house with no mortgage, so she was able to indulge herself with an interesting part-time job and quite a lot of very satisfying charity work in the community.

Right now, it was the niggling little question that was occupying her. She liked puzzles. She liked mysteries. She liked trying to figure things out, for a story or an article—or just her own satisfaction.

Working for the paper just gave her a legitimate reason to express her curiosity.

To poke my nose into other people's business.

She leaned over and reached into the top drawer of her nightstand, drawing out a notebook and pencil. She turned to a fresh page and made a note to herself, not even sure she could come up with a good reason to ask Emma about the pearls—or her newly tense relationship with her cousin, for that matter.

Not that Vic and Emma had ever been really close, but they'd been at least outwardly casual with each other for as long as Nellie could remember. Even as young people, they'd seemingly gotten along, once the ten-year age difference wasn't really a factor.

So what was going on now? And why did they need to meet at the office of the family lawyer to discuss something? It shouldn't be inheritance stuff; Rayburn House as well as various other properties and funds had been left to Emma and Jessie when their father had died five years back, and Nellie could well recall Vic's surprise that his uncle had left him a treasured classic car (which he now happily drove) because he hadn't expected to be left anything at all.

As far as Nellie knew, Emma had never cared about that car, had certainly never resented Vic inheriting it, and had most certainly had her hands full managing the bulk of her father's considerable estate, especially with Jessie's absence at the time—and since then.

The only change that might have affected the cousins' relationship, as far as Nellie could see, had been Jessie's sudden and—to her, at least—unannounced visit.

So what dust—or dirt—had been stirred up by the return of the prodigal daughter?

Nellie sat there with her knees drawn up, pencil tapping absently against the notepad for a few moments as she thought about that. She could come up with various ideas easily enough, because she had a lively imagination—really too lively for the newspaper business, her boss had told her more than once.

But the problem right now was that her ideas were all over the place, from simple to soap-opera dramatic; without a person or event to start her off, some inkling of what was going on inside the Rayburn family, there was really no reasonable way for her to guess.

Eventually, she sighed and gave it up for the moment, returning her attention to the bathroom door, where steam was emerging thicker now and beginning to crawl across the ceiling toward her. She watched it for a moment, not really thinking about anything until a familiar, idle thought crossed her mind.

If he uses up all the hot water, I'm going to be pissed.

Sighing, she glanced down as she started to close the notebook.

And caught her breath, an icy finger trailing down her spine.

There was her note to herself to find a casual way to ask Emma about the pearls. Her handwriting, of course. Of course.

Beneath that, more than halfway down the page, a series of ragged letters slanted drunkenly across the lined paper. They hadn't been there when she had made her note. She didn't remember writing them, and they most certainly weren't in her handwriting.

HELP ME . . . MURDERED
FIND THE TRUTH. BE CAREFUL.
HE'S WATCHING.
JESSIE . . . THREAT
PROTECT EMMA

The message wasn't written in pencil. It was . . . red. Nellie moved a trembling thumb and slowly tested a letter. It smudged wetly on the page.

Blood.

Nellie stared at the message, trying to wrap her mind around the impossibility of it, her throat suddenly dry as she swallowed, an icy finger skittering up and down her spine. Usually, she enjoyed a good mystery.

This one scared the hell out of her.

WHEN NAVARRO EMERGED from his room after the storm had finally passed and his headache had eased, he discovered innkeeper Penny Willis in the large foyer area that was a central hub for the common rooms, hallways, and main stairway leading to other parts of the house, having a quiet but firm conversation with the three paranormal researchers.

He lurked, still in the hallway.

". . . guests can't be disturbed. I realize that you wish to explore the house but, really, occupied rooms are off-limits, and right now nearly all our rooms are occupied."

The woman, a slender brunette with an earnest expression, said, "The family floor has the greatest reputation for events—if we could just do a walk-through some evening when Miss Rayburn isn't at home—"

"I'm sorry, Miss Templeton—"

"Hollis. We're not much for formalities."

Penny's expression showed a fleeting, wry realization of that, but all she said, firmly, was,

"The family floor is off-limits to guests at all times. Miss Rayburn only allows the sort of investigation you want to conduct when she isn't in residence here. Unfortunately for you, she's here all summer."

"But if we asked her—"

"I'll pass on your request. I give you my word." Penny's voice was even firmer, kind but definitely discouraging any further discussion of the subject.

The one named Hollis looked at her male companions, disappointment on her face. The older of the two men shrugged and said, "We can do some research in the family archives, and I have contacts in other paranormal research groups who've been here. We can at least go over the ground that's already been covered."

The younger, taller man added calmly, "Best to get the preliminary stuff taken care of anyway, and avoid a needless duplication of efforts. Maybe Miss Rayburn will allow us access to the family floor later on. And there's still the town, the other locations known to be hot spots. Should keep us busy for a while."

Hollis still didn't appear happy about it, but shrugged in her turn, clearly leaning toward defeat, however unwillingly. "Yeah, yeah. I guess. But, Miss Willis—"

"Penny."

"Penny, thanks. You will tell Miss Rayburn we have the utmost respect for her privacy and, if allowed access, will certainly not disturb her home or spend any more time there than is absolutely necessary for our purposes?"

"I will."

"Thank you." She looked at her fellow researchers. "Gordon, if you want to get started in the library, maybe Reese and I can take a walk around Main Street and get some preliminary readings. This might be a good time, what with the storm just past."

The older man nodded and headed for the inn's library and family archives without further hesitation. Hollis and Reese, each carrying what looked like a laptop-sized shoulder bag, nodded to Penny and headed for the front door.

Navarro waited until they were well out of sight and Penny heaved a faintly exasperated sigh of relief, then came out of lurker mode and joined her.

"I thought I caught a glimpse of you," she said to him.

"Figured I'd avoid them as long as possible," he said.

"Smart man. Like I said, we've had paranormal researchers here before, even regularly, but this group seems especially keen to visit the family floor."

"And Miss Rayburn doesn't allow it when she's in residence. Yeah, I heard you tell them."

She tilted her head slightly, a definite curiosity

in her eyes. "Do you two know each other, by the way? Yesterday, when she came out of her office, it looked like you might."

Deliberately, Navarro said, "I never met Emma Rayburn until yesterday."

"Ah. My mistake."

Navarro decided she wasn't entirely convinced, but didn't waste his time trying to change her mind; he had a hunch that would only make her more certain that they had, in fact, met before, and that there was some unusual, interesting reason why he was denying it.

He suspected Penny loved a good story even more than the writer he pretended to be loved one.

So he merely nodded and left the inn, bent on doing more exploring to try to satisfy the nagging feeling he had that he shouldn't look to the mountains for his answers, even after finding human remains there.

The answer was closer; he could feel it.

The same way he could feel something dark in the very air of this seemingly peaceful, pretty little town.

POLICE CHIEF DAN Maitland eyed the two paranormal researchers sitting in his office and tried not to register too much disbelief. "You want permission to hike up to where Jane Doe was discovered?"

The woman shifted a bit as if in discomfort, and

said, "You've already given her that designation? Poor soul."

"There wasn't a lot left to identify," Maitland told her. "I didn't have much choice in what designation or name to use."

"But surely dental records—"

"Her skull wasn't recovered."

This time, the attractive brunette looked a bit queasy. "Oh. I see."

Her partner glanced at her, then looked at Maitland. "We've viewed crime scenes before, Chief."

"Far as we can determine, it isn't a crime scene. In all likelihood, either she fell or else her body was dumped there after she was killed."

"So maybe an accident and maybe not?"

Maitland sighed. "Right now, I'm considering it a potential homicide due to several factors, which, as I'm sure you're aware, I can't discuss outside the investigation. But unless and until we get an ID, there really isn't anywhere for the investigation to go."

The man who'd introduced himself as Reese DeMarco nodded. "We don't want to step on any toes, Chief. And we don't want to get in the way. But sometimes we are able to . . . glean bits of information potentially useful to law enforcement."

"You've helped the police before?"

"Well, we've provided information. Whether it's

been useful is something we haven't been told. We've found that most law enforcement agencies don't like to admit that any of their leads were obtained through unconventional sources."

Maitland tried to imagine what the people of Baron Hollow would think if he followed a lead offered by a self-avowed psychic. Legend, myth, and reputed hauntings aside, his community was a hardheaded, hard-nosed one, by and large, and he knew very well they weren't much impressed by self-avowed psychics.

He kept his expression neutral, however. Because he didn't see the sense in offending visitors when Baron Hollow depended on their tourist dollars, and because he preferred to at least pretend he was a man with an open mind.

"You can be sure I'll follow up on any lead I get, Mr. DeMarco, no matter where it comes from. As for you two hiking up to where Jane Doe's body was found, I wouldn't advise it. You'd be well off the trails, and in this area even experienced hikers familiar with the terrain can get turned around and not know which way is out."

DeMarco looked at his partner. "If it's likely she wasn't killed at that spot, I'm thinking there probably wouldn't be any residual energy anyway."

Hollis Templeton, still looking a bit queasy, nodded in clear reluctance. "I guess you're right. She could have been killed a long way from here. And she might never have even lived in the area."

"Nobody in Baron Hollow has gone missing," Maitland assured her. "We have transients like yourselves, visitors passing through, but we keep a fairly close eye on them while they're here." He smiled. "Wouldn't want to lose anyone on my watch." Even as he said it, Maitland reflected that he had indeed very publicly lost one on his watch, even if she hadn't turned up on any missing-persons list.

She sighed. "Well, there's still Rayburn House, especially if Miss Rayburn gives us permission to explore the family rooms. And we have two churches and three other downtown buildings on our list to check out."

"As long as you have permission or it's a public building, feel free to explore. With the usual caveats, of course. Be careful, be respectful of the property owners and their property, and if you mean to photograph or video anything or anyone, be very sure you have permission to do so."

"Got it, Chief." DeMarco smiled pleasantly and rose to his feet, offering a helping hand to his partner.

For the first time, Maitland wondered if what he saw in her face was queasiness or real illness. There was something more than a little fragile-seeming in the attractive brunette. He found himself getting to his own feet, and saying, "We have several good doctors practicing here in town, Miss Templeton."

She smiled, if a bit weakly. "Oh, I'm okay. Just jet-lagged is all. But thanks for the concern, Chief."

He didn't escort them from his office or the building, but gazed after them with a slight frown, not even sure why he was bothered.

Outside the small but fairly modern police station, the two paused on the walkway for a moment, then turned to head slowly in the direction of a beautiful old church a couple of blocks away.

"Did you get anything?" Hollis asked.

Her partner half shrugged. "Not much useful, I'd say. A few tidbits. You?"

"No, I don't think I got anything useful. He's more agitated than he lets on, but finding human remains tends to do that to cops."

"You shouldn't have pressed so hard to tune in his aura. I was afraid you'd get a nosebleed."

"I'm fine."

"Are you?"

She sighed. "I keep telling you, I'm stronger than I look." But she didn't object when he firmly took her arm, more supportive than anything else.

"This isn't about strength," he said. "I know how strong you are, believe me. I also know how tired you are. You need to get some serious sleep. We both do. We won't be any good at all if we don't."

"I'm not sure we have time to rest."

"And I'm sure we'd better take time."

"What I feel about time right now . . . You don't have any sense of a ticking clock?"

He shook his head. "Not really the kind of thing I pick up on. The chief isn't happy to have an unidentified body on his hands, and something else was bugging him, something I couldn't quite read, but I don't think he's overly concerned about anything in particular."

His partner drew a breath and let it out slowly, leaning just a bit on his supportive arm. "Well, I think he should be concerned. This whole place . . . it's off somehow."

"Maybe you're just sensing energy left by the storm."

"I felt it before the storm." She looked up at him, blue eyes disturbed. "I felt it as soon as we got here. There's something wrong in Baron Hollow. Something a lot darker than a haunted inn or church. That body . . . I think she was his first mistake. Or maybe his mistake was Jessie Rayburn. Because without her, we never would have known about the woman in the woods."

JULY 3

"You've done a good job of avoiding me."

Emma drew a breath and let it out, trying not to make the action obvious, then turned to face Nathan Navarro. "I have my hands full running a business," she said.

"You weren't here yesterday afternoon."

She wasn't about to be questioned by him, and let him know that by silently lifting her brows and then turning away from him.

"Emma—"

"At least get out of the reception area," she said over her shoulder, walking into one of the common rooms that a glance had told her was empty of guests. She went to a wingback chair near the fireplace, but instead of sitting, stood behind it, leaning casually to face him with the chair between them.

He eyed the chair, only then seeing that she had yet another barrier between them. A Sheltie, standing beside her mistress. Not growling or barking, merely watching him with an intensity he could feel.

"Yours, I gather," he said.

Her expression was thoughtful, nothing more. "Herding dogs. They can stare a hole through you. Yes, she's mine."

He eyed the dog. "Want to introduce us?"

"It's okay, Lizzie," she said, after a moment.

The Sheltie's plume of a tail waved once, but her Lassie-like face remained alert and watchful.

Navarro took a couple of steps closer and knelt to offer his hand, opened loosely and palm down, and when the dog had sniffed it, he scratched her behind an ear briefly before rising to his feet. "I think she's reserving judgment," he offered, still aware of those bright eyes fixed on his face.

"She's reserved with strangers, period. It's a characteristic of the breed."

Small talk. Navarro wondered how long they could keep that up.

"So I guess I call you Nathan now," she said, her gaze meeting his.

Not long at all.

ELEVEN

"It's my name," he responded.

"Uh-huh."

"My real name—Emma."

"Well, you know, that's the thing. I have a town full of people who will tell you I'm Emma Rayburn, people who've known me my whole life. I can introduce you to the doctor who delivered me. You're staying in the family home where I grew up." She paused. "But you? How do I know Nathan Navarro is really your name when it was something else last summer?"

"I can show you identification," he said. "But we both know that can be faked. I can give you my word, but only you know if that's enough."

"I don't know that it is."

It was a not-unexpected response, and Navarro merely nodded. "I get that. But even if I have all the proof I need to convince me your real name is Emma Rayburn, what I *don't* have is an

181

explanation of why you were living under an assumed name last summer."

"That," Emma said, "is a problem we both have."

He shifted position, surprised by his inability to hide what he knew was restless anxiety; as Maggie had said, he was normally quite good at masking his feelings. But not with Emma. And it was made even more difficult when he caught a faint whiff of her perfume. Trying not to get sidetracked by the disturbing jumble of images and emotions triggered by the scent of jasmine, he said, "I will if you will."

"Let's hear it." Her tone was noncommittal.

He had already decided what to tell her, at least initially. "I'm a private investigator. I was in St. Louis looking into the disappearance of Vanessa Faber. You remember—she worked for the same company you did. Then."

"Doesn't explain why you used an assumed name."

"Strangers turning up suddenly with no good cover story seldom get their questions answered. It's a common, useful practice to borrow the identity of a real person with real reasons for being where we—where I—need to be."

"And you always find such people? With every investigation?"

"So far, whenever that was needed."

"And the real people whose names you use? I'm assuming they're compensated?"

"Of course. Zach Allen got an all-expenses-paid vacation to Hawaii. He'd always wanted to go."

Emma lifted an eyebrow. "What about this time? You claim to be using your real name."

"It's a unique situation. I'm borrowing an occupation more than an identity; Colin Sheridan is a pseudonym, and the writer has gone to the extreme of using other fictitious names while traveling in order to protect his real name; he's a very private guy. So if anyone got too curious and tried to find out if Nathan Navarro was his real name, they'd come up against a wall."

"They wouldn't discover that Nathan Navarro is a real person?"

Talk about a loaded question.

He hesitated, then replied, "Unless they were very, very good at researching identity, they'd find just enough to convince them Nathan Navarro is likely a fictional person. If they had access to law enforcement or military data banks, and the right clearance, they could find out easily enough that I am who I say I am, that Nathan Navarro is a real person and he is me."

"My, my." Her tone was mild. "It all sounds very cloak-and-daggerish. I mean, being someone whose background requires a special clearance to learn about."

"I spent ten years in the military, Emma. Naval intelligence. Because of the work I did, the military developed multiple cover identities for me—and

183

pushed my real identity into the background. Deep background." And he hadn't explained so much about himself to anyone for a long, long time. "Working now as a private investigator, that's come in handy more than once."

"Has it? Do you even know who Nathan Navarro really is?"

"I know. I have to know. To live as someone else for an extended period requires it. Otherwise . . . you can get lost."

"And you never have."

"No." *Not yet, anyway.*

Emma nodded slowly. "Okay. The writer is supposed to be here researching for a new book. I talked to him months ago. Did you talk to him months ago?"

"No. But when I needed a cover story, it wasn't hard to find out who had reservations at Rayburn House."

Her eyes narrowed. "Why wasn't it hard?"

"It's a small town, Emma. With a thriving gossip mill. Other people know your business."

He thought she was going to challenge that, but finally she shrugged and said, "True enough."

"Your turn," he said.

She looked at him for a long moment, then said dryly, "Nothing so exciting as investigating what turned out to be a murder. I just like to be somebody else sometimes. Temp summer jobs and different names."

"Emma, with identity theft being the issue it is, companies are careful these days, very careful. They check things like Social Security numbers. It isn't an easy thing to fabricate a background that stands up to scrutiny."

She smiled faintly. "They aren't so fussy with volunteers and interns. About official paperwork, I mean. I don't work for the money, but for the experience. In St. Louis, I was officially a student intern, unpaid."

"They didn't tell me that."

"They didn't need to. I wasn't even a person of interest in the disappearance of Vanessa Faber. My work never connected in any way with hers; we worked different hours and on different floors." She shrugged again. "If you hadn't been a regular at the company coffee shop, like I was, we probably never would have met."

Navarro had to admit that was probably true.

"What I want to know," she went on with hardly a pause, "is what you're doing here. What are you investigating, Nathan?"

He should have been ready for that question from her, but rather to his surprise, he wasn't.

When in doubt, tell the truth. Or as much of it as you can.

He drew a breath and let it out slowly. "My company has reason to believe more than one young woman has gone missing in this area."

Her gaze was fixed on his face, and Emma didn't blink. "You found a body. Remains."

Navarro nodded. "Yes, and she could be one of the women on my list. But—"

"Your *list?* How many women are you looking for? Because according to the official records, there are no young women from this area who've been reported missing."

"I didn't say they were from this area. Just that we have reason to believe they disappeared in this area."

Emma frowned. "So passing through. Tourists, hikers. You have reason to believe these women on your list came through Baron Hollow at some point."

He nodded again. "No evidence to convince the police, unfortunately."

"Except the body you found."

Navarro said, "Identifying that body, even assuming it can be done, is likely to take weeks or months. In the meantime, my assignment is to keep looking."

"For other bodies?"

He hesitated, then said, "As unpleasant as it sounds, that's more or less my specialty."

"Finding bodies?"

"Yeah. I learned a lot about investigative techniques in the navy, but I find bodies because . . . Well, call it a knack. An instinct."

Emma was frowning again. Very slowly, she

said, "The company you work for. It isn't by any chance called Haven, is it?"

Navarro had no idea how much Jessie might have told her sister about Haven, so even though he had carefully avoided any mention of psychic abilities, he'd known she might put the pieces together and come up with the right picture.

She was, after all, highly intelligent. And she knew this small town that was her home; the presence of two investigators, especially when one of them was her sister, was unusual enough that she was bound to look for a connection.

Play it by ear.

That was what Maggie had told him to do if his and Jessie's investigations intersected, or she—or, by extension, Emma—got suspicious enough to ask questions.

"Jessie told you about Haven?" he asked bluntly.

Emma nodded slowly.

"*All* about Haven?"

"Psychic investigators," Emma said.

Which just about summed it up, rather to Navarro's relief.

"Okay. Yes, I'm Haven. No, Jessie doesn't know I'm here. There was no official reason for me to be here when she set out. She came here for personal reasons, as you know?"

He made it a question, because he really wasn't sure how much Jessie had confided in her sister.

"Yes. To . . . face her past. Close the door, so she could move on."

"Yes. Nobody expected anything else to come of it. But . . . in the course of exploring her past, Jessie saw something. A spirit warning her that there's a killer at work here."

Emma stared at him for a long moment, then came around the wingback chair and sat down in it. "Oh, for Christ's sake," she muttered.

The chair had an ottoman in front of it, and Navarro sat there, facing her, almost touching. Every sense he possessed told him that his investigation was about to take a turn. He just wasn't sure in which direction that would prove to be.

"She didn't tell me," Emma said, half to herself. "Spirits, yes, all over the house, all over town. Lots of spirits. Even asked me if there had been any recent murders reported. But she never said . . . Dammit. I never said either."

"Never said what?"

Emma drew a breath and let it out slowly, obviously steadying herself. "Never said I was dreaming about murders."

HE'D LEFT HER in the dark for so long that by the time he entered her prison carrying a very, very bright light, she was literally blinded by it. She could hear herself whimpering, pleading for him not to hurt her, promising she wouldn't scream, wouldn't tell, wouldn't do anything he didn't want her to do.

He turned on other lights, so that she was totally blinded, and even through her pleas she heard strange sounds she couldn't identify but which terrified her. Metal on metal. Scraping sounds. Wet sounds of something being moved and dropped to the ground.

The head. He's moved the head.

The fact that he said not a word only fed her terror.

"Please, oh, please, I'll do whatever you want, I promise. I—"

He slapped her brutally across the mouth.

She still couldn't see because of the bright light, but now her eyes were watering as well, and sobs clogged her throat so she couldn't say anything at all.

He handled her with a casual cruelty, unlocking her wrist manacle and dragging her off the cot, across the short span of hard dirt that scraped her knees.

Wait. I'm naked. I'm naked?

The last time her mind had worked sanely, when she had tried to explore her prison, she had been wearing her clothes; she was sure of it. But not now.

Now she was totally naked, and she had no idea how or when he had managed to get her that way.

She instinctively tried to cover herself with her

free hand, but he was working too quickly, and the moment of modesty fled when she understood what was happening. He was fastening her onto something that was definitely some kind of small chair, and she realized it must have been where she had managed to touch the unspeakable remains of his last . . . victim.

Victim?

Never in her life had she been a victim, not Carol Preston. She was strong, athletic. She had a black belt in karate, for God's sake! Nobody had ever pushed her around.

Ever.

She wanted to fight him, was desperate to at least try, but he never gave her a single opportunity. He was very, very good at controlling her physically, at maneuvering her quickly without allowing her to have even the chance of getting a hand free to scratch and claw, and that told her he had done this before.

She thought of her little gun and the pepper spray, both taken away from her with terrifying ease, and her confident words to the other hikers about being prepared for her hike, and a wave of despair more powerful than anything she had ever felt in her life washed over her.

He wasn't going to hurt her and then just let her go.

She was going to die here.

And nobody would even think to begin looking

for her for another week or more. Looking far north of Baron Hollow.

"Please . . ." she whispered.

From behind the bright lights, his voice finally came, pleasant and almost cheerful. "There are stages to this, you know. Keeping you in the dark was one. People are always afraid of the dark, whether they want to admit it or not. Letting you realize, in your own time, that you can't escape—that's a stage. Now comes the stage where I give you some idea of what's really going to happen to you."

She started when a gloved hand seemed to come from nowhere, holding something so that she could see it.

A huge, wicked hunting knife, with a serrated blade.

Covered with blood.

Carol Preston began to scream.

EMMA ONLY JUST stopped herself from leaning closer as she looked over Navarro's shoulder at the screen of his tablet. They were in his suite because that was where the tablet had been, though Emma couldn't help a fleeting hope that Penny hadn't seen them head in this direction.

Penny could be the soul of discretion. When she wanted to be.

"Your police chief was right," Navarro said. "Nobody fitting the description of the woman you saw in your dream has been reported missing from the area. From the entire Southeast, as a matter of fact. And there's nothing on the name Carol Preston."

"How could there be nothing?"

"I mean nothing on any of the official missing-persons databases. I'll send a request back to Haven, and they'll do an identity search, find out who Carol Preston is, where she's from. And probably where she buys her groceries and gets her teeth cleaned." His fingers were already moving rapidly over the screen keys, sending the request to Haven.

"You can't do that here?"

"I'm not a hacker," he said frankly. "Haven has a lot of clout and even more money because it's mostly funded by a multibillionaire with a lot of very powerful friends and allies, but there are privacy laws, and contrary to what you may have seen on TV, it isn't all that easy to actually get access to official records concerning private citizens. I mean, she probably has a Facebook page, maybe even a blog, but aside from those providing precious little useful info, there are also likely to be a whole lot of Carol Prestons some-where on the Internet. It's not a particularly uncommon name."

Emma moved slowly away and sat down in a reading chair near the little desk in his suite. Her dog moved immediately to sit by her feet, and

Emma leaned forward a bit to scratch behind one of those alert little ears. "Facebook might give us a photo," she offered.

Navarro glanced at her, then did a bit more rapid work on the tablet. When he was done, he frowned at the screen and then turned it so she could see. "The only human faces representing Carol Prestons are considerably older than the woman you saw. The rest—and as you can see, there are many—are using avatars or silhouettes to represent themselves. Not a bad idea, actually. Too many people don't realize how vulnerable they can be when they use the Internet. When they put too much of themselves out there. And out there forever."

"Note to self," Emma murmured.

Navarro turned in his chair and leaned forward, resting his elbows on his knees and linking his hands loosely. "So you've been dreaming of women being tortured and killed."

She nodded. "Not often. Every few months, usually. And just since the accident."

"Which was a head injury."

He wasn't really asking her questions, and yet Emma heard herself replying anyway. "Yeah, a little over two years ago. Knocked me out, cost me a few stitches and a few days in the hospital." She still felt extremely wary of him, and wanted badly to talk to Jessie about him. But Jessie's cell phone was going straight to voice mail, and Emma didn't really expect her sister to return until close to nightfall. If then.

"Why a few days in the hospital for what you're describing as a minor head injury?"

"I have a cautious doctor." She shrugged. "I was out for longer than he liked."

"How long?"

"An hour, give or take."

His brows rose. "Yeah, that would give a doctor pause. He probably scared you silly with all the possible effects of an injury to the brain that would keep you out that long."

"Bad dreams seemed one of the more benign of the possibilities," she confessed. "Until I started remembering more and more details. Very violent, very scary details."

"And it felt real to you?"

"Very real."

"Not so much a typical nightmare."

"Not so much."

Navarro shook his head slightly. "But you aren't psychic."

"No, that's Jessie's deal. You know Jessie?"

"Actually, we've never met."

Emma glanced at him, brows raised. "How big is this outfit you both work for?"

"It's not so much the size as it is the scope. Many of us are based in different areas and rarely if ever visit base. I live in Chicago."

"You don't sound like it."

"I wasn't born or raised there."

Emma sighed. "Well, this is all very stiff and unnatural, isn't it? Talking about anything personal, I mean. In talking about murders and possible murder victims, we're fine."

He ignored the last part of that. "To be expected, I guess, under the circumstances. Last summer was . . . I did leave abruptly."

"But then, you never promised to stay, did you?"

"Emma—"

"Why don't we get back to talking about possible killers."

"We will. But I want you to know first that I did go back to St. Louis as soon as I could, and I did look for you. Obviously, I didn't find you. The alias you'd been using made that all but impossible."

Emma wasn't quite sure what to do with that. Or with her surprise. "Oh. Okay." She frowned. "I'm probably going to hate myself for asking this, but just what did you have in mind?"

"I was going to come clean, tell you who I really was and what I do for a living. After that, the ball would sort of be in your court." He paused, adding, "Which is where it is now."

"Oh, don't you dare," she told him. "There are a million things going on right now, many of them apparently very bad things, and what I don't want on my mind is any thought of restarting a relationship with a man I barely know. Less than barely."

He almost smiled, but murmured, "Got it. Bad timing."

"To say the least." She made a determined effort and pushed all that out of her mind. "I need to talk to Jessie. *You* need to talk to Jessie. If she saw a spirit that warned her about a killer, and I'm having dreams about a killer, bad enough. Then you come to town and right off the bat find a body? A body that matches up in some very unpleasant way with a recent dream of mine? It all has to be connected."

"In which case, you're right. We need to talk to Jessie."

"And I have no idea where she is," Emma said. "Except that she's out there looking for something, for a secret that might very well be what the killer most needs to protect."

TWELVE

Victor Rayburn was parked outside the newspaper office, waiting for Nellie to come out and join him, when he saw Emma, with her dog and a tall stranger, emerge from the inn and begin to walk slowly toward the downtown area. They were a couple of blocks from his position and on the other side of Main Street, but he could see them clearly enough.

The man might be a stranger to him, he decided, but not to Emma. She looked fairly inscrutable, and that meant she was on guard if not actually on the defensive.

He'd seen the look more than once over the years. A very private person, their Emma.

The stranger also wore an unreadable expression, but something about the way he moved told Victor he was more than a little tense. Accustomed to weighing up people, he saw a big man who was physically powerful and comfortable in his skin, with a straight posture that was possibly ex-military—

When that thought surfaced, Victor remembered that Dan Maitland had mentioned that the hiker who'd found what was left of a woman's body on Tuesday was ex-military. A very experienced hiker, way more prepared than most who chose to explore the wilderness around Baron Hollow. But Dan had been most surprised, Victor knew, by the fact that the hiker was the writer staying at Rayburn House.

Dan had supposed out loud that writers surely came in all shapes and sizes, but this one still surprised him.

Surprised Victor too. If, that was, it was the writer he was looking at now.

Frowning, he tapped long fingers against the steering wheel and watched the couple until they passed him and continued on their way down Main Street.

Something to worry about? He wasn't sure.

Wouldn't be sure until he found out just who the stranger was.

He hated complications.

ANOTHER TYPICAL SUMMER storm had broken not long after Emma and Navarro had returned from lunch—that being an excuse both had grasped to get out of the inn and do *something* until Jessie showed up.

"We could go looking for her. I could," Navarro suggested.

Bluntly, Emma replied, "Does your ability help you find the living as well as the dead?"

"No."

"Then looking for her is a waste of time. She took her backpack when she headed out, as usual, and all I can tell you is that nobody seems to see her in town, or up on the trails. I've asked."

"And you still refuse to tell me what, specifically, she's looking for?"

She watched him reach up to rub one temple slightly and decided he wasn't even aware of the action. Clearly, though, storms bothered him. "It isn't my story to tell."

"Emma—"

"It's her story to tell, if and when she wants to tell it. I promised to keep her confidence, and I take my promises seriously."

"Note to self," he murmured, then said, "If she's investigating anything that could threaten the murderer, then she's in deadly danger, Emma."

"Don't you think I know that? But I won't break a promise. Because if you're wrong—and you have no proof you aren't—then breaking that promise could destroy what little trust exists between my sister and me."

Navarro didn't remind her again what that promise could cost; in his experience, family meant complications and illogical decisions based on emotion, and he knew better than to waste his time trying to untangle that.

"Headache?"

He looked at Emma, frowned, then realized what he was doing and stopped rubbing his throbbing head. Since they were alone in this small sitting room, he said, "Psychics are often sensitive to storms. All that electrical energy in the air. It affects us in different ways, but almost always dulls our abilities—and, in my case, also gives me a pounding headache. On the level of a migraine."

"Lying in a dark room might help," she offered.

He wondered if it was concern for him or just her desire to be rid of him that sparked the suggestion, and was afraid he knew the answer.

"It doesn't," he said briefly.

"Meds?"

"No. This sort of headache doesn't respond to anything except the end of the storm." Thunder boomed, and he winced.

Wondering if a distraction might help his headache—and her worries about her sister—Emma said, "You said something about not having your psychic abilities all that long. Not born with them?"

"No."

"Neither was Jessie, I think. At least, she never showed any signs until our mother died."

"Was she close to your mother?"

Emma thought about it, and nodded. "Yeah, she was. Neither of us was close to our father, and I was . . . a solitary child happiest on my own. I guess Jessie was closer to Mom. And she was two years older than me, so Mom's death probably hit her harder." Emma felt a pang when she said that, realizing that she should have known, not merely guessed, how her sister had felt over the loss of her mother.

They had never talked about it.

Navarro nodded. "That trauma is probably what turned her from a latent to an active psychic."

"A latent?"

He gave up the pretense and rubbed both temples, but answered her because talking at least didn't make the headache worse. Much. "Some people believe and some of the science we have strongly suggests we're all born with latent psychic abilities; it's just that we never need them or nothing ever happens to . . . turn them on."

"And trauma does that?"

"Often. Physical, emotional, or psychological trauma. The death of someone close is a common traumatic trigger. Losing her mother may have been Jessie's."

"What was yours?" she asked, unable to fight the curiosity.

"I got shot," he replied matter-of-factly. "In the head."

"WHAT ARE YOU doing here?" Sam Conway, owner and editor of Baron Hollow's one newspaper, *The Daily Ledger*, stood in the doorway of Nellie Holt's small office, frowning at her. "I know you come and go pretty much as you please, but I don't think I've ever seen you here on a Friday afternoon."

Nellie waited out a deep, rolling rumble of thunder, then said, "Well, look out there; it's pouring. Vic had business after we had lunch earlier; then the storm came. I was bored at home and decided I might as well come back in and work."

He lifted an eyebrow at her. "I wasn't aware you had a story going."

"Nothing as defined as a story," she told him wryly. "Just a few questions and an itch on the back of my neck."

Conway's expression turned wary. "The last time you had an itch, I nearly got sued."

"Is it my fault a certain town commissioner had

a conflict of interest and didn't recuse himself from an important vote?"

"No, but it's your fault he got caught."

Nellie smiled. "Yes. It was."

Conway sighed. "So what is it this time? The itch?"

"Jessie Rayburn."

"What about her?"

Nellie gestured toward her computer. "I've been looking into the last fifteen years of Jessie's life, after she left Baron Hollow."

Conway leaned against the doorjamb and folded his arms, deciding not to ask why. Nellie had an itch; that would have been reason enough for her. "And?"

"And she did a damned thorough job of disappearing for most of that time. Far as I can determine, she didn't have a job, a bank account, a home or apartment, or pay taxes for at least ten of those years. She was either totally off the grid or using another name."

"How did you—"

"Don't ask."

He decided not to. What he didn't know he could deny later, and with a clear conscience too. "Okay. And then?"

"Then, a few years ago, she signed on with an outfit called Haven."

"Never heard of it."

"No, neither had I. Not really a company, more

like an organization. They aren't secretive, exactly, but they are . . . discreet. They've done a good job of keeping their activities out of the news. But there's been some buzz within law enforcement, and I have a few contacts. What I found out is that Haven is a civilian organization that more or less mirrors a very specific unit within the FBI."

He blinked. "FBI? Jesus, Nellie—"

"Oh, don't worry. They've teamed up on a few investigations when big task forces were involved, but it looks to me like Haven operates completely independently of the FBI. Sometimes they work for fees, but the whole outfit is bankrolled by a very wealthy businessman named John Garrett. He's kept a low profile, especially for a guy who's worth a few billion dollars."

Conway could feel himself begin to sweat. A nice little newspaper in a nice little town—that was all he'd ever wanted. A newspaper with pleasant articles about nice people doing nice things in that nice little town.

Had that really been too much to ask?

Nellie laughed. "You're regretting offering me this job, aren't you?"

"It crossed my mind. More than once." He sighed. "So Jessie works for this Haven outfit. So? What is it they do?"

Very deliberately, Nellie said, "Well, mostly they investigate crimes. Violent crimes. Like murder."

After counting to ten silently, Conway said, "Last

I heard, we had cops to do that sort of thing. And other law enforcement agencies. Like the FBI."

"Apparently, we've got Haven too. Or can have them, if a case fits within their areas of expertise. I'm not clear on all the details, not yet, but it looks like each of their . . . I don't know, agents, detectives, operatives, whatever, is a licensed private investigator, with at least some law enforcement training."

"You're still talking about Jessie?"

Nellie ignored that. "They're based somewhere near Santa Fe, but with John Garrett's resources, that doesn't mean a thing in terms of how widely their reach extends. They've got about three jets at their disposal, and I've found evidence of their involvement in police or FBI investigations in at least six states. And that's just what I've been able to find today. Since lunch."

"Stop bragging; I know you're fast."

"Just reminding you. I could use a raise."

"Jessie's a private detective?" Conway couldn't get past that. "Jessie?"

"Wild, huh?"

"I'll say. She was a couple of years behind me in school, but even so, I knew she had a . . . reputation."

Interested, Nellie said, "I heard the same thing, but never could trace it back to anything specific. Do you know?"

"No. Just heard she was . . . up for anything."

Nellie made a rude sound. "Well, if that's all it was, I'm betting some guy she turned down before he could get to second base lied through his teeth that he made a conquest. That's how most *wild* teenage girls get that reputation."

"If you say so." He looked dubious, but shrugged.

Nellie frowned. "Well, never mind that. Here's the thing. What makes Haven different from any other outfit of private investigators I've been able to find is their special . . . talents."

"What kind of talents?"

"Psychic talents."

Conway barely hesitated. "Oh, come on."

"Seriously. I mean, the cops I've talked to were guarded about it, but it's clear they believe something paranormal was going on in their different investigations, at least as far as the Haven operatives were concerned."

"Okay, well . . . that's weird, but so what? Just looking around, watching TV or going to the movies, you can see folks seem to be more than a little interested in the paranormal right now. All those ghost hunters and paranormal investigators and groups showing up here are proof of that. Hell, I hear another one of them is staying at Rayburn House right now."

"Really?" Nellie was somewhat irritated that this was news to her.

"Yeah." Conway was frowning now. "Wait—are you saying that Jessie's psychic?"

"I don't know what Jessie is. But she works for Haven, and they're an outfit of psychics."

"Okay, but—"

"So what's she doing here, Sam?"

"She came home for a visit." Conway shook his head. "And to check out her inheritance. The simplest answer is usually the right one, you know."

"Uh-huh. And what about the body that writer found? Jessie comes back here after fifteen years of absolutely no sign she was even *remotely* interested in coming back home, didn't even come back for her father's funeral, and first thing you know we've got an unidentified body?"

"Well, but she didn't find it."

"Doesn't mean she wasn't looking for it," Nellie said stubbornly.

Conway tried to work out her logic and failed. Which didn't surprise him in the least. "I'm not seeing a story in it, Nellie. Not yet, anyway," he added hastily when she opened her mouth to argue with him.

For a moment, Nellie was tempted to show him the piece of paper with its bloody message, and explain her own coldly frightened response to it. But she knew Sam Conway very well, so all she said was, "Maybe there won't be, when all's said and done. But it's an itch, Sam, and I have to scratch it. Do you mind?"

"Would it do me any good to say I did?" Without

waiting for a response, he added, "Just for God's sake be careful, will you? Dan Maitland hates amateurs nosing around his business."

"I'll be careful."

Conway let out a snort of disbelief, but also shrugged in resignation and went on about his business.

So, Nellie had his tacit approval to continue scratching the itch. Part of her didn't want to, though, because every instinct she could lay claim to was telling her that what she might pry open in the attempt wasn't a can of worms but more likely something a lot worse.

She opened her brief bag and pulled out a copy of the note—the original was in her safe-deposit box—glanced around and listened a moment to make sure she was alone, then opened the folder and stared down at the note.

HELP ME . . . MURDERED
FIND THE TRUTH. BE CAREFUL.
HE'S WATCHING.
JESSIE . . . THREAT
PROTECT EMMA

Since she knew Emma, however casually, Nellie had started with the only named unknown in the note: Jessie. And she had found plenty, though far more questions than answers. She'd also done a bit of snooping around town, only to discover that nobody was seeing much of Jessie, including her sister.

Which, to Nellie's mind, added weight to the idea that Jessie was here investigating something.

But what?

Was there a murderer watching? Who was he watching? Jessie? Or Emma?

Who was the threat? Who was being threatened? And who could Nellie trust with any of this?

HE HADN'T REALIZED how angry he was until she made a wet gurgling sound and went limp.

He stood there, panting, riding out the surge of pleasure for several long moments. But then, all too soon, the pleasure ebbed, and he was left staring down at what was left of Carol Preston.

He hadn't intended to kill her so quickly. He liked to play with them, cut them up slowly so he could listen to them beg and see the stark terror in their eyes.

But he was still angry about the one who had escaped him. And he was angry because things were happening in Baron Hollow, things he couldn't seem to control. And that anger, he told himself in a rare moment of clarity, was pushing him.

He'd meant to spend more time with Carol, his June Rose. But his anger . . .

He sighed regretfully, and stepped aside to lay his bloody knife on the workbench. He thought the storm was probably still pounding the countryside, but couldn't hear it down here; this place was very effectively soundproofed.

He didn't especially relish planting his June Rose in the garden in the rain, but he also didn't want to have to store her—and he wasn't certain when he'd be able to get free long enough to get back here.

He checked his watch, swore under his breath, and got to work. He moved a couple of the big lights back into the storage room, leaving himself only one to work with. In the storage room, he double-checked the freezer, and smiled at the disembodied head of—what had her name been? Catherine something. The one who had escaped him.

He had left her where he'd found her—but taking her head, though he admitted to himself he had done it in anger, had proven very useful. Arranging it on the chair just within reach of his June Rose, for her to find in the pitch-black darkness, had quite effectively terrified her.

He had watched the tape from his infrared camera.

He was still smiling about that when he sensed something.

In the cabin above his head.

THIRTEEN

Jessie had returned to the cabin again and again, watching, listening, but not daring to get closer. It was only now, Friday, that she finally convinced herself no one lived there.

The cabin was used, but it was not occupied.

Not, at least, on a regular basis.

Still, she might not have chosen this day and time to finally explore the cabin if it hadn't been for the storm. It rumbled up out of nowhere, as storms so often did in the mountains, and one look at the sky told Jessie that this one was going to be rough—and long.

She approached cautiously as always, and circled the cabin completely just to reassure herself that it was empty today. She saw nothing that made her think otherwise, even though she still had that skin-crawling feeling of dread, of unease.

Oh, get on with it.

She had managed during the last few days to shore up her walls even more, so that very little got through now. And, as always when she got near the cabin, her own unease seemed to make the walls even stronger; she doubted even another psychic would be able to sense her when she was near the cabin.

Still, her instincts kept telling her to leave, or at

least to call for help before exploring whatever lay inside that innocent-looking cabin. But the last thing Jessie wanted to do was call Haven in, maybe even the SCU, when she didn't have anything other than the words of a spirit that something bad had happened, was happening, here.

Especially when Maggie had specifically told her to get on with her vacation and leave the investigating—other than of her own past—to others.

She needed more before she called in the troops.

Satisfied that the cabin was as empty today as it had been the day before, Jessie finally left the cover of the woods and walked across the well-kept yard and up the steps to the front porch.

Which was just about the time the storm hit.

Ignoring the rumbling thunder and driving rain, Jessie went to the front door, which she tried only after donning a pair of latex gloves.

Locked.

Not too surprised, she dug into her backpack for a small, zippered leather case and took from it the tools she needed to pick the lock.

"So we're going to be breaking the law?" she had asked her boss, Maggie Garrett, when this particular lesson began.

"It's likely we'll have to bend it from time to time," Maggie had replied calmly. *"If you have reason to believe an innocent may be at risk, or can convincingly argue you suspected something*

was wrong, then a locked door can and should be breached." She had paused, then added dryly, *"Kicking a door down may be all well and good for TV and the movies, but as often as not we'd rather no one knew we got inside in the first place. So—you learn to pick locks. Problem?"*

"No. No problem at all."

As it turned out, Jessie had learned her lessons very well.

The cabin's front door was almost ridiculously easy.

It made her a bit wary, so once inside with the door closed, she left her backpack beside it and did a quick search, gun in hand.

Empty.

The cabin had, basically, two fairly small rooms. There was a living room with a kitchenette, and there was a bedroom and tiny bathroom. Everything was neat and clean, with a colorful quilt on the double bed and a number of locally made rugs scattered on the weathered wooden floor. Both the quilt and the rugs were old, and she had a strong hunch it would be difficult if not impossible for her to find out who had bought them.

But she had a digital camera she had fully charged the night before in anticipation of today and this search, and she was able to take numerous pictures of the space and close-ups of the rugs and quilt before the camera died on her.

Definitely a downside of being psychic.

With a smothered curse, she returned the camera to her backpack, then stood just studying the space. It was, she thought, a man's space, and yet it was oddly impersonal. No photographs or artwork, and the small bookcase in the living area held a dozen or so rather pointedly generic books on hunting and fishing and gardening.

A rapid check showed her there was no name written in the front of a sampling of the books, no bookplates or other indication of ownership. None of the books was new or recently purchased, she judged.

Several kerosene lanterns sat about: one on the kitchen counter, one on the bedside table, one on a rustic coffee table between the leather couch and the rock fireplace.

A gun rack hung above the fireplace, but no rifle or shotgun occupied it. In the kitchen were basic pots and pans and flatware, mostly old, nothing special about them or the plates and cups and glasses also in the cabinets. The place settings were for four, but Jessie didn't take that as significant; she knew very well that most "starter sets" of dishes and glassware and the rest came in fours.

Again, however, everything showed signs of age and wear. Even the checked curtains at the windows looked as if they'd been hung in place years before.

Both the kitchen and bathroom faucets worked,

and the water ran clear, which told her that either there was a well somewhere near with electricity run to it, or else whoever built this had managed to pipe through a lot of land to connect to the town's water supply. Or perhaps the church's, since it was, by Jessie's estimation, the closest building. She assumed a septic system for the toilet, but if the owner had tapped the town's water system, or the church's, she supposed he could have tapped the sewage system as well.

But not electricity. Because that usage was monitored, and somebody would have noticed.

Okay, suspicious—but squatters were experienced at staying off the grid, and maybe it was just that. Land gone unused for decades, remote and difficult to get to, so why not make a home of sorts here?

Because nobody was living here; she was sure of it. Visiting, yes. Staying a weekend or a couple of days now and then, sure. But not living here.

"Think, Jessie," she murmured aloud. "Is there any sign a killer uses this place? Because there are always signs . . ."

All she had to do was find one.

HE COULDN'T HEAR her moving about above his head, but he knew she was there. He could feel her, just as he'd been able to feel her years before. Sense her. It was why he had made the choice he had made that night. Well, one reason, anyway.

He wondered idly just how much she remembered about what had happened. Not very much at the time, obviously, or so it had seemed. Afterward. Maybe not anything at all.

Or maybe just enough to cause him problems.

Why else would she be here?

Unconsciously, he made a clicking sound with his teeth. "Oh, Jessie," he murmured. "You should have stayed away. You should have left well enough alone. I had the others under control. Everything was going along just fine.

"Why did you have to come home and spoil it?"

QUICKLY BUT METHODICALLY, conscious of her inner clock ticking away the time she'd have until the end of the storm and approaching darkness forced her to head back to town, Jessie began to search. She found nothing unusual in the kitchen or bedroom—the latter holding only a bed and a bedside table with no drawers or shelves.

There were no toiletries in the bathroom beyond a very generic bar of soap on the sink. Old and worn—but clean—towels, otherwise nondescript.

Returning to the living area, frowning, she began a more careful search, tapping walls that felt solid, lifting chair and couch cushions to look beneath them, checking the books—all of them, this time.

She found it on the bottom shelf, a thick book whose title proclaimed it to be *The Complete Book of Gardening*, but whose pages had been cut to hollow out an opening for a small wooden box.

It looked handmade, and reminded Jessie instantly of other boxes she had seen just that morning, locally carved with various original designs by artists who loved and understood wood.

Jessie carried the book a few steps away so she could sit on the couch and lay the book on the coffee table. Carefully, she pried the wooden box out of its hiding place. It had a tiny lock.

Child's play. Jessie had that open in about three seconds.

She didn't know what she had expected to find. Such a hiding place was, after all, not particularly suspicious in and of itself; ready-made "safe" books were easy to buy, with velvet compartments fashioned in pretend books so a homeowner's small valuables could be hidden in plain sight.

But this box didn't hold small valuables.

It held trophies.

Jessie knew what they were as soon as she opened the box, even though she had never, in her work for Haven, been on a case involving a serial killer. She had studied, as every Haven operative did, the cases investigated by the SCU in recent years. And despite a fair noninterest in the sciences, she had a solid working knowledge of the basics of law enforcement investigative techniques, including profiling.

Most serial killers kept trophies, reminders of the victims they had slaughtered.

There was a part of Jessie that told her she should have felt shocked, or sickened, by what she found, and she was bothered by the fact that what she felt was only intense interest. Until she really looked at what the box contained, and it hit her with the force of a blow that she was looking at the representations—in some cases *pieces*—of people. People who had lived and laughed and thought they had a normal life ahead of them.

Until they encountered a monster wearing a human face.

Jessie set the open box carefully on the table, swallowed hard, and began removing the items it held one by one.

Half a dozen tiny locks of hair: blond, brunette, coppery, and shades in between. A dozen driver's licenses, all belonging to young women, the oldest issue date going back seventeen years, the issuing states covering the Southeast and up the Eastern Seaboard. Half a dozen student ID cards from colleges and universities, two from as far away as California and Nevada. A small gold cigarette lighter. Two silver charm bracelets. Four gold stud earrings, each with a different semiprecious stone in the center. And—

Jessie saw her gloved hand trembling, and had to try twice before she was able to pick up the final item lying at the bottom of the box. It was another earring, but unique: a small, handmade dream catcher with a fringe of three tiny, beaded rawhide strips dangling from it.

Dear God.

Her free hand lifted to her ear, and Jessie had a flash of memory. That night, that hot night, fingers fumbling at her ear, pain when the earring was roughly taken from her as so much had already been taken from her.

The mate to that earring had been lost at some point that night as well, and Jessie was glad.

She stared at the earring, thoughts and memories tumbling through her mind. Just a few weeks after her mother's death in a car accident. She and Emma still numb. Their mother's jewelry box held open before them, and their father telling them with matter-of-factness that each of them, Emma and herself, could choose one piece of their mother's jewelry to keep as a memento. The rest, he'd said, would be offered to Sonya Rayburn's favorite charity, sold to raise money for a worthy cause, like her clothing and most other possessions.

Not a bit sentimental, their father.

Jessie, the elder, went first. She'd known what Emma would choose: the strand of pearls their mother had almost always worn. Not because Emma, only eight then, knew the value of pearls, but because her mother had often let her borrow them when she played dress-up.

But Jessie, who had always sensed beneath the poised and proper surface of Conner Rayburn's wife a suppressed and perhaps half-forgotten bohemian side, had chosen the earrings she had never even seen her mother wear.

If her father had been surprised by the choice, he hadn't shown it, merely accepting it with a shrug.

Jessie had treasured the earrings, wearing them only on special occasions.

Like that "party" when she was seventeen, when everything changed.

The ticking of the clock in her head grew louder, breaking through the memories and her absorption with a literal crash of thunder, and a glance toward one of the windows told Jessie that despite all the noise, the storm was beginning to wind down. And it was getting late.

She barely had time to get back to town before dark.

For just an instant, she was tempted to keep her earring, but in the end she returned it to the box with all the other . . . trophies. Then she closed and relocked the box, returned it to its book hiding place, and put the book back on the shelf.

The evidence had to be here. She couldn't afford to alert the killer to the fact that someone had found his trophies. That someone understood what he had been doing for years.

And, nagged by more than one unanswered question, Jessie knew she had to come back here again before she raised the alarm. At least one more time.

She had to know where he was doing the killing.

AT FIRST, HE was disappointed that Jessie had slipped away before he could get his hands on her. But a moment's thought convinced him that it would be more fun to hunt her.

Tomorrow, during the festival. That would be perfect. There would be so many people around that no one would notice her disappearance. Or his, for just long enough. And since the festival went on into the night, finishing with fireworks, he would have plenty of time to bring her back here and finish her off.

He wouldn't be able to spend a great deal of time with her, unfortunately, because the real trick was going to be planting all the evidence necessary to strongly suggest Jessie had merely run away.

Again.

Satisfied with the plan he would embellish later, he got back to the work at hand. He went into the cabin first, just to carefully check and make certain Jessie had not discovered anything she shouldn't have. The cabin looked untouched, and his prize box was where it was supposed to be, so he felt certain she hadn't found it.

He left the cabin and went around to the cellar, down into it, then deeper into his trap. He freed his June Rose from his special chair and wrapped her in a plastic tarp. He hadn't removed any limbs this time, so it was easy enough to toss the bundle over his shoulder and leave his secret room, climbing up out of the cellar.

It was still raining, though only lightly, and thunder rumbled faintly as the storm moved off to the east. With the sky still overcast, darkness was coming sooner, but he still had time enough.

He had already prepared her place in his garden, taking care as always to select the perfect plant to complement all those already in the ground and thriving.

His garden, densely planted and filled with meandering paths and small benches and the occasional tasteful statue, was his delight. He had taken care to plant it so that it was screened from any but the most determined visitors—and that was a kind of visitor he never had out here.

His secret garden.

It took a great deal of effort, and though he had to steal time from a busy schedule, he didn't need much sleep, so he worked out here every chance he got.

He was either manicuring his garden, preparing it for another lovely rose—or preparing the rose.

He used his time wisely, and today even had the foresight to dig the hole and cover it with a tarp hours ago. He laid his Rose gently on the ground, then removed the tarp that covered what would be her final resting place.

He unwrapped her from the plastic tarp, and laid her naked in the place prepared for her. They had to be in their purest state, his roses, when he planted them, naked and baptized in their own blood. He arranged her carefully, folding her bruised and broken hands over the gaping wounds in her breasts.

He lingered there for a moment, even bending down so he could gently brush a strand of blood-sticky hair away from her temple.

Perfect. She was perfect.

He looked at his left forearm, where a rolled-up sleeve left the skin bare, and studied the tattoo there. A rose all wound about within a thorny cage.

"I said I'd keep you with me," he murmured. "I promised I'd keep you safe."

He got to his feet and, whistling, began to shovel rich, dark, wet earth over his June Rose until the depth was right and he could plant above her a lovely pink-blooming rosebush.

FOURTEEN

The passenger door of Victor's Camaro opened and Nellie got in, bringing with her a wave of faint perfume and bright cheerfulness. "Hey. Did I keep you waiting too long?"

"Not at all." He paused, thinking rapidly. "It's still early, but do you want to grab dinner before we go back to my place or yours?"

It was their usual Friday evening routine: dinner and then back to his house or hers, one of them almost always staying overnight.

"Dinner," she said promptly. "I'm starving, and there's nothing more in your pantry or refrigerator than there is in mine."

Victor shrugged as he started the car. "We both prefer restaurants and takeout. Single people can afford to opt for convenience."

"Single people with a decent income," she countered dryly. "I have a couple of single friends who're learning how to cook. Much cheaper to eat at home, and they're tired of soup and scrambled eggs."

"I'd get tired of that after a day." He shrugged again. "So, where do you want to eat?"

There were three good restaurants in Baron Hollow, two downtown and one about five miles away, near the highway that bypassed the little town. There was also the usual assortment of fast-food restaurants and a couple of pizza places, but neither Victor nor Nellie considered them especially satisfying for the evening meal. Even if that meal was a bit early.

"Let's just go over to Mario's," Nellie suggested. "I feel like Italian, and even though it won't start for another hour, the music is best on Friday nights."

The restaurant in question was only two blocks down from the newspaper office, but she didn't suggest that they walk. Nellie knew very well that he liked to be able to see his classic car from wherever he was seated while out in public, not out of any fear that it would be stolen, but simply because he enjoyed looking at it.

He also enjoyed looking at Nellie, of course, but he'd taken care to leave her wondering just which he enjoyed most. Not to play mind games, but because he didn't want to hurt her, and rejection hurt; as long as she thought he might prefer his classic car to her, she was unlikely to get too serious for his peace of mind.

He did *not* want to settle down, even in theory, and in practice he found himself inevitably bored with any woman after a time.

Nellie had lasted longer than most, probably because she was no more interested in marriage or long-term relationships than he was, because she had a healthy sense of humor and a robust enjoyment of sex, and also because she got him.

Thinking about it, he wasn't sure any other woman he'd slept with really had.

"Hey, you missed an empty space," she pointed out.

He dragged his mind back to the task of driving, forced to circle the block because that empty space was the only one in front of the restaurant.

Friday nights meant downtown Baron Hollow was as busy and crowded as it was ever likely to be—except for Saturday afternoon, which, typical for small towns, was the busiest time of the week.

And, of course, the festival on the Fourth would bring in hordes.

"Something on your mind?" Nellie asked, looking at him with raised brows while he maneuvered the Camaro into that vacant parking space.

"Tell you inside," he replied absently, concentrating on parking just so for the maximum amount of space between his baby and the cars on either side. He didn't like dings.

Nellie waited patiently until he was satisfied and they could go inside the restaurant. Inside, of course, he had to greet several people he knew, regulars who tended to come a bit early on Fridays to grab the best tables.

Victor always got the very best table, at the front window, whether he came early or came late.

He flirted mildly with the young waitress, with Nellie looking on in amusement, and she waited until the slightly flustered Allison had gone to fetch their drinks before asking again.

"Something on your mind?"

Victor glanced out the window at the Camaro, then looked across the table at Nellie. "Yeah. Know anything about the writer staying at Rayburn House?"

"Knew there was one staying there. And that he's the one who found the body on Tuesday."

"Gossip, or your source inside the police department?"

Nellie laughed. "That makes it sound so . . . Big City. My source inside the police department. Yeah, Vic, when I ran into Melissa at the coffee shop this morning, she told me all about him. Well, what the rank and file know about him, at any rate, since Dan tends to use her as a glorified secretary."

He wasn't interested in the lot of glorified secretaries wearing police uniforms. "So what did she say?"

"Not a lot. He's a writer, nonfiction, and he's here researching local legends and reputed hauntings. Supposed to be writing a book about that sort of thing."

"There's enough of that in Baron Hollow to fill a book? News to me."

Nellie shook her head. "Not just in Baron Hollow. The Southeast. Word is, he's looking for the lesser-known stories and legends. We're far enough off the beaten path to provide more than a few of those. We've been written up locally, even regionally, but not nationally. At least not until the ghost hunters discovered us in the last couple of years."

"Some of those stories have made their way onto the Internet," he pointed out.

"Yeah, but nothing's gone viral. Books by legitimate writers and researchers are going to get more attention than Internet blogs or fans-of-the-paranormal sites; you know that."

"Maybe. I also know that with national exposure comes a lot more interest in Baron Hollow. And that means more visits by earnest 'researchers' anxious to catch a ghost on video or—what do they call it? When they supposedly get a recording of a spirit speaking?"

"Jeez, I don't know. And I'm surprised you know anything about this sort of thing."

"Hard not to know a bit, what with all the TV programs on now." Victor shrugged, then frowned. "Interesting that a paranormal research group showed up at the same time as the writer."

Disgruntled, Nellie said, "Why is it that everybody but me knows about them?"

"Answering only for myself, I saw their van when they arrived," Victor replied, his thoughtful gaze turning once more to the window. "It has the name of their outfit on the sides. And one of those weird logos."

"Weird how?"

"Oh, you know. Obvious that somebody tried to come up with symbols for paranormal research without making it look like they were in search of Casper the Friendly Ghost. What this outfit came up with was one of those double loops I seem to remember symbolizing infinity, and above it flames and a bird coming out of them. Weird."

Nellie dredged into her memory and said, "The

bird and flames could mean the phoenix. Symbol of destruction and rebirth." She made a mental note to research the group later.

"Well, whatever it's supposed to mean, I just find it very interesting and not a little odd that we have paranormal researchers *and* a writer looking into local myth and legend descend on us at the same time. Especially since practically the first thing the writer does is hike up into the mountains and find a body."

Nellie waited while their waitress—with another girlish blush for Victor—delivered their customary drinks, took their meal order since neither one of them needed to even look at the familiar menu, and then retreated.

She also waited while two passing customers, newly arrived, stopped to have a few words with Victor. Nellie knew that he enjoyed the social pleasantries but, even more, enjoyed the fact that people stopped to talk to him or waved to him across the room.

Somebody Special in Baron Hollow.

"It's a nasty subject to discuss over dinner, I suppose," she said when they were finally alone again, "but what do you think about that body?"

"I don't think anything," he replied, brows lifting. "At least, not unless and until Dan has an ID or some idea of how or why she was killed."

"But you do think she was murdered."

"I think it's unlikely, but that seems to be the

prevailing theory, since she was found without clothes or hiking equipment. Did Melissa tell you anything different?"

"No. But she did say they'd be lucky to get an ID."

"Without a skull, very lucky."

Nellie had wondered whether he knew about that, but wasn't too surprised that he did. Word had gotten around. It always did.

She said, "Even with so little to work with, the medical examiner in Chapel Hill will eventually be able to give them an approximate height, weight, race, age—that sort of stuff. Maybe even cause of death, if she was shot or stabbed or something else happened that could leave evidence on what bones they found. But without dental records or anything else to identify her . . ."

"She stays a Jane Doe." He shrugged. "At least nobody we know is missing."

"There's that," Nellie said.

"Yeah," Victor said. "There is that."

"WHY ISN'T SHE answering her cell?" Navarro demanded, using his own to talk to his boss.

"I don't know," Maggie replied frankly. "We've tried pinging it, and get nothing. Either the battery is drained or it's off. I'd be more alarmed by that, but her cell goes dead on a regular basis, and she frequently doesn't notice it right away. Or even for days if she's involved in something."

"What about the GPS in her car?"

"The car's parked at the inn. Wherever she is, she's on foot or using some other wheels. Or horseback, I suppose."

"This late? No, all the stables require the horses to be back well before dark, and they're all accounted for. I checked." He sighed. "She's not supposed to be investigating anything here other than her past, right?"

"Those were her orders." Maggie's voice turned wry. "But Jessie has been known to . . . go off the reservation. Fairly often, as a matter of fact."

"So if she stumbled across something more interesting, she'd start following a different trail?"

"Probably."

"Without reporting in?"

"It's possible, Nathan. Maybe even likely. She has a way of . . . justifying her actions after the fact."

"Now's a fine time to tell me that."

"Sorry. For what it's worth, I really did believe that uncovering whatever it is that's been blocking her abilities and causing her nightmares these last couple of years was the most important thing on her mind. And maybe it still is. Do you know for certain that she's investigating possible murders?"

"No. She asked her sister if there had been any murders in the area—presumably after her encounter with the spirit—but as far as I know, she didn't even exhibit much beyond normal interest in the remains I found."

"Then maybe her absence has to do with exploring her past and nothing more than that."

Navarro hesitated, then said bluntly, "Is she okay? Can you feel that?"

"Everything I feel tells me she's fine," Maggie replied. "Physically, at least."

"So I shouldn't worry."

"I didn't say that. We both know things can go south in a hurry, and with a likely killer operating in or around Baron Hollow . . . I don't know. Can Emma shed any light?"

"I'm working on that," Navarro answered, his gaze on Emma.

"Good luck. When you do see Jessie, tell her I said to call base, pronto. No excuses." Her voice was as gentle as it always was, but Navarro heard the steel.

"Copy that."

"Don't miss any of your own check-ins, okay? Remember, I worry."

"I won't forget." He ended the call and returned his cell to its special case on his belt.

Emma immediately said, "So she thinks Jessie is okay? Even though it's nearly ten at night and she hasn't shown up yet?"

Navarro sat down in a chair across from hers. "Maggie forms a kind of bond with just about any operative who stays at the main compound, especially over time. A psychic connection. Jessie has lived there the last few years."

"Okay. And so she can feel Jessie is okay?"

"Physically okay. Not in immediate danger. But part of the reason Jessie is here at all is because nobody could get a solid read on her, not Maggie, not even some of the more powerful telepaths. And that's a bit unusual, especially for psychics without a lifetime of control or control training behind them."

"She can read me," Emma said, frowning. "In fact, she told me that my thoughts kept slipping through her walls even though she was making them stronger here. Because of all the spirits, I mean."

Navarro frowned as well. "Is that the only reason she was making her walls stronger?"

"She said . . . it was protection. From negative energy. Said bad guys were as likely to be psychic as good guys, and that the first thing all of you were taught was how to protect yourselves."

"True enough."

"I don't know if she felt threatened, if that was one reason she made her walls stronger. She's just seemed . . . unsettled. Distracted."

"And you don't know why."

"It could be normal for her, as far as I know. I don't know what's been going on in her head. She's been seeing spirits, here and all over town. Maybe some of them were bad or dangerous and she just didn't want to tell me about it. Isn't that reason enough?" Emma knew she sounded defensive, but couldn't seem to control that.

"Sure," he said mildly. But his eyes were intent, and they never left her face.

Emma and Navarro had the small sitting space that was one of the inn's common areas to themselves, which wasn't all that unusual so late at night. Some guests were out at one of the two restaurants that offered live music and late hours on Friday nights, but the majority of guests tended to retire to their rooms by now.

Emma was seated where she could watch the reception area and see if anyone came in, hoping to see Jessie, and her gaze kept turning that way even as she said, "How did you manage to survive being shot in the head?"

"It wasn't a psychic bullet."

She looked away from the reception area to stare at him, startled, then had to smile. "Sorry. I guess that question did sort of come out of nowhere."

"So did the bullet." He shrugged. "Classified mission, so no details about it, but I can tell you I was a courier with no reason to expect violence."

"Is that why you got out of the navy?"

"Not because I was shot. My recovery was remarkably fast and easy, according to the doctors; the bullet literally did no damage even though it passed through an area of my brain."

"You mean . . . from one side to the other?"

He indicated with his index finger a point several inches behind and slightly below his left ear. "Went in here." Then he moved his finger to just above his left temple. "Came out here. My hair covers the scars." He shrugged. "The docs said the bullet could have just skimmed over the skull and under the scalp; they've apparently seen that before. But this bullet cracked through my hard skull and actually traveled through the brain before coming out again."

He had Emma's full attention now. "How could it pass through your brain without damage?"

"The docs didn't have an answer for that. At the very least, given the trajectory of the bullet, it should have damaged one or both of my optic nerves, affecting my eyesight, but it didn't. Far as they could tell, it didn't do any damage at all except for the entry and exit wounds. They had me in a medically induced coma because they expected my brain to swell, but it didn't. When they brought me out, I was fine. No memory issues, no physical issues—nothing."

"Until you discovered you were psychic?"

"Yeah."

"How did that happen?"

Navarro shrugged. "It dawned on me, gradually, that I knew things I shouldn't know. About people around me, about things that had happened. Small things, mostly. At first, I didn't know what the hell was going on. I asked my doctor, who was kind enough not to either laugh at me or lock me away, but he just said the brain was a landscape largely unknown to medical science, and maybe that bullet had . . . sparked something in me."

"That doesn't sound like any doctor I've ever heard," Emma said, thinking of her own doctor's dismissal of her dreams.

"Yeah, that struck me too. Then, a few days later, I got a visit from Special Agent Noah Bishop of the FBI's Special Crimes Unit. He wanted to talk to me about being psychic and what it could mean."

"How did he know? I mean, did he read somebody's mind or something?"

"Simpler than that. I gather Bishop has spent years building a huge network of friends and allies all over the country, including some in the military and government, who simply notify him of little oddities like my bullet in the brain and subsequent medical report."

"Your doctor? Violating privacy laws?"

"I'll probably never know. But it seems most likely. In any case, Bishop's agenda has always been clear: He's looking for people with psychic ability. People suited for the work and open to being recruited. For his unit and for Haven."

"So how did you end up in Haven? It sounds like you would have fit easily into the FBI."

"Yeah, I'm qualified. But after so many years in the navy, I wanted a bit more freedom. Haven offered that, and the jobs have certainly been . . .

varied. I like the travel and I like the long stretches off when I feel like I need to recharge."

"So no roots?" She thought about her own, deeply set.

"I'm from a military family, Emma, and went in straight out of college; it's the life I know. But I will admit that sometimes the idea of having a home rather than just a home base has its appeal."

Emma felt the need to veer away from the personal. "So you found a job that allows you to use your abilities. What's the other one called, by the way? Sensing things you aren't supposed to know?"

"Clairvoyance."

"Are you picking up anything now?"

Without even thinking about it, Navarro replied, "There's a honeymooning couple in the inn, doing what honeymooning couples usually do; your chef is having problems getting to know his new stove, so you might plan to send out for tomorrow morning's pastries; that group of paranormal researchers—" He broke off with a frown.

"What?" Emma was unconsciously fascinated.

"Something off about them. Can't quite pin it down. Anyway, they're in their rooms going over paperwork. Or records. Historical stuff about the town." He frowned again.

"What?" Emma repeated.

"Nothing. I could just swear I was being blocked, sensing only what they want me to."

"And that's unusual?"

"Very."

"Maybe they're bad psychics," she suggested, more tongue-in-cheek than anything else.

"No, it's not negative energy I'm sensing." He shook his head as if to shake off whatever it was, then looked at Emma and said, "I'm also sensing that you keep your mother's pearls as a memento only because your only memories of her are that she allowed you to borrow her clothes and jewelry to play dress-up when you were very young."

FIFTEEN

The storm had brought nightfall earlier than usual, since the skies remained cloudy, and Jessie found herself less than halfway back to the inn when it became difficult to see her way.

She had a flashlight in her pack, and didn't waste much time getting it out and turning it on. The problem was, as familiar as she was with the shortcut she'd been using to reach the cabin, she had never been out this far after dark.

Everything looked different after dark.

So she picked her way cautiously, aiming for accuracy rather than speed; if she went off her course and got lost, she could easily find herself wandering around out here all night.

At best.

She didn't think about the worst that could happen.

To say that she felt wary and uneasy would have been an understatement; the fine hairs on the nape of her neck were literally standing out, and she felt cold despite the warm humidity left behind by the storm.

So she was half-braced for something to happen; she just didn't expect her flashlight's beam to fall on the almost transparent form of the spirit she had encountered before.

Jolting to a stop, she muttered, "Shit."

"You've gone off the path," the spirit told her gravely.

"There isn't a path. That's the problem."

The spirit looked around, as though noticing for the first time where they were, then returned her attention to Jessie. "I don't mean here. I mean you've gone off the path you have to follow to get all the answers you need. To stop him."

"I found where he keeps his trophies," Jessie said, hearing the defensiveness in her own voice and reminding herself she was talking to a spirit.

"I know. But you're running out of time. And you haven't asked the right question yet."

"What's the right question?"

"What really happened that night fifteen years ago?"

"I know what happened. At least . . . I'm remembering."

"You can't trust your memories," the spirit said. "Your guilt and shame are too strong. They're blocking you."

"I know that. I'm working on it."

"Are you? Then why are you out here?"

"Because—"

"Why are you out here when you should be talking to Emma? And listening to her?"

UNTIL THEN, EMMA had been telling herself that everything he'd mentioned could have originated from something overheard or surmised logically. But the pearls . . .

"Good guess," she said finally.

Navarro's smile was faint. "You have no problem at all believing that Jessie sees spirits, and you have firsthand evidence that she sometimes reads your thoughts, and yet my clairvoyance has to be a 'guess'?"

He had a point. Dammit.

Emma sighed. "Okay, okay. Yes, that is why I keep the pearls. I loved them as a kid, but I didn't really grow up into a heels-and-pearls sort of woman, so they stay in the house safe."

"You don't have to defend your choices, Emma. Especially not to me."

She half nodded, but changed the subject with determination. "I know you trust this Maggie you guys work for, that you believe her when she says Jessie isn't in danger—"

"At the moment," he qualified.

"Yeah. Yeah, at the moment. Even so, it's getting late, and she still hasn't come back here. Assuming she shows up and you guys are able to talk tonight, how is she going to react to you being here?"

"I have no idea," he replied frankly. "It probably depends on whether she's still probing her past or has changed course and is on the trail of a killer."

"If she had done that—found evidence of a killer—don't you think she would have reported it to Haven?"

"She should have. But according to Maggie, she's shown a tendency in the past to strike out on her own during investigations." He paused, adding, "Which, in my experience, is an indication of a lack of confidence in her own judgment. My bet is, she wants to make very sure she has a strong reason to call in the troops before she does it."

"So calling in the troops is a big deal."

"Depends. Some cases just call for one other operative. But if Jessie has found or is looking for evidence pointing to a serial killer, then it gets really tricky. Haven isn't a law enforcement agency; we can work with locals, but only if they ask. We can and do work independently of them as private investigators, but unless we're deputized, we can't act as cops. And, when it comes to the really big monsters, we want the biggest guns we can get, and that's the FBI and the Special Crimes Unit. Which has to be invited in unless there's evidence of a federal crime."

"So . . . Jessie could be looking for evidence of a federal crime, but not necessarily a murderer."

"Maybe. Or maybe just enough evidence to go to the state cops; they tend to get jumpy whenever anyone says 'serial killer,' and tend to be quicker to act on that sort of information than locals. Locals tend toward denial, in my experience."

"Not in my backyard?"

"Yeah, something like that."

After a moment, Emma grimaced. "What's in Jessie's own past . . . that was bad enough to drive her away from here, and keep her away nearly half her life. It was what she was fixated on remembering, uncovering, when she got here. She was really, really determined. If she thinks something else is going on, and it's got her focused on it instead of her past, then it almost has to be a killer."

Navarro said, "I really wish you'd tell me what it is in Jessie's past that she came here to settle."

"I told you, it's not my secret."

"And not just hers? It involves others?"

"I'm not going to play twenty questions with you."

He sighed. "Well, it was worth a shot."

But Emma didn't like the way he was frowning. "What's wrong?"

"Something else I'm picking up. Emma, has it occurred to you that the fall from the horse, the head injury, might have awakened latent psychic abilities in you?"

"How could it have occurred to me? I didn't even know that's the way it works sometimes until you told me." She hesitated. "My nightmares, that's what you're thinking about? What you're . . . picking up?" She didn't much like the idea of having information about herself seemingly plucked out of thin air, especially by him.

He didn't answer the implied question, just the obvious one. "Maybe they're more than nightmares. Maybe they're visions."

"You mean of the future?"

"The future. Or the present. There are some psychics in both Haven and the SCU who can do that. Not really seers because they don't always see the future; sometimes what they see is in real time, happening somewhere else even as they're experiencing a vision about it."

"Just seeing oddball things for no reason?"

"There's almost always a reason. A connection of some kind."

It was Emma's turn to frown. "How could I have a connection to murders happening? Assuming they are, that is."

"It could be as simple as you knowing the killer."

She didn't like the sound of that. At all. The

alternative sounded much better. "I have dreams."

"Sometimes visions come in the form of dreams." His gaze was still intent. "We're less guarded when we sleep, and our unconscious minds are . . . freed from conscious constraints. Sometimes the conscious mind doesn't want to accept abilities that might frighten us."

Emma felt uneasy, though she couldn't have said precisely why. "I don't like my dreams because they're filled with violence," she admitted. "With . . . unspeakable things."

He hesitated, then said, "I'm not too thrilled with my own abilities sometimes. The finding the dead part, I mean. It means I have to accept going in that there's absolutely nothing I can do to save that life. It's already gone. The only thing I can do is try to bring closure to a family or help bring a murderer to justice."

"That's no small thing," Emma offered. "Some people never know what happened to their loved ones. And plenty of murderers get away with it because their victims are never found."

"That's what I tell myself."

"It doesn't help?"

Navarro shrugged. "Sometimes. Sometimes not. But at least working for Haven means I have people I can talk to about it. People who understand and accept what the rest of the world generally views as freakish abilities. At least, as well as they can be understood. And that means a lot."

"It doesn't seem to have helped Jessie," Emma noted, trying to keep her voice neutral.

"From what I've been told, it actually helped her a lot. Word is, she was in pretty bad shape when Bishop found her and got her to Haven."

Emma frowned. "Because of her abilities?"

Again, he seemed to hesitate, but then said, "I'm sure that was part of it; otherwise Bishop wouldn't have known about her, much less been able to find her. Look, we try to keep as much of our private lives as private as we need them to be, and that's not always easy when you work with psychics. We pick up things without intending to, so we try to be on guard with each other if we have part of ourselves or our pasts we want or need to protect."

"What are you trying to tell me?"

"That Jessie apparently went through some rough times after leaving Baron Hollow. I don't know the details; it isn't any of my business. All I do know is that Jessie is—or was—one of the damaged psychics. Whether it was because of her abilities, her *in*ability to manage them, or whatever was going on in her day-to-day life, from what I heard, she was about one psych evaluation away from being locked up somewhere."

THE MORE HE thought about it, the more angry he got. Not only because she was nosing around where she didn't belong, but because he was all too aware that she, of all people, could ruin him.

And, clearly, she intended to do just that.

If he gave her the chance.

She hadn't been part of his plans, and even after she came home he'd been willing to let her place in his life stay in the past. He even honored her, in a way, because if it hadn't been for her and that hot summer night all those years ago, he might never have discovered who he really was.

In her own way, she'd been his kingmaker.

Still, as angry as he was, he realized after thinking it through that there was a certain rightness to taking her now that she'd come back home. A certain elegance of timing.

If he'd tried to track her down, there might have been trouble. But this way, she had come to him. And that was just about perfect.

Because nobody believed Jessie Rayburn was going to stay in Baron Hollow. Nobody. Sooner or later, she was going to leave, just as she'd left fifteen years before, and her absence now would cause no more of a ripple than it had then.

Baron Hollow would go on.

He would go on.

And in time, everyone would forget that Jessie Rayburn had ever existed.

WHEN JESSIE DID return to Rayburn House, she passed through the reception area and was halfway up the stairs before Emma could react, and by then she would have had to yell to get her sister's attention.

To Navarro, she said, "Look, I need to talk to her before you do. I need to tell her about my dreams."

"I get that. But I need to talk to her too, Emma, and as soon as possible. For her own safety, we need to know what she's been investigating. She needs to know she has backup here, another Haven operative."

Emma nodded. "You won't get an argument from me. I'll tell her about you. Maybe she'll be knocking at your door in half an hour or so. But if she doesn't . . . Well, it's late. Tomorrow will be crazy, with the festival, but if not tonight, I'll tell her to meet you in the dining room for breakfast in the morning so you two can talk."

Mildly, he said, "If the dining room is crowded, we'll need more privacy to discuss the situation."

Sighing, Emma said, "I'd invite you for breakfast upstairs, but Jessie has been up and out before me these last days. Just be in the dining room early, around seven or so, order coffee or something, and I'll do my best to get her down here. Then you two can find a place to talk. Good enough?"

"I guess it'll have to be."

"Okay." She rose but hesitated, adding, "I hope you can convince her to stop all this running around on her own. I'll try, but . . . like I said, we aren't close and she's keeping her thoughts and feelings very much to herself with me. Anyway, I'm sure I'll see you at some point tomorrow. Maybe during the festival."

He nodded, silent, and watched as she left the room, her patient Sheltie at her heels as usual.

She left Navarro with a lot to think about. He was, for one thing, reasonably sure that Emma was indeed psychic. But whether her dreams were of things to come or things happening as she dreamed them, he couldn't say. The dream of the woman running naked through the woods argued for visions of something happening at the time she dreamed them, but she had been reluctant to go into detail about other dreams and, without any certain knowledge of when and where those other women she had dreamed of might have died, knowing more wouldn't have done him much good anyway.

But there was something else, something he hadn't mentioned to Emma because it was so . . . nebulous in his mind. He couldn't even explain it to himself, really. He looked at Emma, talked to her—and was conscious of the nagging feeling that there was something important he was missing. He just didn't have a clue what it was.

He returned to his suite, restless, wondering if Jessie would pay him a visit tonight, either on the defensive or with blood in her eye.

· · ·

UPSTAIRS, EMMA WAS wondering the same thing.

"Maggie should have told me she sent in another operative," Jessie was saying to her sister, frowning.

"I gather your cell phone is dead, and has been for a while."

Jessie glanced toward her bedroom and, presumably, her backpack, but didn't go to check out the phone. "I'll charge it overnight," she said.

"I think your boss wants you to check in, and tonight rather than tomorrow."

Jessie's frown deepened. "Don't worry about it, okay?"

Emma tried to hold on to her patience. "The settling with the past business not going so well, huh?"

A ghost of a laugh escaped Jessie. "You could say that. Things can get awfully . . . tangled . . . when you look too far behind you. Things you don't expect get uncovered."

"Things?"

"Feelings. And connections."

"To family? Have you talked to Victor?"

"He doesn't like remembering unpleasant things."

"Unpleasant?"

Jessie frowned again. "Egging on a seventeen-year-old cousin to drink too much. And maybe . . . I don't know, Em. The memories are still fuzzy. Flashes of faces . . . I'm still not sure what happened at that last party, but I know something did. Something bad."

"How can you find out what it was? Jessie, what have you been doing all week?"

Jessie looked at her sister almost as if she didn't see her, and spoke slowly. "There's more to it all than I can bring into focus. The more I remember or find, the more there *is* to remember or find. I think something started that night, something that was triggered by what happened to me."

For some reason, Emma couldn't bring herself to raise the subject of a possible killer. "And you don't know what that might be?"

"I have . . . a suspicion. I need to pin it down."

"A suspicion of what?"

Jessie hesitated visibly, then shook her head. "If I'm right, you'll find out soon enough. And if I'm wrong . . . I don't want to put into your head what's in mine right now."

"I doubt you could put in anything worse than what's there now." Emma hadn't intended to, but she heard herself blurt, "I've been having nightmares. Nightmares about women being murdered. Tortured and murdered in ways too horrible for me to even describe. Only they might not be . . . just nightmares."

Without reacting in any visible way to the information, Jessie merely said, "What makes you think that?"

"I had an accident a couple of years ago, got

thrown from a horse and hit my head. Nathan seems to believe I might be psychic now."

Jessie didn't seem surprised. "One thing they told us at Haven was that these things often run in families. Me being psychic increases the likelihood that you are at least a latent. And trauma is a major trigger in turning a latent into an active. A head injury could have triggered your abilities to go active."

"So, doesn't that change things? If what I'm seeing in my nightmares has happened or will really happen . . . then this killer is real. He's a monster. He has to be stopped."

An odd little smile twisted Jessie's lips. "And he will be. I can promise you that."

"Jessie, you're beginning to scare me. What the hell?"

Shaking her head again, Jessie said, "Just remember your promise. Whatever happened that summer is my secret to uncover. My baggage to deal with."

"But Nathan—"

"Especially not Navarro. He's a fellow Haven operative; leave him to me."

"Jessie—"

"You swore. Don't forget."

Emma nodded reluctantly, but said, "Jessie, *are* you looking for this killer? A serial killer?"

Jessie lifted an eyebrow. "On my own? Without backup? That wouldn't be very smart."

"Jessie—"

"I think I'll find out what I need to tomorrow, at the festival. All the missing pieces. There are people I need to talk to. Information to . . . fill in the gaps."

"What about Nathan?"

"What about him? He isn't here investigating my past; he's looking into the murders that spirit told me about and your nightmare visions apparently confirm. That is what you said, right?"

"Don't you think there's a connection? Between what happened to you and what's happening now?"

"I don't see how there could be." Jessie's gaze slid away from her sister's. "Listen, it's been a long day and I'm beat. I want to take a shower and go to bed. I'll talk to Navarro in the morning, before the festival starts and things get crazy. Good enough?"

"I guess it'll have to be," Emma responded, very conscious of repeating Navarro's words from earlier.

JULY 4

They had ended up at Nellie's house, which told her more, perhaps, than Victor realized. It told her he had somewhere to be on this very warm Saturday morning, that he needed to be there early, before the festival, and that he didn't want her asking any questions. Easier and simpler for him to leave her bed than for him to maneuver her into leaving his.

Forgoing morning sex, he was gone when she woke up, leaving a note on the pillow saying he'd see her at the festival.

Nellie could smell coffee, and knew he had left it hot for her. She stretched languidly in bed, not yet ready to rise even though she was wide-awake.

And thinking.

About that other note she had, the very scary note written by someone or something unknown and possibly in blood.

HELP ME . . . MURDERED
FIND THE TRUTH. BE CAREFUL.
HE'S WATCHING.
JESSIE . . . THREAT
PROTECT EMMA

Nellie had done what research she could on Jessie—though she was waiting for a callback from a friend who owed her a favor. She had found out what she could about Haven; she was reasonably sure she knew most of the details about Emma's life. Here, at least.

Those summers traveling, not so much.

Nellie's lively imagination could conjure up all kinds of trouble Emma might have gotten herself involved in while away from Baron Hollow, but murder wasn't one of them.

So why did Emma need protecting?

And from whom?

SIXTEEN

Who would think Nellie could protect Emma? How could she? By finding this "truth" the message spoke of?

Nellie sighed in frustration. There was murder and there was a truth for her to find, and Jessie was either a threat or *being* somehow threatened, and she was supposed to protect Emma.

Piece of cake.

He. Who was he? Surely someone she knew, or else why would the note have been . . . delivered . . . to her?

Still grappling with the notion that a ghostly hand had left her a note possibly written in blood (she had sent scrapings to a friend in the town clinic's small lab, but hadn't heard back yet), and not quite ready to believe it just yet despite the evidence, Nellie preferred to ponder a more human puzzle.

So to speak.

A murderous *he* who might have some connection to her. She wanted to believe that whatever was going on in no way involved Victor. Wanted to be able to assure herself firmly and with utter conviction that Victor didn't have it in him to hurt a fly. But . . .

But. You couldn't know a man most of your life, sleep with him on a regular basis for the better part of a year, and not know him awfully well. And what she knew about Victor Rayburn was that he could be ruthless if he felt the need to be. He had a temper, and even if she'd never seen him resort to physical violence, something in his eyes on the rare occasions when she'd seen him furious told her that it was, at least, possible.

And he seemed to be at odds with Emma, something he avoided talking about, at least to Nellie.

Was it because of Jessie? The tension between them had seemed to increase when Jessie came back to Baron Hollow. Why? Because Emma knew something she hadn't known before? Maybe—but that didn't explain whatever discussions they'd been having only in the office of the family lawyer.

The problem, Nellie decided finally, was that she didn't really know how things stood between Victor and Emma, and until she did, she couldn't rule out that line of inquiry and move on.

Frowning, Nellie threw back the covers and got out of bed, heading for the shower. As she got ready for the day, she considered and dismissed several possible ways she could go about finding the information she needed. The Rayburn family lawyer was out; Trent Windell was the soul of discretion and nobody *ever* learned about his clients' business from him or from anyone on his staff.

Victor had already shown a disinclination to talk about his relationship with Emma, and Nellie didn't want to awaken his suspicions by pressing the matter.

Just in case.

She walked a fine line with Victor, knowing better than to show too much interest in either the parts of his personal life that didn't involve her, or, indeed, anything other than their casual dinner-and-bed relationship. As the latest in a long string of lovers, she'd had ample opportunity to observe which of the women in Victor's life had a longer run, so by the time his attention had turned to her—with a nudge or two from her, of course—she'd known to keep things light, casual, amusing, and undemanding.

So far, it was working.

And she didn't intend to rock that particular boat unless and until she absolutely had to.

She would regret losing Victor as a lover. He was very skilled.

So she couldn't ask him what she needed to know, not unless she had no other choice. He'd made it clear he didn't want to talk about it, and pushing him was not a good idea.

Emma was the logical answer. And Nellie knew

just where Emma would be today at the festival. Crazy busy most of the time, so Nellie would have to time her approach.

That was fine. Vic clearly expected to meet up with her at some point, so she needed to be flexible.

Nellie debated, the whole time she was showering and getting dressed and drinking her morning coffee with a piece of toast, whether to confide in Emma about the note. It might cause her to open up. Or it could just as easily have the opposite reaction.

Play it by ear.

IT WAS EIGHT a.m. when a note was delivered to Navarro's table in the dining room. A note from Emma saying simply that she was sorry but Jessie had slipped out even earlier than usual. She knew about Navarro's presence, and Emma had tried to convince her to talk to her fellow operative, but she had the uneasy feeling that Jessie was hell-bent on finishing whatever it was she had started.

Navarro sighed, not very surprised. Jessie was on the loose, and from everything he'd heard, all of Baron Hollow would be crazed today with the festival.

Well, shit.

She had picked a perfect time to be deliberately elusive.

Navarro had been in the dining room for nearly

an hour, and had gone ahead and had his breakfast because he'd had a strong hunch that Jessie wouldn't show. He forced himself to open up his senses—all of them, in a trick Bishop had taught most of the operatives—searching for any sign that danger, to Jessie or anyone else, was threatening.

The SCU agents had chosen to call it, at least among themselves, their "spider sense," this heightening of the normal five senses to a point far beyond what most people could achieve. Even among agents and operatives, the ability varied greatly in strength and, as with all abilities, it wasn't something every psychic could master.

Navarro had mastered it.

It was, in a way, like opening a door; sight, hearing, touch—all the senses became exquisitely sensitive, sometimes painfully so, and the sensory input could be overwhelming.

He kept his gaze fixed on his coffee because if he looked up, he knew the room would seem uncomfortably bright. Besides, he was trying to focus, to reach out beyond this room. But for the first minute or two, he was busy pushing through the suddenly loud chatter of everyone in the room and out in the reception area, and the scents of the flowers on the tables and the perfumes and colognes worn by fellow guests, never mind the scents of bacon and eggs and onions . . .

He pushed through that, concentrating.

And on the extreme edge of his awareness, almost beyond his reach and for just an instant, he sensed something cold and dark.

Then it was gone. His ears popped as though he were coming down from a high altitude, and he felt a faint throbbing in his head that he knew from bitter experience would torment him for a few minutes and then gradually lessen and disappear.

Great. Just great. He sensed something cold and dark—which he already knew existed here. Somewhere. In someone.

Way to go, champ.

He needed to find Jessie. He needed to know what she knew or suspected.

So far, he hadn't seen Emma, but he was reasonably sure she was also already up and gone, helping prepare for the festival that began in only a couple of hours.

The tables in the spacious room were far enough apart to offer privacy if a guest wanted to eat in solitude, but he had chosen a table for two, positioned so as to provide an unobstructed view both of the room and the foot of the stairs visible through the wide doorway to the entrance hall.

Resigning himself to having to track both Jessie and Emma down in what promised to be an extremely crowded downtown Baron Hollow, he sipped his coffee, giving himself time until his head stopped throbbing, and looked around at his fellow guests of Rayburn House. Until now, he really hadn't paid much attention to most of them.

About half the tables in the dining room were occupied; though the inn had a full house, it was clear some guests either preferred the breakfast room service offered or else chose to eat somewhere in town. Or they slept in.

There were several couples, mostly older and talking to each other or sipping their coffee in companionable silence, with the contented air of retirement and time pleasantly on their hands. One young couple was obviously on their honeymoon.

Very obviously; they could hardly keep their hands off each other. It struck him only then that they must have been the couple he'd picked up on the previous evening.

Navarro averted his eyes from what he supposed they believed was a private caress hidden by the tablecloth, and continued to study the other guests in the room.

There were two other singles he had noted earlier: an older woman who always seemed to be reading a book, and an older man who apparently divided his time outside his room between the library when it was hot outdoors and one of the rocking chairs on the front porch when it was cooler, usually with a newspaper.

Neither appeared to have any wish to be sociable, as far as he could tell. So at least

Navarro wasn't the only one who had kept pretty much to himself.

The three paranormal researchers were at a table across the room, talking quietly among themselves. Navarro thought the woman still looked tired, but she was bright-eyed and smiling, so he supposed she was just one of those people who always looked frail even when they weren't. Either that or she was determined to pretend she was fine when she wasn't.

Then she turned her head slightly, went visibly pale, and he saw her eyes widen.

Without even thinking about it, he looked in the same direction, and thought later that his eyes had probably widened too.

There was a woman standing in the doorway of the dining room. She was tall, slender, fair-haired. Early twenties. Dressed casually but definitely for winter. She might have been another guest, or someone from town who had stopped in at Rayburn House, inexplicably wearing a quilted jacket in July.

Except that she wasn't.

Navarro could see the stairs—through her.

He didn't recognize her.

As he watched, his coffee cup half-raised, he saw her take a step into the room, then another, her gaze fixed on the table where the paranormal researchers sat. By the third step she took, everything about her had grown hazy, and by the fourth step it was as if a slight breeze had dissipated something formed of mist. She was gone.

When Navarro turned his gaze slowly toward the table where her attention had been fixed, it was to see the brunette woman smiling and talking to her companions as though nothing had happened.

Nothing at all.

"BISHOP."

"Navarro. Listen, I have another question for you."

"Which is?"

"Do you have somebody down here in Baron Hollow?" Navarro was in the fairly large garden behind Rayburn House, strolling along a brick-paved path that wound among planters and beds and pots overflowing with summer color. He was alone in the area, and he was far enough from the house to avoid being overheard.

Besides, he doubted anyone could hear a quiet conversation going on back here when only a few blocks away it sounded like Armageddon. Or the festival getting under way. One or the other.

Bishop said, "You know we can't just send FBI agents into situations without evidence of a federal crime or an invitation from local law enforcement."

"That," Navarro said, "was not an answer."

261

"Why do you ask?"

Navarro knew Bishop, and knew he'd get an answer when the SCU chief was ready to give him one and not before.

Dammit.

"I ask because the paranormal research team staying here at Rayburn House has at least one genuine medium among them. She saw a spirit a little while ago."

"You're certain?"

"Oh, yeah."

"How?"

"I saw her too."

Bishop didn't seem nearly as surprised by that information as Navarro had been.

"Her?"

"Young, blond, dressed for winter. So not likely to belong to the remains I found. I'm told the inn is very haunted, so it's at least likely she's one of the resident ghosts. The point is that this medium definitely saw her."

There was a moment of silence, and then Bishop said thoughtfully, "You don't see spirits."

"I never have before. But I saw her. And so did the medium, even if she pretended afterward that she hadn't." Navarro paused, then added, "I'd been trying out the spider sense just a minute or two before, trying to get a bead on this place; maybe this time I opened a door on a sense I didn't realize I had."

"That," Bishop said, "is more than possible. You can locate the dead and you're clairvoyant; maybe it was only a matter of time before mediumistic abilities manifested. It's the sort of thing that tends to happen during an investigation, when we're all on . . . high psychic alert, as it were."

"That's reasonable, I suppose." Navarro pushed that possibility aside for the moment. "But, like I said, this paranormal researcher saw her too. She's a genuine medium."

Again, the silence stretched for a long moment. Until Navarro broke it.

"Maybe I'm wrong, but I don't think many of these paranormal research outfits boast genuine psychics. Not of that caliber, at any rate. And I think that if any of them do, you know about it."

"There are a lot of paranormal research outfits," Bishop said, his tone noncommittal. "Just check the Internet."

"Bishop, I just saw a spirit. And so did this medium. I'm asking you straight out if she's one of yours, an SCU agent or investigator, or whatever it is you call auxiliary members of your unit."

"We haven't been invited in," Bishop said, calmly.

Navarro drew a breath and let it out slowly. "Look, all I want to know is who might get in my way in the likely event that things turn nasty. I prefer to work alone, I already have another Haven operative to worry about, and I don't want to trip over one of your people while we're both looking for the same thing."

"I don't think you'll do that." Hardly pausing, he added, "You've found no further evidence of a serial operating in Baron Hollow?"

"No, nothing solid."

"Well, if Jane Doe was murdered, that's definitely a crime the local police know occurred."

"Yeah, but with no way to ID her, and no locals or transients reported missing within the right time frame, I doubt they're doing much investigating. In fact, the chief as good as told me that much. The state ME won't even be able to give them a decent basic description of Jane Doe for weeks, maybe months, if what the chief said about the backed-up lab is accurate."

"He'll have the report sooner than he expects."

"How much sooner?"

"By Monday."

Navarro was unwillingly impressed; it was hell to get anything official done over the Fourth of July weekend. But all he asked was, "Will it help me?"

"You'll have to let me know about that," Bishop replied.

"HIGH PSYCHIC ALERT?"

"Don't start with me, Tony. I'm not in the mood." Despite his words, Bishop's voice was almost absentminded.

"One of these days," Tony said in a musing tone, "somebody's going to do you a mischief. Before now, my money would have been on Galen. Now I'm thinking Navarro."

Bishop sent him a look but didn't respond.

"Seriously, Boss, you do have a maddening way of putting things, especially to agents or operatives trying to investigate in the field." Tony thought about it for a moment, adding, "Or not putting things, as the case may be."

"Navarro is a big boy," his boss said calmly. "He'll figure things out on his own."

"I'm not saying he won't. I'm just saying he might come after you when it's all over and done with."

"That," Bishop said, "depends on how things turn out."

Tony cocked a curious eyebrow at him. "You mean you don't know?"

"I didn't see the end of it."

Catching the faint emphasis on the pronoun, Tony said, "But somebody else did?"

"Pass me that file, will you, please, Tony?"

Sighing, Tony did so, but he couldn't help adding, "At least tell me all the secrets down there aren't going to get somebody else killed."

"I wish I could, Tony." Bishop's voice was sober. "I really wish I could."

IF EMMA HAD been given to outbursts due to frustration, she would have been ready to scream by the time the Arts Festival was in full swing. But it wasn't her nature, so despite what had become increasing anxiety over Jessie, and frustration because her sister had been even more maddeningly elusive and enigmatic, she buried her own feelings and went about the business of being the Arts Festival Band Nazi.

The festival really was a major event for Baron Hollow, and it drew quite a crowd to the downtown area, with people coming from miles away. Rayburn House was full, as were the half dozen smaller B and Bs and the larger chain motel out on the highway.

Main Street was closed off at either end, the street lined with tents and booths and tables displaying the local artwork the town was famous for, and more tents and tables and trucks and carts provided every sort of food and (nonalcoholic) beverage possible. There were also both an ice cream truck and another selling flavored ices.

Since it was the Fourth, there was always a patriotic element to the celebrations, taking the form of red, white, and blue bunting draped over anything stationary—and over a few people and dogs on leashes as well. (Emma's Lizzie, who disliked loud noises, was back at the inn with Penny—who also preferred peace to the semi-organized chaos of the festival.) There were American flags flying proudly *and* displayed on hats and T-shirts and painted on skin, and rather amazingly varied interpretations of the national anthem were played at least once by every band.

Small-town America, celebrating the Fourth of July.

It was also clear, sunny, and about as hot as Baron Hollow ever got, which was pushing ninety-five. Which meant that tempers less even than Emma's got more than a little frayed now and then.

"Hey, Emma, did Three Pin say we could borrow their amp? Ours just blew, dammit."

"Emma, our drummer got sick; who can we use?"

"Emma, you've got to tell Mayor Sharp that, no disrespect, but we can't keep playing the national anthem! The audience gets tired of standing at attention, for one thing."

"Emma, some kid just threw up in Bo's guitar case!"

"Emma—"

The Band Nazi. It was a fun gig. Most of the time.

Experienced, Emma coped. She had to stay fairly close to the courthouse for the most part, but she did her best to keep an eye on what else of interest was going on during the festival.

Such as her sister.

Jessie had not offered to help with the festival and was most certainly avoiding her sister, but she was at least presenting a public display of interest and enjoyment as she wandered around Main Street all during the morning. Emma saw her once eating a hot dog, much later enjoying an ice cream cone, and at some point she had allowed one of the artists offering the service to paint a small flag on her cheek.

Emma also saw her sister talking, with what looked like some intensity, to several people. Victor was one, and whatever was being said between them, neither looked happy about it. Later in the morning, Emma also saw her sister speaking to Nellie Holt, and then, some minutes later, to Nellie's boss, Sam Conway.

Since she kept losing sight of those . . . encounters . . . because of the shifting crowd, Emma had no idea how long each lasted or even whether Jessie and whomever she was speaking to parted amicably. But there was something about her sister's posture that made Emma believe that the specific encounters were planned on her part, that this was Jessie seeking out the puzzle pieces of information she needed.

For her missing memories?

Or to help point her toward a killer?

Emma didn't know, and it was maddening not to know, to be always conscious of the uneasy feeling that there were undercurrents here she felt she should understand—no matter how much or little Jessie was willing to tell her. Busy as she was, she kept trying to figure that out, to understand why her fear for Jessie was coupled with an odd, cold, and nervous anxiety that was more about herself.

At least, she thought it was. It felt like something at the extreme edge of her awareness was . . . settled there, waiting for her to look at the right person or thing or in the right direction in order to see and understand what she needed to.

But whatever it was remained elusive.

She didn't see Navarro at all, which made her even more uneasy, because she had assumed he'd be looking for Jessie. And though she had a hunch he had a talent for blending in when he chose, she thought she should have caught at least a glimpse of him at some point.

But she hadn't.

Just before noon, Emma saw her sister speaking to Dan Maitland, and a few minutes later to local bad-boy-grown-to-drunken-failure Peter Troy.

She had no idea what any of the conversations were about, but none of them looked casual, and that was troubling to Emma. Especially since she lost Jessie in the crowd sometime just after noon.

And as the festival wore on, hard as she looked, she could see no sign of her sister.

SEVENTEEN

Not long after noon, Jessie slipped away from the festival. Everyone in town was busy celebrating; she'd never have a better chance to return to the cabin.

She was reasonably sure she had time for one last visit to the cabin undetected. It hadn't been part of her original plan to go back there; the original plan was to leave Baron Hollow and get only far enough away to be clear before calling in the troops.

Not that she didn't want to be part of catching this monster; she most certainly did. But her concern was for Emma. Because monsters weren't easily caught even when their lair was known, and just in case he escaped and had time to do more damage, Jessie didn't want him to connect what was about to happen to him in any way to Jessie— and, by extension, to Emma.

He'd been smart up to now, and careful, but once he knew someone had discovered his secret, he would probably stop being careful and just be enraged.

Jessie didn't want the target of his rage to be her sister.

Hence the ruse she had concocted. She was leaving town, called back to work. Simple, reasonable, believable. She had slipped back to the inn to grab her already-packed bag, leaving a note for Emma to find later on. She had managed to move her car without, she believed, being noticed; there would be so many cars parked at either end of downtown for the festival, in every possible parking spot, that she doubted anyone would even notice hers missing.

She even stopped by the pharmacy early to buy some cough drops for her "scratchy" throat, telling Patty the clerk—and the most notorious gossip in Baron Hollow—that she'd been called back to work and would be leaving town that afternoon, even before the fireworks.

And, no, she didn't know when or even if she'd return.

Groundwork laid.

All that had been according to plan.

The plan made before she'd known about Nathan Navarro.

Jessie had spent a sleepless night trying to decide what difference his presence made. She should have met with him, confided in him; she knew that.

She knew it.

All her training, all her experience, told her that. Logic and reason told her that. She argued inwardly with logic and reason that one thing she absolutely needed to do was return to the cabin just long enough to hide his trophy box, leaving it in the cabin as evidence, but making sure he wouldn't have the chance to destroy it while she and Navarro were busy calling in the troops.

That made sense. That was even, in its way, logical.

But something else was nagging at her, an uneasy sense of something she still didn't know or hadn't realized or found. And whatever it was, it stopped her whenever she thought about meeting up with Navarro or confiding in him. Or in Emma.

No, as careless and irresponsible, as dangerous as it seemed, Jessie's deepest instincts urged her to do this on her own, and now. She had to.

She had to . . . atone.

That was what she felt, as baffling as she found it.

Atone for what?

Jessie didn't know, but she did know her time was limited and that she had none to waste in going back over her decision one more time. It was made, and that was that. Now she had work to do.

All she had to do was one final bit of verification—and leave at least one very subtle signpost for the right people to find. Navarro, probably. He'd know what to look for. They were taught that at Haven, to leave signs for other operatives. Because you never knew when someone might be right behind you and need the edge of information you hadn't had time to share.

She did have preliminary information for the

troops when they were called in, a point of professional pride with her. On her tablet was a report that contained a list of the names on those driver's licenses; using his "trophies" to compile evidence against him was something that gave her grim satisfaction. And she'd made a start, working long into the night searching missing-persons databases for names on the driver's licenses and ID cards. On her tablet.

And a backup on a thumb drive she'd left in Emma's jewelry box.

However, she couldn't remove the trophies themselves from his cabin; the evidence needed to remain there. But she was also worried that he might—just—have time before the troops could catch or kill him to destroy it, or move it, and that was not a chance she was prepared to take.

That was what she kept telling herself. It was logical and reasonable, after all. They didn't know what he'd done with the bodies—though she had a hunch she almost wanted to be wrong about— and without the bodies *or* the trophies, they might well have no case.

So she had to preserve the trophies. She had to.

Besides, she really did want to take a look inside what she suspected was where he imprisoned his victims for a time.

How often, after all, was an investigator given the chance to get a good look into a monster's lair?

. . .

"EMMA?"

She turned with relief to find Navarro at her side. "Where have you been? It's the first I've seen of you all day."

Rather grimly, he said, "Trying to connect with Jessie. I saw her half a dozen times during the morning, but she has an uncanny knack of slipping away into the crowd. Still not answering her cell phone, either; it's going straight to voice mail."

They were both speaking a bit louder than normal, because a band was playing enthusiastically only a few yards away. With sizable amplifiers.

"So you haven't talked to her yet?"

"No. Christ, I thought this was a small town; how many people can there *be* in an area like this?"

"They come from nearby towns. The festival is one of the best in the Southeast," Emma replied automatically. "I'm worried about Jessie. She wouldn't say much last night, but there was something odd about her, something I couldn't put my finger on."

"Probably pissed that I'm here."

"She didn't seem angry. Just . . . set. Like she'd made up her mind and there was no turning back."

"Made up her mind about what?"

"I don't know."

"Confronting whoever hurt her in the past?"

Emma was startled. "How did you—?"

"It had to be a trauma of some kind, or it wouldn't be interfering with her abilities, especially after so many years. Emma, you've got to tell me what happened to her."

Emma looked around, spotted a guitar player from the upcoming band heading toward her with panic on his face, and said quickly to Navarro, "We can't talk here and now. Keep trying to find Jessie. I'll find somebody to relieve me and catch up with you."

"Hurry," he said. "I have a feeling I don't much like."

SHE HAD EARLIER parked her car quite a distance from downtown, nearly halfway to the highway, discovering a handy dirt road she suspected was used by young lovers since it faded into nothing about a hundred yards from the main road. It was close to the shortcut she had been using to get to the cabin, but since she'd had to make an appearance at the festival, and talk to a few people, she still had quite a hike to get back to the car later.

The information she had gathered had done little to solve the mystery that was her past, that summer party so long ago. If anything, the reactions she'd gotten had only confused things. Nellie had proven the most useful; Jessie hadn't even remembered that the other woman, the same age as Emma, had been at the party briefly and had been able to offer up two names Jessie hadn't even considered.

And their reactions to her casual questions had been . . . odd. One had displayed a flash of panic and the urgent need to be somewhere else, and the other had coolly denied being there.

At all.

I don't have time to think about that now. I'll think about it after I've done what I have to and get out of here.

It was an unsatisfactory realization, but one she had to accept.

She hiked to where she'd left her car, reasonably sure no one had noticed her leaving the downtown area. She had locked up all her stuff in the car earlier, carrying only the car key and some cash in her pockets while she was at the festival. She hadn't bothered to carry her cell. She had tried to charge it overnight, but apparently the battery had taken all it could of psychic energy or her own carelessness; it had remained dead despite being plugged in all night. And she hadn't brought a spare.

Now the only things Jessie took with her from the backpack she normally carried on her hikes were her small tool case of lockpicks, her weapon, and a flashlight. She unholstered her weapon and stuck it inside the waistband of her jeans at the small of her back to make it less obvious that she was armed; she slid the small tool case into the front pocket of her jeans, and carried the flashlight, then locked up her car and slid the key into another pocket.

She wanted to travel light, just in case she had to move fast. Even though she had taken great care to leave no sign behind, there was always the chance the killer had realized someone had been in the cabin.

A slim chance, Jessie believed.

She followed the footpath from the road only about thirty yards, then veered off toward the east, and the shortcut she had found. It wasn't a path or a trail, just a very faint track she thought might have been made and maintained by deer and other wildlife passing through the woods.

Whatever had made it, she had yet to see any human footprints along the way, and she had followed the track several times by now. Before and after fairly heavy rainstorms. And still no sign anyone else had walked this way. Even though she moved quickly, she also moved cautiously, allowing her senses to flare out and probe her surroundings.

As she neared the cabin, she had to pull those senses in a bit, because what she always felt near and at the cabin was a sense of dread and darkness so absolute she had never been able to bring herself to just let it wash over her.

She wasn't strong enough for that. She didn't have to think about it; she just *knew*.

She had stopped beating herself up about it. It was something she just couldn't do. Fine. Everybody had their limits. What she *could* do was help stop the monster, and that was what she intended to do.

To give Emma her safe little town back, so she wouldn't . . .

Wouldn't . . .

That was always as far as the thought went. No matter how hard Jessie concentrated, she couldn't find the rest of that sentence. It was weird, and it bothered her on a level deeper than thought. She pushed it out of her mind, but this time for a very good reason.

She couldn't afford to be distracted.

She reached the cabin just then, circling warily as she always did, just to be safe, then went straight to the front door and unlocked it. Inside, she set her tool case and the flashlight on the coffee table, then took the time to check the bedroom and bath quickly, just to make sure nothing was different. Finding everything as it had been on her last visit, she went to the bookshelf and removed the book that secreted the box of trophies.

Aware of time passing, she resisted the temptation to do more than unlock and open it quickly just to make sure the contents were there and the same. They were, and as far as she could tell, nothing new had been added.

Good. That was very good.

She had considered long and hard about where she might be able to hide the box here in this very bare cabin; she had to assume that if he discovered it missing, he would suspect it had been taken away, not merely moved to a new hiding place. So the hiding place had to be one he wasn't likely to stumble upon, or even find easily if he *did* somehow suspect it was still here.

If all went according to plan, the next time he went for the box it would be in desperation, because the hunters were closing in on him.

Jessie returned the pretend book to its place on the shelf, and then went directly to the open fireplace. In the heat of summer it would never be used, or at least that was what she prayed would be true. She leaned into the opening and reached up inside the chimney, touching nothing with her fingers but allowing the box she held to slide along the rock until she felt the narrow ledge she had found.

The box fit perfectly.

She eased her arm from the chimney and looked at the logs piled on the iron grate, at the hearth, making sure there wasn't even a little soot knocked loose to drift down and catch his attention.

She didn't have to be a profiler to know that this

monster was neat to the point of being obsessive-compulsive; the extreme neat order of this place was proof enough of that.

There was no sign of soot.

Jessie reached back to get her lockpick kit from the coffee table, and unzipped it, removing a sharp tool. Then, very, very carefully, she scratched a tiny, almost invisible lightning bolt in the center of the flagstone hearth, pointing toward the fireplace. Only someone looking for a sign would see it.

She hoped.

THE PROBLEM WITH trying to find Jessie in Baron Hollow—anywhere in Baron Hollow—during the festival was, as Navarro observed, that it appeared every man, woman, and child within two hundred miles had decided to attend.

The problem was compounded by the fact that they didn't have a clue even where to start looking.

"Still can't ping her cell phone," Maggie reported briefly when Navarro pulled Emma into the recessed doorway of one of the few downtown stores that were closed and placed the call.

"GPS on her car?"

"Well, there we might have something. But you're not going to like it. I know I don't."

"What is it?"

"Her car moved early this morning. From the

inn, where it's been since she arrived. It was parked downtown near several stores."

"They've blocked off downtown for this damned festival," Navarro said.

"I know. This was early. Around seven. The car was parked near the corner of Main and Oak streets. Then about ten minutes later, it vanished."

"It what?"

"The GPS signal just stopped. Went dead." Maggie's voice was grim. "Jessie knows how to disable one, but it beats the hell out of me why she would. And if it wasn't her . . ."

"Then whoever she's after could be on to her." Navarro saw Emma's face whiten, and did his best to be positive. "Look, we all know those systems are prime targets for thieves. Maybe it was just stolen out of her car and she didn't notice. Or didn't care."

"According to the police history, that sort of crime really doesn't happen in Baron Hollow," Maggie said.

Navarro didn't ask how she knew that. "Okay. Then where she was parked . . ." He mentally went over the map of downtown, since he could see little of it due to the congestion of the festival. "The only thing open that early, around seven, would be the pharmacy. They have a breakfast counter, and open up early, even on holidays." He lifted his brows at Emma, and received a nod in return.

"Casual enough place to visit," Maggie said. "You and Emma both saw her later in the day, right?"

"Yeah, she was among the crowd right up until sometime around noon. It's nearly two now. We've been looking for at least an hour, and haven't seen a sign of her"

"So we can last place her car near a pharmacy, but that doesn't help us much. Would she have gone—wherever—on foot?"

"Emma says she's been leaving the inn every morning for days with a backpack, and you say her car was there up until this morning. I'm betting she'd definitely be on foot, if she's investigating. It's just too damned hard to maneuver a car anywhere around town with this festival going on."

"A good opportunity to check something out, if you knew whoever you were interested in was attending the festival."

"Yeah. Unless he's on to her. Then the festival becomes really good cover for someone else to also . . . vanish into the crowd. And we don't even know who else to look for."

Maggie's sigh was audible. "It could be innocent enough, or at least not dangerous, if it's her past she's probing. Depending on what's there, of course."

"Which I intend to find out ASAP," he said, his gaze fixed on Emma.

As she so often did, Maggie seemed well aware of what he meant. "Secrets can be burdens; don't make Emma's heavier, Nathan."

"No. No, I'll try not to. But if we're going to find Jessie, I need all the information possible."

"To decide whether she's investigating her past or a killer."

"Maybe both. I think we need to visit the pharmacy and find out if she talked to anyone there."

"Report back," Maggie said. "If you become unreachable for more than an hour, I'm calling in the troops. Understood?"

"Understood." He ended the call and slipped the phone back into its case on his belt. To Emma, he said, "I'm assuming you know everyone at the pharmacy?"

She nodded. "I could hear what your boss was saying, or at least some of it." She winced as the band currently playing finished their song with a rousing drum solo, then said, "Why would Jessie have moved her car? I mean, if she's been on foot all this time? The pharmacy is only a few blocks from the inn."

"I don't know why," Navarro said, taking her hand. "Let's go ask."

As always at such open events, there were numerous currents within the crowd, and it took them a while to find one moving in the general direction of the pharmacy. Emma said hello to several people, but they didn't stop for introductions, and she was all too aware that more than one curious soul had noticed their linked hands.

But she had more important things to worry about than her reputation, and when they crossed paths with Dan Maitland, she didn't hesitate to ask, "Hey, have you seen Jessie?"

He'd been working on a corn dog, and dabbed at his mouth with a napkin before replying, "Saw her this morning. Talked to her for a few minutes. Why?"

"We're looking for her," Emma answered without further explanation. She saw his gaze drop briefly to her hand, still linked with Navarro's, and wondered if he'd comment. They had dated from time to time, casually, more as friends than anything else.

But all he said was, "In this crowd you could lose the Pope. But I'll keep an eye out. If I see her, I'll tell her you're looking for her."

"Thanks."

As they went on, Navarro said, "I saw them talking. Neither one looked very happy."

"I know. I saw them too. But I also saw her talking with at least three other men, and though I can't be sure, all those conversations looked less than casual."

"Who was it?"

Emma didn't have to think about it; she'd been so focused on Jessie when she caught glimpses of her that those images were burned in her mind. "Our cousin Victor. Sam Conway, who owns and manages the *Daily Ledger*. Peter Troy, a local bad boy from our high school days and a fairly useless alcoholic now. I also saw her talking to Nellie Holt."

"Who is?"

"A casual friend from school, though more mine than Jessie's since we're the same age. Nellie writes feature stories for the *Ledger*. And dates Victor."

"Dates?"

"They're lovers. Months, at least, which must be a record of sorts for Victor."

Quick to pick up on a note in her voice even with all the noise around them, Navarro said, "From what I've overheard and . . . sensed . . . local gossip says there's a new tension between you and Victor. I'm guessing it has nothing to do with your friend being his lover."

"Of course not. Nellie's a big girl, no fool, and she knows what she's doing."

"Local gossip also says Victor wants to buy land you don't want to sell, and that's causing the tension."

Emma frowned at him as they paused to allow a cluster of people blocking their path to go on their way. "Well, you've really had your ear to the ground, haven't you? I know our gossip mill is second to none, but I wasn't aware there were so many people interested in whether Victor wins what he wants or I keep it. But it isn't just local gossip you've . . . picked up, is it?"

"No," he admitted. "I've been sensing bits and pieces. But either way, I don't believe the tension between you and Victor is about land. Or, at least, that's not the major cause. It's about what happened to Jessie, isn't it?"

"We can't talk about that out in the open," Emma said, continuing on toward the pharmacy.

Navarro bit back a sigh, then said, "So, basically, Jessie is touching base with people from the old days. Specific people."

"That's what it looks like. She could be pretty sure of seeing everyone today and being able to speak to whoever she wanted or needed to and make it look casual. More or less."

"She ambushed them," Navarro said. "If she had tough questions to ask, it would be the best way to catch someone off guard and possibly get a truthful—or at least honest—response."

"I'm just afraid—"

"Afraid of what? That she asked the wrong person the wrong question?"

"Some secrets are dangerous," Emma said finally. "And some people would do . . . a lot . . . to protect them."

EIGHTEEN

Aware of time ticking past, Jessie hesitated for just a moment, asking herself whether she really needed to do this.

Yes. She did.

She picked up her flashlight and left the cabin the way she had entered it, locking the door carefully behind her and then sliding the tool kit into her pocket.

She went around to the end of the cabin farthest from the almost-road that stopped on the other side of the stream. It wasn't the logical place to find the entrance to a cellar, and he had camouflaged it very effectively with raised flower beds on either side of it, but once she had started looking, it had been easy to find.

It looked like a typical cellar entrance from this perspective; she didn't even need a lockpick. She had opened the hatch-like door the day she'd found it, her last day exploring the exterior of the cabin, but had been running out of time and had been forced to stop there.

Even so, the sense of dread she felt from this place was all here, all down in the earth beneath the cabin, and she *had* to see what was down there. Even though she knew.

The lack of a lock on the exterior door troubled her, but she assumed there would be another door once she made her way down the steps that appeared to have been cut out of the hard earth. These old-fashioned cellars had been cut so there was a cool place to store vegetables and other perishables in the days before electric refrigeration came along.

Jessie turned her flashlight on and aimed it down the steps, hesitated only a moment, and cautiously began to go down. At the bottom of the stairs, she found—a root cellar.

At least to the casual glance.

The area smelled of the earth, and it was cooler than outside. But to Jessie it felt cold. Very cold. She had to force herself to ignore that chill, to stand her ground and shine her flashlight around the small space. Rough shelves with what looked like canning jars of various vegetables and soups; a neat rack of gardening tools; a couple of stacks of clay pots for plants or flowers. And—a door.

It looked newer than she had expected it to, but that was probably because it was a steel door, its surface smooth and reflective. Jessie had to move toward it several steps before she could really make out any details in the glare of her flashlight's reflected beam.

It was solid except for a two-foot-by-two-foot piece of heavy steel mesh, closely woven but not so closely as to prevent air from, presumably, reaching the space beyond it. And it had what looked like a simple door handle, with a simple keyhole beneath it. That was all.

She wasn't surprised to find the door locked. Nor was she surprised that the lock was more difficult to pick than might have been expected from its appearance. So much so that after a good ten minutes of careful effort she felt a decided sense of triumph when she finally heard the *click,* and got to her feet to open the door.

Pain. Terror. Pain. Terror. Pain.

Jessie drew in a breath, realizing only then that the force of the emotions battering her had literally stopped her breathing, and for long enough that the first breath she drew was actually painful.

In more ways than one. Because when she did breathe, all she smelled was death.

Somehow, she managed not to drop everything and run as she wanted to do, as all her instincts and senses insisted she do. Instead, she shored up her walls even more, with desperate strength, and stepped through the door.

It felt like she was entering hell itself.

Her flashlight showed her that this part of the cellar was intended to store something other than vegetables or tools. This space was lined with lumber walls and ceiling, and the metal racks fastened to those walls held . . . implements . . . that were tools of horror. Knives and other bladed instruments like saws; whips of every kind; straps ending in buckles and spikes; heavy cudgels, their ends horribly stained.

Everything was stained. With blood.

If he was neat to a fault upstairs, down here he allowed his inner demons their absolute freedom. Because nothing had been cleaned, not even of bits of human tissue and hair caught in sticky blood.

Sickened, she turned her flashlight's beam away from that tool wall, and wished she hadn't. Directly in front of her was a chair contraption that was also stained with blood, and beyond it was a cot—with a heavy chain with a cuff at one end and the other end bolted to the wall.

The mattress on the cot was stained.

Again, Jessie wanted to run, but there was a closed door on the left-hand wall, and she took a step farther in, turning her flashlight so she could see—

She felt something against her ankle, and in the instant before it happened, she realized that she had fallen into his trap.

The trip wire was rigged to what was probably a simple pulley and weight system that slammed the steel door shut behind Jessie, and when she whirled to shine her light on the door, she went cold to her marrow.

This side of the door was smooth, featureless except for the heavy steel mesh ventilation panel.

There was no handle.

There was no lock.

There was no way out.

"WHAT DO YOU mean she left town?" Emma was staring at Patty, a clerk at the pharmacy who insisted she had talked to Jessie that morning before the festival.

"It was early and I'd agreed to pull a split shift," she explained, more to Navarro than to Emma. She tucked a strand of coppery hair behind one ear and smiled at him winningly. "So I could spend at least part of the day at the festival. I was here early. And so was Jessie."

"What did she say?" Navarro asked.

"Not a lot, really. Said her throat was scratchy, allergies probably, and bought some cough drops. I asked her if she was looking forward to the fireworks tonight, and she said she'd be gone by then. Said her work had called, and she had to head back to New Mexico. Have you ever been to New Mexico? Because it really sounds gorgeous, and—"

"Did she say when she was leaving?" Emma asked.

"Said she'd probably stay for a while, maybe until lunchtime, but then she had to hit the road."

"You're sure?" Emma sounded baffled, and wore the expression as well.

"Well, I'm sure that's what she said. Had her car

outside, said she was going to park it way down on the end of town closest to the highway so she could get out when she had to."

"Thanks," Navarro said briefly, drawing Emma, unresisting, away from the counter and toward the door. As soon as they were outside the store, he said, "Would she lie about something so . . . trivial to her?"

"Patty? No, I don't think so. She's known as one of the biggest gossips in town, but she's also—sometimes uncomfortably—accurate in what she says." Emma shook her head. "But it doesn't make any sense. Why would Jessie leave without so much as a word?"

Navarro looked at the length of crowded street between their position and Rayburn House, blocks away, and said, "We can work our way to the inn and see if she packed up. I doubt anyone else could have done that given the extra security on the family floor."

Emma didn't ask how he knew about that. "But to just leave without a word? Knowing you were here and wanted to talk to her? Knowing she was supposed to report back to Haven?"

"Maggie said she had the knack of justifying her actions after the fact; maybe this is one of those times."

"But it doesn't make any sense," Emma said as she walked beside him—as best she could—along the crowded sidewalk. "I *know* she was close to finding whatever it was she was looking for, because last night she had that look she used to have when we were kids and she was about to do something to get herself in trouble—"

Even as the words left her lips, Emma felt a chill of understanding. "Dammit, that's *exactly* what she had in mind. She intentionally avoided meeting up with you, and ducked both of us all day because she had some cockeyed plan she was hell-bent to see through."

"A plan that included leaving Baron Hollow? Or just making it seem as if she did?"

"I don't know."

Navarro's fingers tightened on hers, and he kept his voice as low as he could, given the crowd all around them. "Either way, Emma, you're going to have to break your promise and tell me what happened to Jessie fifteen years ago. If she's crossed paths with a serial killer, that's an investigation she is *not* trained to handle, not alone."

"I know," Emma said.

JESSIE STOOD THERE staring at the door, her flashlight's beam running over it as though searching for something she knew damned well she would never find.

Goddammit to hell.

Stupid of her, she realized now. He'd been getting away with this for a long, long time, and she should have understood what that meant.

She shouldn't have underestimated him.

Because of course he would have set a trap. Even if she hadn't raised his suspicions, just as a matter of self-preservation he would have set a trap. She should have realized that.

Too late now.

It was a trap she had fallen into.

Panic surged through her, and she pulled her weapon from the small of her back and aimed it roughly at where the lock and handle were on the other side. And pulled the trigger.

Only a hollow clicking rewarded her efforts.

She stared at the gun and, her training finally taking control, checked it. The clip was empty. In juggling her tool kit and flashlight with the gun, she hadn't noticed the difference in weight.

Jessie felt her heart pounding, her stomach churning.

Bastard. Bastard.

Somehow, he had known it was her. Known she was hunting him. Because she had cleaned and reloaded her gun the previous night, and put it straight into her backpack.

The backpack that had been locked in her car all day while she'd been at the festival—and this morning it had been parked near the pharmacy.

Had he done it then? Had the son of a bitch, unobserved or just unnoticed, unlocked her car and found and unloaded her gun? Had there even been enough time for that? Or had he followed her to where she had left her car all morning, and taken his time getting in and unloading her weapon? Not that it really mattered now.

Bastard.

Bastard.

She was well and truly trapped. Trapped behind a door with no lock she could pick despite her tools, and a gun that was useless without its bullets.

Trapped.

There was no space for her to stand behind the door and try to ambush him whenever he came. He might wait until her flashlight's battery died and she was in total darkness when he came after her. And despite all the killing tools around her, her bet was that he would come through that door either with a gun of his own or a Taser. Something that would bring her down quickly and easily despite whatever she managed to arm herself with.

Hell, for all she knew, he had the place rigged to fill with gas.

As soon as that thought occurred, Jessie began to shine her light around the horrible space, this time searching for some chink in the trap, something she could block, or plug up, or otherwise render useless. Her flashlight pierced the pitch darkness of the room, and she forced herself to move it slowly, methodically.

Anything to occupy her mind, to try not to think about how terrifying her situation was.

Trapped.

Helpless.

And no one, absolutely no one, knew where she was. Her car was well off the road in an area not likely to be searched. That was if anybody bothered to look for her after she'd taken such pains to seemingly leave Baron Hollow. She would be missed eventually, of course, when she didn't turn up back at base, and they'd send somebody to look for her. Maggie would make sure of that if nobody else did.

But . . . she hadn't reported her suspicions, much less her findings. Hadn't confided in her sister. Had, as during her most irresponsible days, gone her own way alone, hell-bent to figure it all out for herself and damn the consequences.

Even Maggie would consider that. Even Emma. Especially Emma. And anyone else in her life.

She had, after all, a history of just driving away whenever life got to be too much to handle. That was what they'd say.

What even Emma would say.

Jessie wasn't a defeatist. Never had been. But if the past few years had taught her anything, it was that some things had to happen just the way they happened.

She had fallen into his trap.

Okay, then. Ignore the terror. Don't think about that. Think about your training. Survival—that's what you think about. Think about whatever you can use. There's plenty here.

Surely I can fight him. Hurt him.
I can do something.

At the very least, she could give the bastard a hell of a fight.

Before he killed her.

HE SPENT SEVERAL minutes watching her on the small screen of his cell phone, idly wondering if she would find the infrared camera placed high above the doorway and giving him an excellent view of her careful, seemingly professional search of her prison.

She was good. Quite methodical.

He wondered when it would dawn on her that she would never leave that place alive.

Smiling, he cleared the screen and slipped the phone into his pocket even as he slipped back into the festival crowd, secure in the knowledge that his camera would continue to record and that he could watch it all later.

Technology was amazing.

There was an app for everything.

EMMA HANDED THE note to Navarro, vaguely surprised to see that her hands were steady. "It's her handwriting. And the way she'd word it, short and sweet. 'Gotta go, it's work, call you soon.'"

"And you're sure she packed up all her belongings?" They were in the foyer of the family suite.

"Everything's gone." Emma sank down on an upholstered bench and absently petted her dog, who had joined them as soon as they'd come into the inn.

Navarro was frowning. "It all feels very carefully planned to me. Jessie intended people to think she had left Baron Hollow."

"But why would she, if she *was* on the trail of a killer? Wouldn't she want to be here when he was caught?"

"I'd think so. Unless . . ."

"Unless what?"

"Unless her being here posed some kind of threat. Or if she was convinced that the killer had to believe she'd left town, maybe because she suspected he was on to her, and wanted to make very sure he believed he didn't have to worry about that anymore. To give us time to call in the troops before he could panic and run, or destroy evidence. Or do something worse."

"It makes as much sense as any other possibility, I guess. But why the hell couldn't she tell one of us that was what she was going to do? Why just make damned sure neither of us could talk to her beforehand? Afraid we'd screw up her plans?"

"Maybe." Navarro shrugged, still frowning. "From everything Maggie said, I gather Jessie does tend to go it alone. And, honestly, being the one to locate a serial killer is a pretty big feather for anyone's cap—if that matters to her. If she's looking for validation. Could that be one of her motives?"

Emma shook her head. "I don't know what to think anymore. But . . . the GPS system in her car, that bothers me. If she wanted the killer to believe she was leaving, why disable that? I mean, I don't know if he could have used it to track her—" She stopped, lifting fingers to massage her left temple. "Or could that be it? She's not *really* gone, just waiting somewhere close by, out of town, but just in case he could track her, she disabled the system?"

Navarro looked like he didn't want to say what he had to. "Maggie hasn't called. Which means Jessie hasn't called in the troops. Not yet, at least."

"Maybe she's waiting until after the festival. Waiting until she's really sure he believes she's gone."

"Maybe."

"You can't sense anything?"

"No."

Emma eyed him uncertainly. "You've tried?"

"I've been trying all day. There are just too damned many people crammed into this town. It's like listening to white noise." His head was pounding as a result of the effort.

"I have a splitting headache," Emma muttered.

Navarro wondered whether Emma had unconsciously reached out herself, psychically, trying to find her sister.

Maybe.

He hesitated, then said, "Look, I know you're still not comfortable breaking your promise to Jessie, but I need to know what you know. Whether her plan is a good one or a bad one, there's always the chance something will go wrong, and I'm handicapped if I don't know what's driving her."

Emma looked at him for a long moment, then got to her feet. "I'm going to take a few aspirin for my head and get some caffeine. You want anything? It may be a long story."

He nodded, following her into the sitting area of the suite. "Something cold would be good. Emma . . ."

She stood at the fridge and looked at him inquiringly.

"You have to realize that something could have already gone wrong with Jessie's plan. The note and the absence of her things, what she told Patty at the pharmacy, even moving her car, all that shows planning, and tells us she meant to leave, or at least get some distance away. But the fact that she hasn't contacted Maggie . . ."

"I know." She handed him a cold drink, then murmured again that she needed aspirin, and headed toward her bedroom.

Navarro sat down on one end of a comfortable sofa, rather surprised to find that Emma's dog had remained rather than following her mistress; she sat a few feet away, watching him with an intentness he could feel almost like a touch.

"Did Jessie bother to tell *you* where she was going?" he asked the dog dryly.

She cocked her head to one side in a quick gesture, as if hearing something unfamiliar.

Navarro decided that talking to someone else's dog was a bit like talking to himself. He pulled out his cell and made a call.

Maggie heard him out, then said, "You're right; she hasn't called here. Not even a text message."

He could hear it in her voice. "But?"

"I was just about to call you." She drew a breath and let it out slowly. "I've never had a really strong connection with Jessie, but I can tell you she's in trouble."

"Any idea what kind?"

"She feels trapped. And panicked."

Navarro didn't have to look at a clock to know that the day was rapidly winding down. "It'll be dark in a few hours; even in summer this valley loses the sunlight early. We don't even have time to launch a search. And not a clue where to start looking; from all appearances, from witnesses to what she said to a note in her own handwriting, Jessie just left town. I've got a hunch the chief isn't going to be all that concerned, especially if we report Jessie missing with no evidence except our feelings and hunches."

Steadily, Maggie said, "Then you're on your own,

at least until you have some evidence she's in trouble, or you can convince the police that's true despite the lack of any proof." Maggie drew another breath. "John and I can report her missing, no contact, no GPS on her car, say she was supposed to check in and didn't . . . but she's an adult."

"With a history of just taking off," Navarro added grimly. "Especially from this town."

"Yeah. Look, find out what you can, talk it through, try to figure out what Jessie was really up to, but you and Emma be careful. Jessie may have asked the wrong person the wrong question, and you two could do the same thing."

"You believe this killer is somehow connected to whatever happened to Jessie fifteen years ago, don't you?"

"I don't believe in coincidence," Maggie replied. "And neither do you."

NINETEEN

Jessie had no way of knowing how much time had passed, but she was certain it was hours, because she had explored every inch of her prison, and had broken her lockpick tools spending what felt like forever trying to unlock the door along the left-hand wall.

She suspected he had somehow booby-trapped that lock, because she was careful and she was good—and tools like that didn't just break. He was just toying with her; that was what she thought. Toying with her, allowing her to believe there might be a way out, and then making certain she would be defeated.

Bastard.

Jessie's bravado lasted a long time. Refusing to waste time thinking about what would happen to her if she couldn't escape, she concentrated fiercely on finding a way. She explored, and she thought, and when she finally had to admit to herself that there was no way she could escape on her own, she methodically considered and rejected various plans of how she might get the upper hand whenever he came for her.

She refused to give up.

When she spotted the infrared camera, she went to get the horribly bloody chair so she could stand on it and smash the camera, only to find that the chair was somehow fastened to the hard dirt floor. Her guess was concrete underneath, but she didn't bother to confirm it.

Refusing to give him the satisfaction of seeing her panic—because surely he was watching or recording her—she kept her face expressionless as she nerved herself to pick up several of the blood- and tissue-covered implements until she finally found one she was able to throw at the camera and smash it.

"Fuck you," she muttered, feeling a surge of triumph.

Her bravado lasted a long time.

And then she realized her flashlight was growing dim.

"Oh, shit," she whispered.

NAVARRO WASN'T NORMALLY a pacing sort of man, but he prowled around the sitting room like a restless cat in a cage. Outside, darkness had finally fallen, and they could hear the sounds of the fireworks of the festival getting under way.

Neither of them felt very festive, and Emma had a lapful of Sheltie who hated fireworks.

"I should have told you sooner," Emma said. "Promise or no promise." Her eyes were still a little red, as they had been when she had finally returned to tell him what she knew of Jessie's mission, but her voice was steady.

He gestured slightly, as though pushing that aside. "You say she was still claiming she didn't remember what happened to her, but was certain something had."

"That's what she said. She was focused on Victor, at least in the beginning, and said she definitely remembered him egging her on to drink too much. But, later . . . if anything, she seemed less certain as time went on, more baffled. Distracted."

Curled up at one end of the couch, stroking her trembling dog, Emma watched him prowl and tried to remember every nugget of information Jessie had shared. "She seemed to think she'd find the answers she needed during the festival, when she talked to—whoever it was she suspected. She was so closemouthed about it all, especially these last few days. Dammit, I don't even know for sure if—if she was hurt, or how many men she suspected. She—she never actually said there was more than one, or at least I'm not sure she did, but thinking back I got the impression there was."

"We both saw her talk to a lot of people today, Emma."

"I know, I know." Emma chewed on a thumbnail for a moment, then said, "It was so hard to tell, at a distance and with so many people around, how many there were or even who some of them were. But she *did* talk to Victor. And Sam, and Dan, and Peter Troy. Others. And we have no way of knowing which one mattered."

Navarro stopped pacing and looked at her. "Jessie is not dead—you realize that, right?"

"You mean not yet."

"She's alive."

Holding her voice steady, Emma asked, "Trapped and panicked, according to your boss?"

"She's alive," Navarro repeated.

"Will you feel it when she dies?"

The stark question hung in the air between them for a long moment, until Navarro said reluctantly, "You're more likely to feel it—to know—than I am. At least at first. Have you given up already, Emma?"

She wanted to say no, but Emma found she couldn't give him an answer at all. Because somewhere deep inside herself, she had a terrible feeling that Jessie's life could be measured in hours.

And there wasn't a damned thing Emma could do to save her.

HE USED A Taser on her.

That was all it took, a blinding light fixed on her the moment the door swung suddenly open, and the darts of a Taser shooting out to stab her.

The next thing Jessie knew, she was trying to shake off the effects of the mini-electrocution even as she realized she was duct-taped to the bloodstained chair.

Naked.

At first, the lights blinded her, and she didn't recognize his voice when he spoke to her from somewhere behind them.

"What I don't get is why you came back here at all. You never gave a shit about this place, and couldn't wait to shake the dust of it off your feet."

"Fuck you," she said.

Sounding amused now, he said, "Defiant to the end? Hey, I don't really care, you know. Why you came back. And I am grateful that you set the stage so well for a repeat performance of your dramatic departure fifteen years ago. All you left for me to do was ditch your car."

"It's hard to ditch a car these days," she managed.

"Not when the GPS system is disabled. I disabled yours before you drove it out of town. The same time I emptied the clip of your gun. I had a feeling you wouldn't notice either one. You always were a little careless with details."

"Fuck you," she repeated.

He actually laughed. "And before I destroyed your tablet, I checked to make sure you hadn't sent any nasty little reports back to that outfit you work for. I didn't have time to work out your password and open that file, but it was easy enough to check the system and know it had never been sent anywhere at all."

Thank God he doesn't know I found his trophy box. That thought was followed by a more desperate one. *Don't let him wonder where I might have left a backup of the stuff on the laptop.*

At least she had that triumph. Because if he had known she'd found the box, he would, undoubtedly, torture her until she told him where she'd hidden it. And Jessie had no illusions; hurt somebody enough and they'd tell you anything.

Anything to stay alive just a little while longer.

Trying to put that off as long as she possibly could, she said, "That doesn't mean I didn't tell someone. What—you think they'd send me here alone?"

"I think you came here alone. To find your past.

Based on the questions you were asking some of us during the festival, that's my guess. All that stuff about one party in a summer full of them. Who was there, what did we do, who was making out with who. Like you thought something unusual had happened, but couldn't remember what it was. And, you know, that's something I find really surprising."

"I don't know what you're talking about."

"Yeah, that. I can't decide whether it's because you're actually a real psychic, or if you're just really good at blocking things out and rewriting your own past."

Unable to help herself, she said, "What the hell?"

He made a *tsk-tsk* sound. "I guess connections matter. Because it must have taken a boatload of guilt for you to carry the burden all these years. Even if you couldn't quite remember, it was still your burden, wasn't it? You ran away, and took it all with you, so she could feel safe here. Sort of ironic that you ended up working for a place called Haven. Because that's what you made sure Emma had here. Haven."

Whispering now, Jessie said, "I don't—you don't—Who the hell are you?"

He stepped in front of one of the lights, in silhouette at first, and then turned another of the lights so she could see him. He was holding a very big knife. And he was smiling.

"I'm the devil, Jessie. Didn't you know? Because Emma knew. Whatever she's forgotten since, Emma knew. Fifteen years ago."

The smells in the room were liquor and sweat and sex, and something burning that could have been incense or grass or something she didn't recognize. But she recognized the smell of his breath, because it wasn't just whiskey; it was rotten eggs. Sulfur.

It was hell.

It was evil.

Jerked around, her face slammed into a door frame, maybe a fist or two, a blow, another, a cracking agony when a rib gave way. And then he was on top of her, inside her, thrusting and grunting, and she could feel her flesh tear even as it cringed away from him as something even more unnatural than the act of violence.

She was being held down for him, her ankles and wrists, and the others were laughing drunkenly, urging him on, daring him to "tear her up" and "teach her what it's all about."

She turned her head to try to escape the whiskey-soaked, rotten-egg smell of his breath, and through tear-blurred eyes she stared at the tattoo on the inside of his forearm.

A rose, wound about by a thorny cage.

Trapped.

". . . show you," he gritted out in a hoarse whisper, thrusting harder, faster. "I'll show you. You won't get away from me this time, Rose. You'll never get away from me again."

Lost in a haze of pain and confusion and terror, she could almost feel a part of herself trying to escape, trying to just . . . go some-where else, somewhere this wasn't happening. Be someone this wasn't happening to.

And when he was finally done with her, dragging himself off her with a brutal laugh, when the others released her, she turned on her side and curled into a ball, hurting so badly she didn't understand how she was even still alive and breathing.

"Hey, maybe we should take her home," one of them said in a voice that was abruptly on the cusp of sober. "Or to a hospital. She looks . . . she looks pretty bad."

Another voice laughed and said, "Yeah, you messed her up real good. The sloppy seconds are going to be—"

There was an odd gurgling sound, and then the evil one said, "Nobody else touches her. Got it?"

A cough, and then, "Yeah, yeah, sure, no problem. You ruined her for anybody else anyway, man, you really did."

"Just get the hell out of here. And keep your mouths shut, both of you."

There were sounds, footsteps, stumbling a bit, then the door opening and closing.

She felt his hot breath on her face again, but kept her eyes closed tightly and tried to be someone else.

"Not a word, you little bitch. Hear me? Not a word to anybody, ever, or I'll make tonight feel like a day at the beach."

She might have whimpered an assent; she wasn't sure. But eventually the sour breath moved away, and there were more footsteps, and the door opened and closed.

She didn't know how long she lay there, hurting, trying to catch her breath when every one stabbed at her. Her face hurt where he had slapped her at some point; she couldn't really remember. Maybe he had punched her. Or one of the others had.

It was getting harder to remember the details. She just hurt all over. And so badly inside.

After a long, long time, she managed to pull herself to the edge of the bed. It was even harder to breathe when she moved, but she forced herself to make the effort. She wanted to get out of here. She wanted to go home.

She wanted to forget this had ever happened.

She wanted to be somebody else.

The bedroom was strange to her, unfamiliar, but the bathroom door was open a crack, and somehow she managed to pull herself off the bed and stagger to it. The light was on, and it was bright. She squinted and avoided looking in the mirror, just hobbled to the sink on legs that felt weak and so, so shaky.

She ran some water and bent over, gasping because of the pain that stabbed her with the movement. She cupped her hands and splashed water on her face. It hurt. And her fingers felt how puffy her eyes were, felt the swelling along one jaw and the pain in her nose.

She slowly straightened, the pain in her middle stealing her breath again. And looked in the mirror.

She saw Jessie's horrified face, staring at her, heard her sister whisper, "Oh, my God, Emma . . ."

Jessie, she realized, was behind her, in the doorway.

Then she looked at her own reflection, and something in her mind and soul turned over with an agonizing twist. Both her eyes were nearly swollen shut, the bruising just beginning. Her nose was obviously broken, her lips swollen, the bottom one split in two places. Her jaw was swollen and turning bluish.

There was a vicious bite mark on her collarbone. And high on her left breast . . .

And that was when Emma Rayburn's mind decided not to remember.

NAVARRO SAT BOLT upright in bed, hardly aware of the light of dawn struggling to push its way into his room. For a long, long moment he couldn't breathe at all, and when he did it was with a harsh sound.

He threw back the covers and got out of bed, dressing quickly. He left his suite without bothering to take his key, intent only on reaching Emma as quickly as he could.

The inn was lit for the night, a few shaded lamps glowing in rooms dawn hadn't yet reached. It was silent.

He went up the stairs two at a time until he reached the family floor, and even as he got there the door was opening and Emma, pale and grave, stood there. She was wrapped in a long, thick robe, and drew it about her even tighter as she turned silently and preceded him into the sitting room.

Lamps were lit in the room. She sat at one end of the couch, and her little dog immediately jumped up beside her and snuggled close with a soft whine.

Much as he wanted to, Navarro wouldn't have dared touch her. Not then. He sat down on the chair closest to her, where he could watch her face, and be as near as he thought she could bear.

She began to stroke the dog, her gaze fixed on it. "You know," she said, her voice curiously still. "Did you . . . Was it the dream?"

"Yes," he said.

She swallowed. "The whole dream?"

"I think so."

An odd smile twisted her lips. "Every summer. Every summer I was someone else. And I never knew why. Even when you asked me, I didn't have a good answer. I just knew . . . I had to get away from here, and be someone else.

"And then I fell and hit my head, and started dreaming about . . . horrible things. And met you in St. Louis. And I started to . . . not want to be someone else anymore. Even in the summer."

"It's going to be all right, Emma. You're going to be all right. You're stronger than you know. You can handle this."

"I didn't remember," Emma said. "Any of it. Even when Jessie came back, when she talked about that night, I didn't remember it happened to me instead of her." She looked at Navarro for the first time, honestly bewildered. "How could I not *remember?*"

"The mind protects itself," he said. "Something it's very, very good at doing."

"For fifteen years?"

"Sometimes for a lifetime." He held his voice steady with an effort, trying not to think about how she had been brutalized. "If you hadn't fallen and hit your head, if your abilities hadn't gone active, if Jessie hadn't come home . . . maybe you never would have remembered."

"Maybe that would have been better."

"You remember now because you need to."

"Do I?" She sounded lost. "Do I have to?"

Navarro hesitated, unwilling to offer platitudes. Instead, he said, "We are who and what our experiences have made us, Emma. For better or worse. You remember now because your mind decided you could handle the memories. Face them. And . . ."

Tears spilled silently from her wide eyes and flowed down her pale face. "And Jessie isn't here to protect me anymore. Not in this life. I felt her go. I felt her die. She suffered horribly. Horribly. And—and she remembered. Right there at the end, she remembered it all. Even though it happened to me and not her, her mind was able to re-create what I endured. Even somehow to feel it herself. As if it had happened to her instead of me. She had carried those *memories* buried inside her since she ran away. But what he did to her tonight . . . it unlocked the door. That's why I remember it now. She can't carry the burden anymore. The guilt. The shame. The . . . overwhelming rage and pain. She carried all that buried inside her for fifteen years."

"Why did she carry it at all?" Navarro asked softly.

"Because she blamed herself. My going to the party was her idea." Emma didn't seem to notice the tears that continued to fall. "She was my big sister, responsible for me. And that *meant* something to her. Dad was out of town for nearly a month on business. The housekeeper pretty much let us do what we wanted; it wasn't her job to parent us, just to . . . be there. Jessie had been to those parties before, but I never had. She picked out my clothes. Did my hair. Makeup. Let me wear the earrings that had belonged to our mother. It was supposed to be . . . fun."

"Emma . . ."

"I had to promise not to drink—that was the only rule. So I promised. And I didn't drink anything but soda. Jessie's the one who . . . Jessie drank. Victor egged her on; it seemed to amuse him. Then . . . then things get hazy . . ." She drew a breath and let it out slowly. "I think someone helped Jessie upstairs. I think I followed them, because I was worried. And she . . . she passed out."

"In that bedroom?"

"I think so. She was out cold. And I was there. He wanted somebody. He wanted . . . *me*. For some reason, he wanted me, and I was there."

Because he had to, Navarro asked, "Who was he, Emma? Who raped you?"

"I—I don't remember that. I don't remember his face. I don't even remember the other two, the ones who . . . held me down. I remember the smells . . . and the sounds . . . and the pain. But I don't remember who they were."

"What about the rose tattoo?"

Emma nodded slowly. "I remember that. A rose surrounded by thorns. But I don't remember ever seeing it again after that night. If he still lives here—"

"You know he does, Emma. Whatever memories and emotions Jessie had blocked for so long, she was beginning to recover. She was asking questions. Threatening him. Her memories were leading her straight to him. And he couldn't let her expose him. Not only for what happened fifteen years ago, but for everything that's happened since."

"Killing. He's been killing women."

Quietly, Navarro said, "There's no way of know- ing when rape stopped satisfying him, but I'm betting when we find him, and uncover his past, we'll find other women he brutalized who survived. Then something changed, and he began to kill."

TWENTY

JULY 5

Emma reported her sister missing early on Sunday morning. And though Dan appeared doubtful, especially when Emma showed him Jessie's note and reported what she'd told Patty at the pharmacy, he at least sent officers out to double-check the story.

It might have been because Emma was so pale and quiet that he was willing to go to the extra trouble. Or it might have been because of Navarro, standing silently at Emma's shoulder.

Either way, by the time the church crowd turned up in a downtown area remarkably clean considering the chaos of the day before, most everyone knew that Jessie Rayburn had left Baron Hollow.

Run away again, some said.

Several people stepped forward to claim they'd seen her drive that little car of hers out of town toward the highway, and though there was some confusion about just when that was, at least two witnesses stuck stubbornly to their story that it was afternoon, during the festival.

"She left, Emma." Dan shrugged. "She told people she was leaving, she left you a good-bye note, and witnesses saw her leave. She's an adult and she left. What can I do?"

Emma looked at Navarro, then quietly thanked the police chief, and they left his office. Outside, she said, "It's a little difficult figuring out how to push him to look for her when he's one of the suspects."

They had figured out, starting with a list of men they knew Jessie had talked to during the festival, doing some math, and looking through high school yearbooks, that there were half a dozen possible suspects in what Emma had endured, given various ages and—as well as she remembered—which boys had tended to hang out together.

Navarro was keeping a close eye on Emma, unwilling to leave her even to look for Jessie, especially when he knew the search would be for her body. Not that he thought his abilities would be of any use to him; he was so focused on Emma that nothing else could get in.

Even though something dark was trying to.

Emma was calm, but it was a fragile, uncertain calm. Uppermost in her mind, what she was hanging on to with fierce determination, was the need to find her sister, and even though she had felt Jessie's death herself, she continued to question that what she had felt was real.

"You don't feel her?" She had asked him that several times already that day.

And he replied as he already had: "I'm feeling a lot of dark energy, but it's . . . diffused. I can't bring anything into focus."

"When you reported in, your boss . . . She knew, didn't she? She knew about Jessie. That she's dead."

Remembering Maggie's voice, Navarro nodded, still wary of pushing Emma too far too fast. He believed keeping her focused on Jessie was the lesser of two evils; the murder of a sister she had barely spoken to in her entire adult life was tragic enough, but it wasn't as likely to break her as the crushing weight of a horrifically traumatic event in her own past, newly remembered.

"She knew. And considering how badly Maggie takes the loss of any operative, much less one she cared about as she did Jessie, I'm giving her maybe twenty-four hours before she calls in the troops."

"You say that like it's a bad thing."

"It's a good thing if we know who we're looking for. I mean, aside from Jessie. Right now, we have no evidence against anyone, and no way of knowing what Jessie had discovered. If more Haven operatives show up, or Maggie's able to persuade Bishop to throw out the rule book and bring his FBI unit in without an invitation, we've still got nothing."

"We have suspects," she said.

"On the thinnest of legal pretexts—if that." Navarro shook his head. "I don't like it, but we can't just start accusing people, or even questioning them, without some good reason. Because if we don't have a good reason, and find evidence later on . . ."

"Jessie's killer could go free."

"Maybe. It depends on what else he's done. The point is, we risk a lot by not following rules of evidence. And if this killer is the serial we think he is, we want him dead or in a prison cell for the rest of his life, and we don't want him killing anyone else along the way."

"I know you're right," Emma said. "But . . . it's hard. Waiting. Wondering if we'll ever find her."

"We'll find her," Navarro said. "I can promise you that."

JULY 6

It took him a while to get away, but after so long at his job—his true job, his vocation—he had gotten very good at making people believe he was somewhere other than where he was.

It was a skill that came in handy.

He drove as far as he could, using an alternate car that wouldn't attract attention, then parked it where it wouldn't be seen and went the rest of the way on foot. It wasn't exactly an easy hike, but it was near enough that it didn't take him very long.

He went directly around to the side and down into the cellar, moving through the dim space easily as one long familiar with it. He used his key to unlock the steel door and went inside, ignoring the familiar tools and implements and going to the other door, which he also unlocked. The tiny room was occupied only by the big lights he used—and a large chest freezer.

Idly, he wondered if she had even guessed that he had tapped into Baron Hollow's power supply. Probably not, since he used that electricity only to run the freezer. And the line was buried all the way to the junction where he'd tapped in.

Shrugging off the musing, along with a lingering regret that he hadn't had the time to really play with her as he'd wanted, he opened the freezer.

She wasn't very big, but she'd been in the freezer for a while, so she was almost locked into an awkward position. Awkward for him, at least. But that, too, was something he was accustomed to dealing with. He had brought a black, zippered body bag—amazing what you could buy off the Internet these days—and once he'd maneuvered her out of the freezer and into the roomy, handled bag, it was much easier for him.

He took her to his garden, again feeling mild regret, this time because he really didn't have the time to let her thaw out before he planted her. He had thought he would have time, and so had dug the hole to the appropriate size and shape the day before.

Well, she'd fit anyway. Might not be too comfortable for her, but there was really nothing to be done about that. He didn't have the luxury of time, not anymore.

Because if he stopped what he was doing and listened, very, very intently, he could hear the warning whispers.

They know.
They'll be looking for you.
They'll be looking for your flowers.

So he shortened the usual ceremony, annoyed by the necessity, merely removing her from the black bag and placing her in the hole prepared for her. Naked.

He always took their clothes. Not as *trophies* the way those profilers talked about, because he burned the clothes. It was just that he needed to enjoy his flowers in their purest form, naked as God had made them.

He wished he'd had more time with this one.

But, conscious of time ticking away, he got his shovel and began to plant his flower, burying the body of Jessie Rayburn.

BREAKFAST IN THE dining room of Rayburn House was very subdued on that Monday morning, so much so that Hollis instinctively lowered her voice when she said, "Considering that the official verdict is that Jessie left town under her own steam Saturday, this place is . . ."

"Depressing?" DeMarco offered. "I'd agree. And, since most of the guests here for the festival have checked out, pretty empty too."

"Yeah, but—" Hollis looked toward the doorway, and her eyes widened.

Familiar with the expression, DeMarco waited until she very softly said, "Oh, shit," before he asked a quiet question.

"Jessie?"

Hollis nodded. "Dammit, I was hoping she really

had left on her own. Or, if she hadn't, that at least one of us could pick up *something* to help find her before the bastard killed her."

"It's certainly not for lack of trying," her partner pointed out. "And at least we can do something now. If you want to take on Chief Maitland, that is."

Hollis smiled grimly. "Let's go."

DAN MAITLAND WASN'T happy to be called to the office; it was supposed to be his Monday off. But he came, because Melissa had sounded baffled and uncertain as to what to do, and when he got there he realized why.

The two paranormal researchers were in his office.

"Gordon is still working in the Rayburn family archives," Hollis Templeton said earnestly by way of a greeting, "or he'd be here too. He's very excited."

"Why?" Maitland asked as he sat down.

"The spirit."

Maitland sighed. "I suppose your cameras or recorders caught something you believe is definitive?" That was usually the case, though all Maitland had ever seen or heard were smudges or reflected light on video and indistinguishable sounds on audio.

That was the "genuine" stuff produced by "serious" researchers.

The faked stuff was a lot more entertaining—and a lot more obviously fake.

"Not quite," Reese DeMarco murmured.

"I saw her," Hollis said. "Less than an hour ago. We didn't have any of the cameras on, but I saw her."

Playing along, Maitland said, "I don't suppose you know who she was?"

"Oh, yes, because there were some pictures stuck in the old family Bible. And I asked Penny, to be sure. Besides, the sisters really do look a lot alike. Though night and day. It was Jessie Rayburn."

The chief had been about to try a sip of the hot, undoubtedly foul coffee their ancient coffeemaker produced, but instead slowly set the cup down on his blotter.

I should have stopped off for a decent cup of coffee. Dammit.

"Jessie Rayburn isn't dead," he said.

Hollis blinked. "But I saw her. I could see *through* her. And then she started to come toward me, and after just a couple of steps, she faded away. That happens pretty often with a new spirit; they don't yet know how to focus and gather energy to come all the way through."

Maitland resisted the impulse to ask the attractive brunette if she'd had a psych evaluation recently. Instead, he said kindly, "I verified that Jessie Rayburn left town safely, Miss Templeton, so—"

Her mouth firmed, and the blue eyes took on an unexpectedly steely sheen. "Chief Maitland, I don't imagine things. And I am a bona fide, certified medium."

He wondered fleetingly how one became certified as a medium. Was there a test? Was there some kind of stamp, like in a passport or from the USFDA?

Government approved. Accept no substitutes.

"I know what I saw, and what I saw was real. Whatever your report says, whatever your investigation discovered, however many witnesses you can find who saw Jessie Rayburn drive out of town, I'm telling you that she's dead."

Maitland dragged his mind back from the brink of frivolous thoughts and focused on the researcher's very serious face. "Then maybe she had a car accident on her way back to New Mexico, or—"

"She was murdered."

"Did the ghost have a knife sticking out of her?" He had wondered that, actually, whether ghosts—assuming they existed at all—were doomed to wander among the living looking as they had looked at the moment of death.

In which case, he supposed car accident and burn victims could account for many a "monster" in a child's closet at night.

"I'm quite serious, Chief. No, Jessie Rayburn did not have a knife sticking out of her, but she *was* murdered."

"She told you that?"

"I felt it."

"I'm sorry, Miss Templeton, but I need a little more evidence before I can declare there's been a crime." He took care this time to keep the condescension out of his voice.

She raised her chin a notch. "I understand from Penny that a missing-persons report was filed by Miss Rayburn's employers when she hadn't arrived back in New Mexico by this morning. That her sister filed a missing-persons report. That nobody has seen or heard from her since sometime in the afternoon of the festival. Since she *left* Baron Hollow. I would think those things together would be enough for you to investigate further."

"Miss Templeton—"

"And then there's the body found up in the mountains last week."

"What's that got to do with—"

"Exactly, Chief."

He found himself speechless for one of the few times in his life, and looked at the woman's silent partner to see a faint gleam of sympathy in eyes occupying an otherwise expressionless face.

"People go missing up here all the time," Hollis said. "At least that's what we hear, what people in town are saying. The average seems to be one or two every year, and that's just the ones people know about. The wilderness just swallows them up, like that poor woman up on the mountain was swallowed up and forgotten, until somebody stumbles over the remains. *If* somebody stumbles over the remains.

"But Jessie Rayburn was from a local family; she was born here. Her sister and cousin are prominent citizens in Baron Hollow. And I doubt very seriously that she hiked up into the mountains and got herself lost, *especially* since you have witnesses who claim to have seen her drive herself out of town."

"Miss Templeton—"

"We haven't spoken to Miss Emma Rayburn yet, but I'm sure that when we do, she'll be interested in what I saw."

Maitland wondered, but all he said was, "So what is it you want me to do, Miss Templeton? However inadequately you believe it was done, there *was* an investigation into Jessie's movements that last day, and there *are* reputable witnesses who stated that they saw her driving herself out of town toward the highway."

"Away from downtown?"

"I'm not sure I understand what you mean."

"I mean, did any of your witnesses see her actually drive onto the highway and head west? Or are your witnesses people who were downtown at the festival and saw the back of her car heading in that general direction? Because it's—what?—a good five miles to the highway from downtown?"

"About that," he said slowly.

"I don't suppose anybody bothered to check along those five miles? Knock on doors, check side roads, look for any signs that she didn't actually make it to the highway?"

Speaking up for the first time, her partner said mildly, "If you don't have anything else pressing, Chief, would it hurt to send a few of your people to canvass along the route out of town? Because, I can tell you from experience, she isn't going to give up."

"WAY TO UNDERMINE my credibility," she complained when they stood outside the police station a few moments later.

"I didn't undermine you. He's sending officers out, isn't he?"

"Yeah. Maybe they'll even find something."

"More important," he said, "we can spread the word that he's looking into Jessie's disappearance again. If I know small towns—and I do—he'll have more volunteer searchers than he knows what to do with in nothing flat. And however motivated the officers are, the locals are really curious about Jessie, and they'll look for her. Hard."

"I suppose." She frowned, then said thoughtfully, "You know, it's a bit refreshing to be a private citizen and try to bully the police without worrying about stepping over jurisdictional lines."

"Yeah, I could see you were having fun." He took her arm as they began to walk in the general direction of Rayburn House. "But that whole 'bona fide, certified medium' thing was a little over-the-top."

"You think?"

"He was wondering if there was a test. And a stamp of approval, like in a passport or the USFDA thing on a side of beef."

She winced. "Oh. Not the effect I wanted."

"I was pretty sure it wasn't."

"But maybe there should be a special ID card."

"You have one of those," he reminded her.

"Yes, but I can't show my credentials here. Not yet, anyway. And when I can, when *we* can . . ."

"Chief Maitland is not going to be pleased with us. At all. Yes. I know."

MAKING A STAB at normalcy, Emma had gone to the park that morning, both to exercise her dog and to breathe fresh air and try not to think too much. And with what she suspected was genuine sensitivity, Navarro, who had been pretty much stuck to her side during all her waking hours since early Sunday morning, had not offered to come along.

She missed him not being with her, which was a disconcerting realization. Even Lizzie was noticeably subdued, for once not interested in chasing her Frisbee. But they walked around the park, Emma trying not to think much, wondering when the numbness would begin to wear off.

Wondering if it was grief for Jessie she was holding at bay, or grief for what she herself had lost that summer. Innocence, certainly. Trust. A soul-deep feeling of safety in the haven that was supposed to be her home. That had been damaged even though she hadn't consciously remembered it, hence her need every summer to escape, to become someone else.

She wondered, now, how the brutal attack that night had shaped Jessie's life. That she had taken on the burden of her sister's memories and pain was remarkable, and yet Emma wasn't surprised by it. Jessie, despite her sometimes flaky outward appearance and actions growing up, had possessed a bone-deep sense of responsibility for her baby sister, probably because she had practically raised her.

Emma was fairly certain it hadn't been a conscious thing, just Jessie's instinct. She had gotten medical help for her sister in such a way that no one in Baron Hollow would know anything about it, and then hidden her sister away at home while she healed, employing amazing creativity and ingenuity to hide Emma's injuries from even the housekeeper. Until Emma had healed. Until the injuries were only scars easily covered by makeup, and bones had knit, and bruises had faded.

Had she begun then to take on the burden of pain and shame and guilt herself? When it had become obvious that for Emma that night was a blank, had Jessie, consciously or not, accepted the burden of what had happened because she blamed herself?

Was that why she had run away? To take it all with her, far away, and leave Emma here, outwardly healed, inwardly with an emotional and psychological block so solid that she didn't even consciously remember that night or even her own injuries?

Had Jessie "run away" in order to leave Emma her safe haven?

Maybe. Probably. But to do that, she had to have believed—at seventeen—that Emma's ordeal had been an isolated incident, boys too drunk to know what they were doing, getting carried away. Boys who would be horrified enough to not only keep the secret for themselves but also never do such a horrible thing again to another girl.

Easy enough for a teenager to be convinced of that. But, grown and working with people who investigated horrible crimes, those buried memories must have begun eating at Jessie. With training had come the uneasy awareness that maybe Emma wasn't quite as safe in her "haven" as Jessie had supposed. And maybe those drunken boys had not stopped doing horrible things.

Maybe that's what had driven Jessie back to

Baron Hollow. Because she knew too much, now, to trust the drunken cruelty had not been pure evil instead.

And she had found her answer.

By the time Emma and Lizzie reached the walkway to Rayburn House, she could see a crowd gathering up the street in front of the police station. She paused for a moment, considering, then said, "Come on, girl," and went with her dog into the inn.

Penny emerged from behind the registration desk almost immediately, saying, "That must have been some workout; it's nearly lunchtime." The words were casual, but she looked worried.

"Peace and quiet after the festival. It was nice," Emma said, totally on automatic. "What's up?"

"Listen, I didn't want to be the one to tell you this—in fact, I'm pretty sure Hollis wanted to tell you in her own unique way, but they took some of their equipment and went out to join the search, so—"

"Penny. What is it?"

"It's Jessie. Dan's reopened the investigation."

"Why?" Emma remained calm.

"Because . . . I'm so sorry, Emma—if it's true, and heaven only knows if she's right or a nut—but Hollis says she saw Jessie here this morning. Or, rather, saw Jessie's spirit."

"I see." Emma wondered if she appeared cold and unfeeling, when all she felt was numb.

Jessie saved me. She let me have a normal life. And paid with her own.

"She seemed really sure," Penny said unhappily. "And she must have convinced Dan, because he's got some of his officers checking out the roads between here and the highway, and volunteers have been showing up for the last half hour to help."

Navarro came out of one of the common rooms, glanced between the two women, then said to Emma, "I think she's a genuine medium. Which means she probably saw what she says she did."

"And Jessie's dead," Emma said. "She's really dead."

TWENTY-ONE

Nellie hadn't been able to catch up with Emma during the festival, and given Jessie's abrupt disappearance sometime that day *and* the fact that Emma and the writer seemed to be working on some kind of relationship, she had felt a bit hesitant to ask all the questions she wanted to ask.

Besides which, the brief discussion she'd had with Jessie during the festival had only raised more questions, and Nellie had been busy running down those answers, reasonably sure Emma would want to know.

A party fifteen years before, one Nellie remembered vividly because her older boyfriend had taken her but made sure neither of them drank alcohol—and left early. And despite all his precautions, her father caught her coming in way past her curfew and had grounded her for a month.

A month without phone and TV privileges tended to brand an event into a teenage mind.

Nellie had made a few calls and did what she could at home on her laptop, but then she drove to the newspaper office, which was open only until noon on Mondays. She took note of the people gathering in front of the police station, but since it was across the street and she felt the need to hurry, she went in and asked the receptionist what was going on.

"Beats me," Ann replied with a shrug. "Somebody said something about a search party. I didn't ask."

Nellie frowned, because search parties were fairly uncommon and she was, after all, a reporter, but then she went on down the hall to her office to find out whether the information she had asked a friend to hunt down for her had arrived, pulled by what she suspected was a much bigger story than a lost hiker.

There was a stack of pages in her fax machine, with a handwritten *You owe me!* scrawled on the otherwise blank top sheet. There was, of course, no signature; her friend had broken a few laws in passing on the information, and both of them knew it.

"Deep background," Nellie had promised. "Nobody will ever know your name."

That was a promise she always kept.

Now, looking through the pages of what was supposed to be a confidential medical report— even if it was fifteen years old—Nellie felt nothing but shock. From Jessie's questions, she had assumed . . .

None of this made sense to her, but the medical report was clear: Emma Baron (Nellie had guessed at the fake surname) had been beaten and raped, and had been brought to this hospital—not Baron Hollow's small hospital, but the huge and impersonal one in the nearest large city—by her sister.

Emma had, apparently, been close to catatonic during the days she spent there, but had refused to either name her assailant or press charges, and though a rape kit had been obtained, whatever evidence it contained was, presumably, in a hospital or police storage room.

Somewhere.

Feeling a queasy sympathy for what Emma must have gone through and dry-mouthed at the possible suspects flitting through her mind, Nellie put the medical report in a file folder and then opened another one, with information she had gathered earlier.

She flipped through the printed-out pages to refresh her memory, then stopped at one, frowning.

It hadn't meant anything to her the first time. But now, with Jessie's questions and her own ringing in her mind . . .

It was information she wasn't supposed to be able to get her hands on, and she had called in yet another very big favor to get it. She wouldn't have dared tell her boss about it. Well, unless and until it paid off.

And she thought, now, that it would.

Nellie bit her lip in indecision, her mind racing. There was no time to think it through, no time to do anything except follow her instincts. And her instincts told her not to share everything she knew.

Not until she had checked some of it out herself.

This, at least.

She put the folder in her laptop bag and swung it over her shoulder, then left her office.

At the reception desk, Ann was flipping through a magazine. "Going for lunch?" she asked, showing mild interest.

"An errand. If anybody asks, just tell them I had to run an errand, okay?"

"Sure. Hey, bring me back a salad, okay? I didn't bring my lunch today, and Sam wants me to work 'til three."

Nellie paused. "Why? Isn't he closing the office?"

"Not 'til three. Said there was too much going on in town."

"Where is Sam?"

"Went out a while ago. Maybe to join up with the search. He didn't say. Just said he'd be back later, and I was to stay 'til three." It was mostly muttered, and more than a little indignant as Ann kept her sulky gaze on the fashion magazine.

There was no use asking the girl just what was going on; Nellie knew Ann would have no more interest or knowledge of that than she had of the crowd outside the police department. An anomaly for Baron Hollow, Ann didn't gossip. Actually, she didn't do much of anything.

Nellie left the building, discovering that the crowd of people had vanished in the time it had taken her to get her stuff and come back outside.

Nellie was again briefly torn between wanting to know if a search party had indeed set out to find someone or something, and wanting to check out information that might lead her to Jessie—or to something Jessie had been searching for.

She didn't even have to flip a mental coin, just got in her car, checked to make sure she had her cell phone and it was fully charged, then headed out.

"WE WERE STRANGERS, you know. Jessie and me. There were too many years gone. Too much life lived away from each other. We tried to . . .

reconnect, I suppose. But it didn't really work."

"You'll grieve, Emma," Navarro told her. "Don't beat yourself up for feeling numb right now. It would be a miracle if you didn't."

Emma reached up to rub her left temple, frowning. "I need to be doing something. And I know damned well you need to be doing something."

After a moment, Navarro got to his feet. "I think it's time we joined the search for Jessie," he said. "Maybe my abilities will finally kick in, or maybe the medium will see something. Either way, two more searching could make a difference."

However much she had put together in understanding the situation, Penny had clearly expected them to join the search, because she had a backpack waiting for them at the reception desk.

"Sandwiches, fruit, granola bars, and juice," she said. "Neither one of you has had lunch. Don't worry about Lizzie; I'll keep her here with me."

"You're a jewel among innkeepers," Emma told her as Navarro picked up the backpack. "Lizzie, stay here and be a good girl," she added, using the customary command that would tell her dog she was leaving for a while.

"We'll be fine," Penny said. "I called the station, and Craig is manning the desk. He has the map with the search grid."

"We'll check in with him. Thanks."

"Don't mention it."

"Thanks, Penny."

As they left the inn and headed for the police station, Emma said, "I'm assuming looking at a map helps point you in the right direction."

"Usually," he agreed. "If the ability is working."

His voice was just a bit distracted, and when she glanced up at him it was to note that there was a distant, oddly familiar look in his eyes. She'd seen that look the previous summer.

Just before the body of a murdered woman had turned up.

"Neither one of us put on hiking boots," she said abruptly.

"We won't be going into the mountains."

"Because you've already been up there?"

"Because Jessie isn't up there." He was frowning now. "None of them are up there."

Emma stopped walking and stared at him. "*None* of them? You can feel there are others?"

Navarro tilted his head slightly, as though listening to some distant whisper. "Jessie did find something she wasn't looking for. All tangled up in her past—and yours."

Emma closed her eyes briefly. "How long? Has he been killing since . . . since me?"

"I'm not sure. But a long time. Scattered out so nobody really noticed the people passing through who got lost somewhere along the way. He's had a lot of practice, and he's learned to hide what he's doing." Navarro blinked suddenly and looked at her, really saw her.

"This isn't your usual way of doing things, is it?" she said in a tone of realization. "This trance-like bit?"

"No," he answered slowly.

"Then why has it changed?"

"I don't know." He took her hand. "But Bishop told me that sometimes it happens. Abilities change during an investigation. Come on. I need to see that map."

Five minutes later, they were leaning over the front desk in the lobby of the police station, studying a map of the area with a clear plastic overlay of the search grid pattern. The blocks were outlined in color all along the main road to the highway, and most of the blocks held cryptic numbers.

"I have a list here of who's searching which grid," Officer Craig Bradshaw told them. "Every team has a number. The chief mostly paired volunteers with cops unless he was sure they were experienced and really know the terrain. Even though all the grids start close in, some of them run pretty deep into the woods."

After a frowning moment, Navarro put his finger on a grid that held no numbers. "Here."

Both Emma and Craig studied the map.

"You own some of that land, Miss Emma,"

Craig noted. "Out there near the Willow Creek Church."

"Yes," she said. "I do. Jessie and I both own parcels."

"That's where we need to be," Navarro said.

"You're sure?"

"Positive."

Emma nodded to Craig. "Okay, assign us a number and list us as checking out that grid, Craig."

"Will do. And good luck." His young face was serious. "I've had a bad feeling ever since I heard about it yesterday. I'm still hoping we find out she's okay."

Emma merely nodded, but once she and Navarro were outside, she said, "I should have told him."

"Best to wait until we have proof."

"Guess so. Still, I wonder how many people are out there searching and expecting to find Jessie's car parked at some house and her inside visiting a friend."

"Maybe a few."

"Yeah. Look, we can stop at the inn and get my Jeep; the grid we need to search is about four miles down the main drag, so we might as well drive as far as we can."

"Makes sense," he agreed. He didn't say anything else until they were in Emma's late-model Cherokee and heading down Main Street toward the highway, then commented, "I noticed the chief had at least three K-9 units searching."

"Search and rescue dogs are used a lot in the mountains, so we have quite a few in the general area. I guess Dan really is taking the search seriously." She paused. "I wonder what that paranormal researcher said to him."

"Probably what Penny said. That she'd seen Jessie and was sure Jessie was dead."

Emma shook her head. "It had to be more than that. What Dan was convinced of was that whatever happened to Jessie didn't happen in or near Baron Hollow."

Navarro wondered if he might have an idea of what had ultimately convinced the chief to take Jessie's disappearance seriously, but since he wasn't sure, he kept the possibility to himself.

They'd find out soon enough, he thought, if he was right.

"HOLLIS, ARE YOU sure you want to follow the creek?" Officer Gerald Neal asked somewhat plaintively from at least half a dozen yards behind her.

"Definitely sure," she said, dividing her attention between the weed-choked creek bank they were forcing their way through and a small box with a gauge and dial she held in one hand.

Just behind her, her partner said in a low voice, "You could have picked an easier path."

"Unfortunately, I couldn't have," she responded, equally low. "Jessie's leading us. And she's getting more and more agitated. Whatever is happening, we're running out of time."

"The church?"

"I don't think so. I mean, whether or not the church is part of this, it's not where Jessie is leading us."

"And I don't suppose she's telling you anything."

"She's tried, but that's one thing I still have trouble with—hearing them. Besides, I think she realized she needed to save her energy to lead us. Right now, she's waving us to hurry."

"Okay, then," her partner said. "I just hope I can get my weapon out of this bag fast enough if I have to. It's a damned nuisance not being able to wear holsters."

"Hey, at least you don't have to carry this useless, stupid box and pretend. What is it again?"

"Supposed to detect surges in energy. I think."

She made a noise under her breath. "And to think some people count on these things. Jessie's aura is getting brighter. I think we're getting close . . ."

BY TACIT AGREEMENT, they left the backpack in Emma's Jeep. And though she gave him a look when he produced a pistol from an ankle holster she hadn't noticed until then, she didn't object. But she did comment.

"Do you always go armed when hunting the dead?"

"Pretty much. The dead I hunt seldom got that way by accident."

Realizing suddenly, she said, "You know who it is, don't you? Who the killer is."

He hesitated, then said, "I had a lot of background information provided to me, Emma. And once I knew what had happened to you, and realized there was a killer here, one name kept jumping out at me."

"He's on our list of suspects?"

"Yeah. And I'm sorry, but—"

She was about to ask, but just then, still a good fifty yards away from the creek, they came out of the woods and upon a parked Baron Hollow Police Department Jeep.

"Nobody's supposed to be searching this grid," she said slowly. "Nobody but us."

Navarro, eyeing the tire tracks the Jeep had clearly followed, said, "This road has been used, regularly. But it hasn't been kept up to look that way. What's at the end of it, Emma? We're still a good hundred yards from the church."

"It's . . . a cabin, I think. It's on Victor's land, but I think Dan leases it from him. Something like that. My and Jessie's parcels are on this side of the creek."

"Did she know that? I mean that she owned land up here?"

Emma nodded slowly. "I told her Victor wanted to buy it. She had a list from our lawyer, and was using it as an excuse to wander around town and out here. Said the gossips would believe she was sizing up her inheritance. Nathan . . . the Jeep. Is it him? All these years, and it was *him?*"

"Let's go find out." Navarro immediately moved forward, following the track toward the creek and moving fast but also as quietly as possible. "Stay behind me," he breathed. "I think someone else is in that cabin with him."

Realizing even as he had, as she'd heard the sounds of raised voices, Emma fell in behind him, keeping her own voice low when she said, "That's Nellie's voice. But how would she know?"

"If she has the right connections, she could get cell phone records. I saw three towers ringing this area on the map; I bet cell reception up here is remarkably good. If Maitland was on her suspect list, I'll bet she wondered why he was spending so much time up here."

Emma wondered where Nellie would have parked her car, but didn't waste much time or energy thinking about it; Nellie knew this area as well as just about anyone.

They came within sight of the cabin, and Emma followed his lead when he left the road before they reached the shallow stream. They worked their way through the trees, then crossed the creek without even getting their feet wet, thanks to all the flat stones.

As they climbed the other bank and reached a surprisingly cultivated part of the land, Navarro glanced over his shoulder at her long enough to whisper, "Listen."

Emma could hear it much better now, as they moved cautiously through what cover they could use as they approached the cabin that was nestled into a sizable clearing twenty or so yards ahead. Nellie half shouting something that sounded like, "Wait, wait! Just listen!"

And then the sound of a male voice rising and falling, using language so filthy and filled with hate that it almost sounded inhuman.

Evil.

She had known it, recognized it, fifteen years ago.

It had attempted to destroy her life, and it had destroyed her sister's life. And all those other lives horribly taken, snuffed out . . .

By an evil straight out of hell.

TWENTY-TWO

If Emma hadn't been with Navarro, she would have turned and run as fast and as far as she could to get away. Instead, she swallowed hard, reminded herself that she had to face her past as surely as Jessie had been forced to, and followed.

Navarro was moving faster as they approached

the cabin, clearly believing that a preoccupation with his latest captive was blinding the killer to possible danger.

The cabin sat on a yard that sloped down to the creek in front of it, with a great deal of cultivated plantings all around it, and they had just reached the ring of trees when Emma saw three other people on the other side.

Two of the paranormal researchers and a cop. The cop looked dumbstruck, even horrified, but both the so-called researchers carried weapons they clearly knew how to use and wore grim determination on their faces.

The brunette woman spotted Navarro and took one hand off her gun to make a quick gesture.

He nodded, turning his head to whisper. "We're going around back. For God's sake, stay behind me."

Emma didn't feel the need to protest. She stuck close as they circled the cabin, hearing Nellie's frightened voice.

"Dan, you know you don't want to do this—"

"You had to stick your stupid goddamned nose into it, didn't you? Had to be the one to figure it all out, the one to come looking for my flowers. And what did you do with my treasure box? Huh? I know you know where it is. Did she hide it? Or did you?"

"Dan, I swear to God, I don't know what you're talking about!"

"Snooping. Trying to find my flowers. My roses. Just like the other stupid bitch came looking, her for a past she couldn't even remember right, and you for a fucking story. Both of you thinking you're smarter than me—"

"Dan, no!"

Emma saw Navarro move faster than she'd ever seen a man move, reaching the back porch of the cabin, then the door, and kicking it in even as she heard the crash of the front door also giving way beneath someone's determined foot.

He disappeared through the doorway.

Gunshots, terrifyingly loud.

So many.

Emma didn't realize she was holding her breath until, in the stark silence, she heard Nellie speak.

"Well, it's about goddamned time. That son of a bitch was planning to cut my throat and stuff me in his freezer!"

Emma hurried to the rear doorway of the cabin, seeing nothing at first except Navarro, standing just inside, his gun lowered.

Safe.

She took a deep breath, so utterly relieved that it told her everything she needed to know.

"You're lucky we got here at all," the brunette "researcher" told Nellie severely. "Next time tell somebody where you'll be when you decide to go off and look for a killer."

"Pot, meet kettle," her partner murmured.

"I did *not* go off looking for that killer," she said to him. "I just found him, is all."

"Uh-huh."

Nellie frowned at the enigmatic byplay. "I didn't know he was a killer. Jesus. I just came up here because I was pretty sure it's one of the last places Jessie was. She'd asked me at the festival if I'd ever been to Victor's cabin, and I told her it was really Dan's, something that seemed to shock her. So I came up here to look around. He came in not two minutes later and surprised the hell out of me." She sat down suddenly on a rustic chair behind her.

She was very pale, Emma realized. Taking several more steps into the cabin, she felt her own face drain of color.

Dan Maitland, a knife in one lifeless hand and his service revolver lying not far from the other, lay only a few feet away from her. He had been shot at least three times in the chest.

The male "paranormal researcher" said to Navarro, "Did you have to kill him?"

"Yes," Navarro said. "I did."

The blond man studied Navarro for a moment, then nodded and said calmly, "Good enough for me."

Officer Neal was also just inside the cabin's front door, his gun drawn, face ashen. "I saw," he said hoarsely. "I know . . . he would have killed Miss

Holt. Or one of you. But . . . I don't understand."

"Yeah," the blond man said, still calm, "the report's gonna be a bitch. But everybody'll know the truth in the end."

Steadily, Nellie said, "Thank you—Hollis, isn't it? And Reese?"

"Hollis Templeton. He's Reese DeMarco."

Navarro said, "And they're FBI. Special Crimes Unit. Damned Bishop. I specifically *asked* him if he had agents here."

"And I'm sure he neatly avoided the question," Hollis said with sympathetic understanding. "He's like that, you know. Even with us. Never shows anybody the cards up his sleeve."

Emma was baffled by that, but all she could think to say was, "I didn't think you guys had jurisdiction."

"Hence the undercover jazz," Hollis told her. "We're here very, very unofficially. But our list of missing hikers covers people who came here across state lines, so assuming we find the bodies Chief Killer here must have buried somewhere about, I expect Bishop will fix things so it's all nice and legal."

"Bishop?" Emma finally thought to ask. Her mind seemed to be working very sluggishly.

"Their boss," Navarro explained. "Remember, I told you about him. Special Crimes Unit chief. And a man who usually gets what he wants."

"Oh." Emma decided to let that sink in.

351

Nellie said, "Well, whoever you are, thank you."

"Thank Jessie," Hollis said. "She led us here."

Emma was more than a little startled. "You saw her? Is she here? Can you still see her?"

Hollis shook her head. "Afraid not."

"Then where is—"

"Out here." Navarro was standing on the small back porch, moving to make room for Emma as she joined him. "They're all out here."

She stood beside him for a moment, utterly motionless. And then her hand crept into his, and she leaned into him.

"Oh, my God," she murmured. "Is every one—?"

"I think so. No . . . I'm sure. Every one."

Stretching out before them, covering almost all the clearing between the cabin and the woods, was at least an acre filled with rosebushes of all colors, blooming gloriously.

"His flowers," Navarro said. Every one a grave.

IT WAS NAVARRO who found the box, searching the small cabin until he found the tiny lightning bolt scratched into the flagstone hearth. He immediately reached up into the chimney and brought out the box filled with trophies.

"What's the lightning bolt mean?" Nellie asked, almost absently, as she looked at what the box contained.

"Haven," Navarro said. "A sign we all use."

"She must have slipped in here again and again

to search," Emma murmured, looking at the box that was filled with driver's licenses and student ID cards, locks of hair and pieces of jewelry.

So many trophies. So many innocent victims.

She saw the little dream catcher earring and caught her breath, a sudden memory slamming into her. Jessie letting her borrow the earrings because they'd belonged to their mother, one of them torn from her earlobe in the attack and the other lost somewhere . . .

Low, Navarro asked, "Are you okay?"

"Yeah." She cleared her throat. "Just . . . remembering something. Tell you later."

He nodded.

Still studying the trophies, Hollis mused, "I wonder if he caught her in here, or went after her somewhere else? This isn't where he held them; that's obvious. There has to be another place. But whichever it was, Jessie had time to hide the box. It must have driven him crazy to realize his trophies were missing. And I'll bet it never occurred to him that she'd hidden them right here in his own cabin."

Emma drew a breath. "I don't want to know if he tried to make her tell him. Before he was done with her. Don't anybody tell me that, okay?"

"No," Navarro said, reaching for her hand. "Nobody will tell you that. Just remember that, in the end, Jessie stopped him. And she brought us here to find them. All of them."

"IT WAS A favor," Victor said, his face still gray with shock, and maybe something else. "Years ago, he asked me if he could put up a cabin out here, just for . . . fishing. A place he could get away from town, where he could be alone. He said—"

Guessing, Emma said, "He said you owed him. For keeping quiet about what you did to Jessie."

Navarro looked at her, but kept his mouth shut. They were all three standing off to the side of the cabin, watching the swarm of state police crime scene people and FBI agents and God only knew who else.

Excavating Dan Maitland's rose garden.

Victor half nodded, but said defensively, "All I did was keep filling her glass. It was wrong as hell, yeah, I admit that, and worse because I did it just for fun, because it amused me to watch her get so drunk she could hardly talk—but I didn't know what they planned to do later. I never would have been a part of that."

"But you were a part," Navarro said. "She was barely seventeen and you got her drunk deliberately. Then you watched them take her upstairs."

"To sleep it off, I thought. I swear. It wasn't until a few years later when Peter got drunk one night and started rambling that I realized they had raped a girl upstairs. Him and Kenny and Dan. He kept saying Jessie would never forgive him for it. That you would never forgive him."

Emma shook her head and spoke steadily. "Peter was one of Jessie's friends. He never would have . . . done that on his own."

"Like dogs in a pack," Navarro said. "People do things in a group they'd never do alone."

Emma wasn't sure if she was strong enough to admit that it had been her who had been brutalized that night, so she kept up the fiction that it had been her sister, for now, at least. In a way, honoring the burden Jessie had carried for her.

"But you never checked on her that night. Never saw to it that she got home all right. Did you even think about her the rest of the night, Victor, or did you go off with some other girl who was maybe a little bit older and a little less drunk and not your cousin?"

He let out a rough sigh, but didn't look away from her accusing gaze. "All right, I was eight kinds of a bastard that night, and I should have been looking out for Jessie. And for you—though I at least made sure you weren't drinking anything but soda. Then, later . . . I sort of lost track of you. I thought you'd gone home. I told Jessie that, and told her how sorry I was, when she finally confronted me about it."

"At the festival," Emma said.

Victor nodded. "I didn't ask her forgiveness, but I did tell her I was sorry. I told her I believed, for what it was worth, that the men who had hurt her all those years ago had paid in their different ways, for what they'd done. Kenny killed himself just a couple of years afterward, and nobody will ever convince me that wasn't why. Peter became an alcoholic, and his life pretty much went to shit; his liver's shot now and it's only a matter of time. Only Dan . . ."

"Only Dan Maitland seemed to have put it behind him," Navarro said.

Victor frowned. "Yes. And no. He didn't seem to think about it, to let it affect his life, yet there were times, like with the cabin, when he . . . used it. Not often, maybe half a dozen times in fifteen years. He didn't say in so many words that I owed him, or that I was just as guilty as he was in what happened to Jessie. But he somehow made me remember, and feel guilty.

"This time, it was something that didn't matter to me anyway. The land was good for nothing, really; I needed Emma and Jessie's acreage to add to what I had to make a parcel large enough to maybe appeal to developers. Emma was emphatic in saying no, and I had no reason to suspect, then, that Jessie would ever come back to Baron Hollow. So I told him he could put up a cabin if he wanted."

Navarro said, "And how long was it before he hinted that you should deed this bit of land over to him?"

"Couple of years." Victor's mouth twisted. "I

probably would have done it, if Jessie hadn't come home. But I'd been stalling him, hoping I could convince Emma to sell out. Then Jessie came home, and I figured I had a shot at getting her land."

Emma stared at him wonderingly. "It never occurred to you that she might be scarred by what happened to . . . her . . . fifteen years ago—and blame you for it?"

"Not until we talked at the festival. I didn't know her memories had been fuzzy, Emma, that she thought that *I'd* been the one that night to . . . attack her. Hell, I didn't know she blamed me for anything other than egging her on to drink too much."

Emma shook her head, but said, "So you gave permission for Dan to build the cabin, and never bothered to visit it later?"

"No. When the tax appraisal came in higher than I expected, I asked the appraiser, and he said there was a pretty nice little cabin on the land, close to the creek. So, higher value, higher taxes. I wasn't happy about that, and I told Dan if he was going to use the land, he was damned well going to pay the taxes. I expected him to get pissed about it, actually, but he just wrote me a check, and cheerfully too."

"He didn't want you focusing on the land," Navarro said. "Didn't want to make trouble, make you curious. As long as he believed he could persuade you to deed it over to him, it was in his best interests not to make waves."

"Yeah, I realize that. Now. And if I'd had any idea at all what the sick bastard was doing out here, I never would have told him that I expected to be able to persuade Jessie to sell me her land. *Or* that I already had a developer interested."

Navarro said, "You threatened his secret. But he still believed he had some power over you—as long as Jessie was out of the way."

"I thought she'd just leave," Victor murmured. "Sell the land to me and leave. She never really belonged here. This place, this town, was too small to hold her."

Emma was silent for a long moment, watching the crime scene technicians work, then brought up a last, baffling point. "Victor, what do you know about that tattoo of Dan's?"

"The rose tattoo on his forearm? He told me once it was to honor his college girlfriend, but it was a pretty creepy homage—which is more understandable now that I know what he's been doing all these years." Victor shook his head. "A rose encased in a cage of thorns. Very distinctive."

"He didn't show it off," she murmured.

"No, he usually wore long sleeves," Victor agreed. "Even in summer. I never asked him why."

Emma exchanged looks with Navarro, and she

knew he was wondering what she was herself. Because surely, in all the years since, she would have seen Dan Maitland's bare forearm. Had her mind protected her to the extent that she had been literally blind to it?

"It's a powerful thing, the human mind," Navarro said. "It knows how to protect itself."

"It was that simple," she murmured.

"It usually is simple, when you get to the truth," Navarro said. "Jessie went looking for the men she believed had scarred her life, but the skills of a trained investigator sent her off on a different path."

"And she found a killer," Hollis said, joining them. "Happens to me all the time."

JULY 10

"The forensics team will be here for days if not weeks," Navarro reported. "And it's only the cops and a dozen private security guards keeping the media at bay. More or less."

"How's Emma doing?" Maggie asked.

"She's . . . holding it together," Navarro replied. "With so much hitting her at once, I half expected her to just shut down, but she's stronger than that. She still isn't sure about going public, but . . . horrific as it all is, she wants to remember, and face it all, and then put it behind her."

"You know I can help," Maggie said.

"I know. And I'll tell Emma about that. But my hunch is that she'll want to go it alone."

"Not quite alone. You're staying, aren't you?"

He answered immediately, calm. "I've decided to take some of my leave time. A few weeks, maybe. We'll see. With Maitland gone, maybe Baron Hollow will turn out to be a nice little town, after all."

"Okay. Keep in touch."

"I will. Thanks, Maggie."

Maggie Garrett hung up the phone.

And smiled.

HAVEN OPERATIVE AND SPECIAL CRIMES UNIT AGENT BIOS

HOLLIS TEMPLETON, FBI SPECIAL CRIMES UNIT

Job: Special agent, profiler-in-training

Adept: Medium. Perhaps because of the extreme trauma of Hollis's psychic awakening, her abilities evolve and change much more rapidly than those of many other agents and operatives. Even as she struggles to cope with her mediumistic abilities, each investigation in which she's involved seems to bring about another "fun new toy" for the agent.

JESSIE RAYBURN, HAVEN OPERATIVE

Job: Investigator

Adept: Medium. Also shares an uncertain one-way telepathic link with her sister. Jessie is not especially strong as a medium, and so is unnerved by all the spirits she sees when she returns home in search of answers about her past.

JOHN GARRETT,
COFOUNDER OF HAVEN

Job: Oversees the organizational duties of running Haven, and makes certain all equipment, information, and assets are ready when his people require them.

Adept: He is not psychic, but possesses a unique understanding of those who are.

MAGGIE GARRETT,
COFOUNDER OF HAVEN

Job: Handles the operatives and investigators who work for Haven, overseeing their training and, even more, monitoring their emotional and psychic welfare, both at base and when they're in the field.

Adept: An exceptionally powerful empath/healer, Maggie has the ability to literally absorb into herself the emotional and even physical pain of other people, in a sense speeding up their healing processes and helping them to cope with extreme trauma. The act of doing so requires that she give of herself, give her own energy and strength to the person she's helping.

NOAH BISHOP,
FBI SPECIAL CRIMES UNIT

Job: Unit chief, profiler, pilot, sharpshooter, and trained in martial arts

Adept: An exceptionally powerful touch-telepath, he also shares with his wife a strong precognitive ability, the deep emotional link between them making them, together, far exceed the limits of the scale developed by the FBI to measure psychic talents. Also possesses an "ancillary" ability of enhanced senses (hearing, sight, scent), which he has trained other agents to use as well. Whether present in the flesh or not, Bishop always knows what's going on with his agents in the field. Always.

REESE DEMARCO,
FBI SPECIAL CRIMES UNIT

Job: Special agent, pilot, military-trained sniper; has specialized in the past in deep-cover assignments, some long-term

Adept: An "open" telepath, he is able to read a wide range of people. He possesses an apparently unique double shield, which sometimes contains the unusually high amount of sheer energy he produces. He also possesses something Bishop has dubbed a "primal ability": he always knows when a gun is pointed at or near him, or if other imminent danger threatens.

TONY HARTE,
FBI SPECIAL CRIMES UNIT

Job: Special agent, profiler

Adept: Telepath. Not especially strong, but able to pick up vibes from people, particularly emotions.

PSYCHIC TERMS AND ABILITIES
(As Classified/Defined by Bishop's Team and by Haven)

Adept: The general term used to label any functional psychic; the specific ability is much more specialized.

Clairvoyance: The ability to know things, to pick up bits of information, seemingly out of thin air.

Dream-projecting: The ability to enter another's dreams.

Dream-walking: The ability to invite/draw others into one's own dreams.

Empath: An empath experiences the emotions of others.

Healing: The ability to heal injuries to self or others, often but not always ancillary to medium-istic abilities.

Healing Empathy: An empath/healer has the ability to not only feel but also heal the pain/injury of another.

Latent: The term used to describe unawakened or inactive abilities, as well as to describe a psychic not yet aware of being psychic.

Mediumistic: A medium has the ability to communicate with the dead.

Precognition: A seer or precog has the ability to correctly predict future events.

Psychometric: The ability to pick up impressions or information from objects.

Regenerative: The ability to heal one's own injuries/illnesses, even those considered by medical experts to be lethal or fatal. (A classification unique to one SCU operative and considered separate from a healer's abilities.)

Spider sense: The ability to enhance one's normal senses (sight, hearing, smell) through concentration and the focusing of one's own mental and physical energy.

Telekinesis: The ability to move objects with the mind.

Telepathic mind control: The ability to influence/control others through mental focus and effort; an extremely rare ability.

Telepathy (touch and non-touch or open): The ability to pick up thoughts from others. Some telepaths only receive, while others have the ability to send thoughts. A few are capable of both, usually due to an emotional connection with the other person.

UNNAMED ABILITIES INCLUDE:

The ability to see into time, to view events in the past, present, and future without being or having been there physically while the events transpired.

The ability to see the aura of another person's energy field.

The ability to channel energy usefully as a defensive or offensive tool or weapon.

Center Point Large Print
600 Brooks Road / PO Box 1
Thorndike ME 04986-0001 USA

(207) 568-3717

US & Canada:
1 800 929-9108
www.centerpointlargeprint.com

X